EMPTY NESTS

NESTED HEARTS BOOK ONE

ADA MARIA SOTO

ROOKERY

Published by
Rookery Publishing
PO Box 300280, Albany, Auckland, 0752, New Zealand
http://rookerypublishing.com/

Empty Nests First Edition (published by Dreamspinner Press)

Empty Nests Second Edition

Cover Art

http://www.paulrichmondstudio.com

ISBN: 978-0-473-51846-2 [Paperback]

ISBN: 978-0-473-51847-9 [epub]

ISBN: 978-0-473-51848-6 [kindle]

ISBN: 978-0-473-51849-3 [ibooks]

For my parents, whom I will never let read this, but who started with nearly nothing and still managed to put two kids through college.

CONTENTS

I started writing this book somewhere around 2010, maybe 2011. By this point I could not tell you what the inspiration was or even the particular motivation. I was working a night shift job that gave me a lot of free time, and living with my boyfriend in a one-bedroom apartment with his ex-girlfriend's cat. Now I am typing these words in my home office in early 2020 and things have changed. Just yesterday the New Zealand government shut down the boarders. It's Friday and I will not be surprised if I am home-schooling my child by Monday. When I wrote the story of single father James I was sure I'd never have kids of my own for a whole stack of reasons.

When I got the rights back to this book I hadn't read it through in several years. I know this is an absolute comfort read for some people but for me it was just cringe inducing. I found things that should have never got through editorial. I found bits of language that I would never use now but in 2010 I simply didn't know better. I found some sentences that were just badly written.

Everything I could find I have now fixed. If you're reading

this story for the first time know you are getting the deluxe edition. If you're picking this up again you probably won't notice any difference and if you do, you're probably one of the people who called me out on something I couldn't fix until it was back under my control. It's fixed now, I think.

AUTHOR'S NOTE

FIRST EDITION

This book takes place in 2011, when it was still sort of possible to do big international business in Russia.

Several real places and organizations are named or appear in this book. No money or gifts have changed hands. In fact, they would probably be surprised to find themselves here. That said, if you live in the San Francisco Bay Area, you should take the time to check out your nearest not-for-profit music venue, if you haven't already.

ACKNOWLEDGMENTS

With thanks to Roane, who cleaned up the disaster of a first draft. Thanks to Cooper West, who managed to pry my finger off the big Delete button. And a big thank you to Nick for working hard to give me the space to make this happen.

January 13, 2011
  _N 46° 03' 36.0", W 150° 55' 48.0"_

GABE JUAREZ WANTED TO DIE. No, he was sure he was dying. It was impossible to feel the way he did and come out the other end alive. The hum of the Gulfstream engines felt like a dentist's drill somehow pressed into every tooth simultaneously. He scraped his fingers through his black hair and felt the crunch of day-old hair gel. He wanted to be sick, but he'd already done that; now he was curled up in a ball, praying for death to come quickly. If it wasn't for the fact that he loved his PA, he'd pray for the plane to drop out of the sky and vanish into the Pacific.

"Frank wants to talk to you," Tamyra yelled from across the narrow cabin, her voice raised against the whine of the engines.

"Tell him to fuck off." He felt too wretched to put any effort into speaking with his overly perky business partner.

"Not an option."

He crawled away from the toilet. His company logo, woven in rows across the carpet, swam inches from his face until he squeezed his eyes shut. He found a workstation seat from memory and leveraged himself up into it while Tamyra held out the phone and watched. Some days he quietly hated her in much the same way he'd hated his mother when he was fourteen.

Gabe grabbed the phone. "Frank, fuck off."

"A little hungover?"

He could hear Frank laughing under the words. "I'm never going to Japan again, I swear. Send anyone else—I don't care who. I am never going back."

"It's a major account." Frank was still laughing.

"I know exactly how major this account is down to the last yen. I know this entire deal ten times better than you do, and I don't give a shit." Gabe didn't care if he sounded on the verge of tears. "Sake does bad, bad things to me, and you know it."

"Tell you what, next time we can bring them out here, and you can introduce them all to tequila."

Gabe's stomach lurched at the word, but he filed the idea away. He knew he could handle tequila. "I am going to hold you to that."

"I'll bet. Now, I'm going to put you on speakerphone with the rest of the gang, and I want to hear the good word straight from your mouth."

He pressed his cheek to the table in front of him and was thankful for its blessed coolness. "Half the school children of Japan under the age of fifteen will be using the TechPrim 9Plus hardware/software bundle within the next three to five years, with a ten-year support and rolling upgrade accounts."

Gabe held the phone away from his ear as *whoop*s echoed down the line. It might as well have been gunfire for the way it made his head feel like it was splitting open.

"Frank, I'm going to hang up now before I'm sick again."

"Not a problem. Try to get some sleep."

Gabe didn't even answer that, just hung up.

Tamyra took the phone from his hand and replaced it with a glass of soda water. "Try to keep that down. It'll settle your stomach."

He squinted up at her, not raising his head from the table. She looked immaculate, but then she always did, with her tailor-made business suits and subtle red-gold jewelry lying perfectly against her dark amber skin. "Why aren't you hungover? You went out too."

"I'm not hungover because I talked the girls into taking me to one of those all-night malls. By the way, you bought me my birthday present last night."

"Your birthday isn't until July."

"And I've seen your schedule between now and July. Besides, you got me exactly what I wanted. You have excellent taste in jewelry."

Gabe gave her a thumbs-up. "Good to know. Now can you please kill me? Please?"

She dropped a couple of shiny white pills onto the table. "Sorry, but you've got that presentation as soon as we're back. We're landing in Oakland and going straight from the airport."

He tried to sit up, but his head began to spin. He dropped it back to the table with a *clunk*. "Oakland?" He could think of nothing he needed to do anywhere near Oakland. "What fucking presentation?"

"The UC Berkeley Future Hispanic Business Leaders Group."

"Oh God, those start today?" He hated giving those talks. They were formulaic—any executive on the planet could give an identical one—and he always felt insincere, even when speaking the absolute truth. The fact that the talks were almost always arranged by the PR Department didn't help. "You give the talks. You know my job better than I do, and you've got a better tan."

"You know I could sue you for that comment."

Gabe reached into his pocket and shoved his keys across the table. "If it means I never have to drink sake again, you can have it all."

"You wish you were that lucky."

He groaned and redoubled his prayers for death.

"Come on. I've got your notes and a clean suit. You can grab a shower before we land."

He slowly pushed himself upright, taking deep breaths while trying to ignore his twisting stomach. Tamyra was actually looking a little sympathetic. "What am I going to do when you realize you are so amazingly overqualified for this job?"

"I don't know, but let's hope you don't have to find out anytime soon."

———

THE FOG HAD BRIEFLY SCRUBBED the air clean, and in the late morning sun, San Francisco sparkled, the Bay looked blue, and even the mudflats were hidden under a rolling high tide. Gabe wondered where his sunglasses were. The traffic whizzed by on I-880. The one time he was praying for a three-hour backup, the traffic gods laughed and removed every possible obstacle. He chugged another bottle of water and tried to look at himself in the little mirror conveniently placed on the back of the driver's seat. He looked like he'd been in a fight. He might have washed and shaved, but there were still dark circles under his eyes, not helped by the capillaries that had burst while he was being sick.

Tamyra flipped the mirror shut. "You look fine."

"I look like hell."

"We've seen you look worse," Jared, his driver, called from the front.

"That's not the same as looking fine."

Gabe sipped at another bottle of water.

Jared navigated the surface streets of Berkeley before pulling to a halt in a probably illegal spot, but anything that looked like a parking spot in Berkeley was probably illegal.

Tamyra dragged Gabe out of the backseat and shoved his briefcase into his hand. "Do you need me to walk you to the lecture hall?"

"I am the CFO of a technological giant."

"Do you need me to walk you to the lecture hall?"

"No. Thank you. I'll find it."

"I'll come find you when you're done."

Tamyra got back into the car, which sped off before a ticket could magically appear under a wiper blade. Gabe stretched his legs as he made his way across the campus. Students rushed past him, engrossed in debates on topics they knew nothing about. A few lounged on benches and bits of grass, taking in the sun before the fog crept back in. And as the breeze shifted, he caught a whiff of a controlled substance. Not for the first time in the last week did he wish he was back in college. He wondered if he could steal a hoodie from somewhere and simply vanish into the student population.

A grinning kid who didn't look nearly old enough to be in college ran up to him. "Mr. Juarez?"

"It's Gabe." He held out his hand.

The kid took it eagerly. "David Garcia. It's really an honor to meet you."

"Thank you." Gabe yanked his hand away. The kid was never going to make it in business if he didn't work on his handshake. He made a mental note to add that somewhere in the lecture.

"If you'll follow me? We've got you all set up."

The lecture hall was one of the older ones with pull-down chalkboards and seats upholstered in '80s avocado green. A few posters on the wall announced it was part of the English Department. That made sense. Business departments usually had better-outfitted classrooms. Luckily, there was a projector. There were also five dozen eager young faces watching his every move. He'd once had that look.

Someone had arranged a campus Tech Services guy to be on hand to help set up the presentation. Gabe might have been at the top of a technology giant, but he was glad for the assistance. He could never get his laptop to talk to projectors. They seemed to hate him. While that was being dealt with, he did a quick mental review of his lecture, deciding to put in a bit about handshakes at the beginning of the networking segment.

"Your system's ready to go."

"Thank you." Gabe looked over the Tech Services guy. He always tried to remember something about everyone he met, even in passing, in case they became important one day. White, thirtyish, brown hair, average height—nothing particularly exotic but pleasant-looking, and Gabe's laptop was talking to the projector in record time.

He settled himself at the lectern and cleared his throat. "Good afternoon, everyone. Please forgive my appearance. I just got off a plane from Japan. And here's a word of advice right off the bat. Whenever you can, get the Japanese to come to you instead of you going there. The local sake is an absolute killer, and you will be expected to drink it for the honor of your company. All night long."

That got a laugh. *Lesson two*, Gabe thought, *always start with a laugh.*

Gabe clapped his hands together. "Now, thank you for coming. My name is Gabriel Juarez, and this is everything I know about business."

GABE HAD GLANCED over his notes on the drive from the airport. It was a three-lecture series, all standard stuff about continuing education, and getting internships and feet in doors. It was a talk he could give in his sleep and possibly had been until his mouse froze. He wiggled it a few times, then poked a couple keys. Projectors hated him.

"And this is why I'm on the money side and not the tech side." That got a chuckle.

The Tech Services guy came down from one of the back rows. "The projector in here has a habit of locking up every kind of laptop," he said quietly. "It's not just yours." He pushed a few buttons in sequence, first on the laptop keyboard, then on the projector's control panel. There was a *beep*, a *whorl*, and then everything was back to normal.

"Thanks."

"No problem." The Tech Services guy went back to his seat, presumably to wait for another lockup. Luckily, when that lockup came, it was on the last graphic. The Tech Services guy came back down and worked his magic again. Gabe wrapped up his talk, fielded some questions, shook some hands, then waited for the room to clear out.

"And you have no idea why it does that?" Gabe asked. His laptop had already been shut down, disconnected, and slipped back into its case.

"Nope."

Gabe looked up. The logo on the underside of the ceiling-mounted projector belonged to his company, but it was from a decade earlier. At that age it was well out of warranty, past any service contract, and almost certainly hadn't had any kind of software upgrade in years.

"I'll send out an e-mail to someone in hardware support. If

it's a known bug, there might be a patch. Though I may get the response in Klingon."

The support guy laughed.

"It's happened!"

"I'm not surprised."

Gabe held out his hand. "Gabe, by the way."

"James." James had a good handshake, strong but not overly so.

"James. Thanks for the rescue."

James' face twitched into a quick, polite smile. "Part of the job."

"Are you going to be around next week?"

"Most likely, unless the server room catches on fire."

Tamyra discreetly slid up to Gabe's side. "James, this is the world's finest PA, Tamyra Dorsey. Tam, this is James... um."

"Maron." James held out his hand. "Nice to meet you."

"Likewise."

"James saved my bacon today by magically unfreezing my laptop."

There was another flash of a polite smile that didn't reach his eyes. "Not magic, just practice."

"Yes. I *will* write a memo about that." Gabe turned to Tamyra. "I take it we need to get going?"

"Sorry. Work and four o'clock traffic beckons."

JAMES SURVEYED HIS DOMAIN. A dozen computer workstations, threadbare carpets, no windows, and a lot of Dilbert cartoons. He looked over his team, consisting of the people who just happened to get thrown at him because they wanted to work certain days of the week and would likely not be around for more than a year or two because they still had real futures ahead of them. Except maybe for Dave. Everyone was present, and everything was quiet. He figured he had about a minute before a phone rang again. He unclenched his jaw and took a long deep breath, letting it out slowly, trying to prevent extreme irritation from bursting into full-out anger.

"Hey!" he barked. "Everyone look at me for sixty seconds. Dave!" He raised his voice. "Music off!"

Dave pulled out his earbuds.

James lifted an e-mail printout, crumpled from where he had been gripping it too hard, and tried to focus on remaining calm. "There have been complaints coming down from up high and landing on my desk recently. Apparently this team has an attitude problem." There was much groaning and rolling of eyes. "And there it is. I fully understand that the faculty and staff we service are occasionally morons, despite having alphabet soup after their names. And I know many of the students are intellectual snobs and spoiled brats. However, the faculty and staff have the power to make our lives difficult, and student tuition is what pays our salaries."

There was a fresh collection of groaning and eye rolling.

"Enough!" James snapped, crumpling the paper again. "I let all of you get away with a shitload in here. I let you sneak off-shift early when you have to be somewhere. I turn a blind eye to longer-than-standard lunch breaks. I let you burn university bandwidth on YouTube because I do it too. Hell, I haven't even fired Dave yet."

"Why would I be fired?" Dave asked through a mouthful of something sticky.

James ignored him. "But out there, you need to start behaving a little better. I'm not saying you have to kiss ass or lick boots. I'm not even talking about service with a smile, but at the end of the day, they are the *Upstairs* and we are the *Downstairs*, so let's cut back on the raw sarcasm. Can everyone do that for me? Please?"

Everyone nodded and mumbled assurances, though no one looked pleased.

"Thank you." James dropped the printout in the nearby recycling. "Now get on to whatever you were doing while pretending to work."

———

GABE'S only desire was to go home and sleep in his own bed for at least twelve hours. Instead he was at his desk, still feeling the aftereffects of the sake. There was a quick knock at his office door, and Frank popped his head in, his mass of red hair leading by almost a second.

"Hey, there. Feeling better?"

"Not really."

Frank's face split into the large grin Gabe had long ago learned to fear. "Well, I've got something that'll cheer you up."

"Why do I doubt that?"

Frank dropped a glossy local industry magazine on the desk. There was a publicity still of Gabe on the front, but it was the five words under it that terrified him. *Silicon Valley's Most Eligible Bachelors.*

His gut dropped. "No."

Frank yanked it away before Gabe could throw it across the room. "And guess who's number one this year."

The whine that came from Gabe's throat made him sound like an overtired toddler. He sincerely wished he could throw a tantrum, then take a nap.

Frank flipped open the magazine, the giant grin not leaving his face. "Gabriel Juarez. CFO. Makes shitloads of money. Oh look, they lied about your age. Took off a good five years. Too bad they couldn't take it off your face!"

Gabe grabbed for Frank, but he danced out of the way. "You love the outdoors. You cook. You can cook?"

"I can fry an egg," he snapped.

"And you're looking for someone special."

Gabe put his hands together as if in prayer and squeezed his eyes shut. "Tell me. Please, Frank, please for the love of God, is the word 'gay' anywhere in there? Or queer? Or 'is really not interested in boobs, so please don't send pictures of yourself in a low-cut dress with your résumé'?"

"Sorry, no."

Gabe slumped back in his chair. It was bad enough he had made the list the last five years; being at the top just made him feel pathetic. The fact that he would now have to spend a month fighting off half the eligible women in the industry was not improving his overall mood.

"I have got to get off that list."

"Speaking of getting off—"

"No," Gabe said instantly.

"You haven't even heard what I'm going to say."

"Answer is still no." He'd learned the hard way, when it came to Frank, it was best to start with no, *then* listen to what he had to say.

"My second ex-wife's second cousin. Nice guy. Good-looking. Young but not too young."

"Remember what happened the last time you set me up with someone?"

"That was a freak accident."

"So they keep saying."

"Come on. You need to get out of your condo. Celebrate a little."

"Do you know how much work I have?" He grabbed a random folder and flipped it open, hoping Frank would get the point and leave him alone.

"Do you know how large a team you have? Delegate a little. Relax."

"I am fine."

Frank placed his hands flat on the desk and leaned in. His breath smelled like ham and cheese Hot Pockets. "You are one of my oldest friends, and I'm saying this as a friend. I worry about you dying alone in the Old Executives' Home. Everyone needs someone, and since you are incapable of finding a nice guy, I will find one for you."

Gabe wondered how Frank's third marriage was going, because he only seemed to get interested in Gabe's love life when his own was falling apart. And Gabe really wasn't in the mood to hear it. Not with the evil sake still rotting in his bloodstream.

"I am perfectly capable of finding a nice guy."

"I mean a *real* nice guy. Not your idea of a nice guy, which is easy, pretty, and possessing the personality depth of a damp washcloth. Or, you know, a complete asshole."

A jolt of anxiety and anger shot threw Gabe. His heart began to race, and the edges of the folder crumpled under his grip. Frank usually had better taste than to bring up that particular ex or any part of that entire situation for any reason.

"And what do you suggest I look for?" Gabe all but snarled.

"Someone who's not an asshole, for one. Someone who might look at you instead of your bank account. Someone who is independently functional and willing to call you on your shit. Someone you might consider taking a day off for. Sane, balanced, responsible, nice to you, not an asshole. I think I mentioned that last one."

"And your second ex-wife's second cousin meets all these qualifications?"

"Hell no. But he's pretty, will certainly put out, and until we get you someone nice, we should at least get you laid. Puts you in a way better mood."

There was a point in nearly every conversation with Frank where Gabe had simply had enough and threw him out. This was it.

"Out." He pointed at his door.

"Just think about it."

"Now."

KEYS RATTLED in the apartment door as James pulled the tuna casserole out of the oven.

"I'm home," Dylan called out.

He heard the thump of baseball gear and schoolbooks hit the floor by the door. "How was practice?" he asked as soon as Dylan got into the kitchen.

"Fine." Dylan reached over James' shoulder and tried to pull a bit of the crusty edge off the casserole dish, burning his fingers a little. James had long ago accepted the fact that his son would tower over him. And he would revel in the classic blond-and-blue looks inherited from his mother. At least the towering strength would put him through college.

"How was work?"

"Mostly had to sit through a special business lecture because the projector keeps locking up laptops."

"Interesting lecture?" Dylan set a couple of old plastic plates on the two-person table that took up nearly half the kitchen.

"Wasn't really paying attention." He'd spent most of the lecture on his phone, trying to beat his personal best in *Nibbles*.

He stabbed a large serving spoon into the casserole and moved it to the table. Dylan inhaled about half of it without much more conversation. As much as James was worrying himself sick over sending his son off to university come September, it would do wonders for the grocery bill.

"So," Dylan started as he scraped the last of the noodles from his plate. "Remember that conversation we were having about the new AP English teacher?"

"If you pull a piece of paper out of your pocket right now, I will never forgive you."

Dylan grinned and pulled a tightly folded piece of paper from his pocket. "Saturday after next, if you want, you have a date."

James was pretty sure teenagers were not supposed to be as hung up on their father's love life as Dylan was. "No. No, I do not."

Dylan pushed over a printout from his school's faculty webpage. There was a phone number handwritten at the bottom. "Thirty-five, no kids. He likes music." Dylan had highlighted that line. "You like music, he likes music. When I talked to him, he said he'd love to take you to see a band he likes."

"Goddammit, Dylan! I do not need you setting me up with strangers."

"He's not a stranger, he's the school's AP English teacher, and I wouldn't have to if you'd get out of the house once in a while. Seriously, Dad, I'm out of here in less than a year. I don't want you moping around this place alone. You do that enough as is, and I worry about you turning into a crazy old cat lady."

James gathered the dishes and dropped them in the sink with a little more force than necessary. Luckily they were the plastic ones he'd had since Dylan was ten. "Maybe you should head to your room right now."

"Sure, I have homework."

"You better believe you do."

"Just consider it. Please. For me?"

"Go to your room. We'll talk about this later."

Dylan slunk away from the kitchen, and James tried to relax. Dylan had been trying to set him up with various men since he was seven. He'd never appreciated that his father might have other priorities, like trying to keep food on the table, a roof over their heads, and saving enough to get Dylan through school in case his scholarships fell through.

James picked up the printout. The guy did have a nice enough smile, and in his profile, he emphasized a love of music. The occasional small concert was his one, tiny, very rare indulgence once he'd started making enough to risk having indulgences.

There was a number penciled at the bottom with a note to call any time after seven. James checked the kitchen clock with its bent second hand that stuttered every five seconds. It was 7:14. He supposed it wouldn't hurt. He certainly didn't need to see anyone, but a concert might be nice, and it would get Dylan off his back for at least a few weeks. He picked up the phone and made the call.

2

Gabe stared at the folder that contained all the information for the *Buduŝie tehnologii* deal. There was a very large file he was pretty sure he hadn't put there. It was labeled "BT2ndPhaseProposalDraftFINALforReview." He clicked on it and started to read.

It covered everything: staggered payouts, employee compensation, real estate transfers, international patents, unsold product, and the all-important mineral rights. It was the proposal he had come in early to finalize, except it was sitting in front of him already written. He checked the date. It seemed to be right. He hadn't lost time or something. He tried to recall any point in the last month when he might have had time to sit down, go through the notes and drafts from the lawyers and negotiators, and finish a major proposal. He couldn't think of any, which only intensified the fear that he was having some sort of major neurological incident.

"Tamyra!" he called. He knew he could page her using the button on his phone, but he always felt like a pretentious dick doing that.

She pushed open the smoky glass doors. "Yes?"

"Do you know anything about this final draft Second Phase Proposal file for the *Buduŝie tehnologii* deal?"

She looked a little confused. "It's the final draft Second Phase Proposal for the *Buduŝie tehnologii* deal."

"Yes, I worked that out. I didn't write it?"

"No, I did."

Gabe looked it over. "When did you do this?"

"I had some downtime a couple of weeks ago, then a little more in Japan while you were out getting wasted with the bigwigs. I fiddled with it a bit more on the plane."

"I thought you were shopping and seeing the sights?"

"Shopping is fun for only so long. I figured I'd save you the time."

Gabe scrolled through more of the document. "And this covers everything from the international lawyers?"

"Yep."

"Right." Gabe wasn't sure what to say. "You know I could have done it myself."

Tamyra gave him a sweet smile. "I know."

It was a huge item off his to-do list, but the fact that Tamyra had written it better than he could have, and in her bits of spare time, only made him feel guilty.

"Why won't you let me give you a team—a position that doesn't involve bringing me coffee?" They had this discussion at least every other month.

"Someone needs to look out for you."

Gabe wanted to argue that he could look after himself and did not need a keeper.

"And you pay me better than you pay your VPs."

"That's because I let you write your own contracts."

"And you keep signing them. Anything else?"

"No. No. Thank you. This is a big load off my plate."

"No problem."

"WHAT ARE YOU WORKING ON NOW?" James asked as Dylan flipped through a glossy pamphlet emblazoned with the red S of Stanford.

"Need to pick my residence hall by tomorrow if I want a chance of getting my first choice." James put a bowl of oatmeal in front of Dylan and set down another for himself. "I'm trying to work out where the other economics majors might be hanging out."

"I'm sure you'll do fine, whichever hall you're in."

Dylan looked up at him. "Oh no. You're getting that look again."

"What look?"

"That look you've been getting three times a day since I got in."

"Is it the Insanely Proud Parent look?"

"More the Wallowing in Memories look."

James couldn't deny that hard truth. "I was just thinking about your first day of kindergarten, when you came stomping out with a note pinned to your shirt because you had set yourself up as a problem child."

"That whole thing was not my fault," Dylan jumped in, still defensive more than a decade later.

"You'd picked the raisins out of your oatmeal raisin cookies at snack time—"

"Because raisins don't belong in cookies."

"Then traded them to another kid for a marble, then refused to give the marble back at recess."

"It was a fair trade. Buyer's remorse is not my fault."

"Possibly, but the real point of the note seemed to be that you'd then thrown the marble in the storm drain so no one could have it. Your teacher was very concerned about your ability to share and cooperate."

Dylan laughed, then leaned forward. "Want to know a secret?"

"Do I?"

"I threw a rock down the drain. I've still got the marble."

James put his face into his hands and tried not to laugh. "Promise me you won't get sent home from your first day of college with a note about your ability to share?"

"I'll do my best." Dylan looked over his shoulder at the clock, then wolfed down his oatmeal in half a dozen large bites.

James took a big swallow of his coffee. He needed to get moving as well, if he was going to grab his bus.

Dylan dropped his bowl in the sink. "Sure you don't need the car today?"

"I'll be fine. Have you got all your homework?"

"Yes."

"Do you need me to wrap your ankle before you go?"

"Dad, it's fine. Stop fussing."

"I'm not going to get to fuss for much longer, so let me have this."

Dylan gave him a peck on the cheek. "Have a good day at work, Dad."

"Drive safe."

"I will."

GABE HAD ASKED Tamyra to work an extra half hour into the next day's schedule before calling the number on the UCB Tech Services website.

There were a handful of rings. "Hello, University Technical Services. How may I help you?" Gabe didn't recognize the flat, bored voice.

"Hi. I'm looking for James... Maron."

A slurping sound came down the line, and Gabe heard what

sounded like a TV in the background. "Yeah, he's out on a job. Can I take a message?"

"Yes. If you could tell him Gabriel Juarez called. I have a software patch for him, and if he'd be willing to meet me a half hour early tomorrow, I can get it in place before my talk."

"Sure, I'll pass it on." There was chewing.

"Thank you." The person on the other end hung up before Gabe could give him his number. He tried to remind himself that being a top executive at a major global company didn't mean random people on the phone had any idea who he was.

JAMES WAS LEANING against the door to the lecture hall. "I was told some guy with a Mexican-sounding name wanted to meet me a half hour before something, and there was something about a software patch? I took a guess it might be you."

"I'm surprised that much came through."

James looked exceedingly irritated. "Yeah, I've written up Dave about his message-taking skills more than once. But you've got a patch?"

Gabe held up a USB stick and his laptop. "There's something to be said for being a guy with a window office."

James got the laptop hooked up.

"I was told to attach the thumb drive and stand back."

"And nothing bad has ever come of that?" Gabe heard James mutter.

Gabe slipped it in the USB drive. Nothing happened. "Maybe I need to click on it." Suddenly there was humming from the hard drive, and lights blinked. A series of application windows opened of their own accord. The screen went blue, then black.

It was Gabe's turn to be exceedingly irritated. He began mentally composing his next memo, and it would not be kind.

By the time the students started to arrive, there had been three attempts and several manual reboots. Then the laptop had begun rebooting over and over on its own, the power button having no effect and the hum of the hard drive getting louder and higher.

Gabe was about to declare defeat when James said, "Fuck it."

Gabe and the students watched as James pulled a little cloth roll filled with tiny tools from his pocket. James used it to remove the underside of the laptop, take out the battery, void the warranty, and reassemble the whole mess. He hit the power button. There was nothing for a long moment, then a *beep*, a *whorl*, and the login screen came up and appeared on the large projection screen behind him.

James handed him the thumb drive with a slight shake of his head before grabbing a seat on the aisle.

Gabe managed to get through the lecture with only two freezes, both of which were quickly remedied, but he kept glancing over to the corner, where James had a little amused smile on his face.

After some questions and polite applause, Gabe collected several resumes, many of which were handed over by young women wearing far more fashionable outfits than the previous week, while James shut down the system and packed away the cables.

He felt far more tired than he should for that time of day. He looked around. Tamyra had yet to appear. "Hey, could I get you a cup of coffee or something?"

James smiled, a proper one this time. Gabe decided James' smile was quite memorable, and he should use it more often. It was slightly embarrassed, a little shy, and quite sweet.

"Thanks, but I'm sure you have places you need to be."

"Not really. Besides, I'm desperate for a latte."

James smiled again but still looked shy. "Sure. I could use a bit of caffeine myself."

THE NEAREST CAMPUS coffee shop was busy, but there was still a table for two outside in the sun. Gabe politely nodded to the blue-haired young woman who put two coffees in front of them. A latte for Gabe, and a small drip coffee for James.

Gabe took a sip. "Oh my, I needed that."

He quickly ran through a list of possible topics for small talk. He could work his way through high-end business lunches, country club cocktail hours, and major corporate events without breaking a sweat, but sitting across from a normal, non-work-related person required a bit more thought. He was pretty sure he hadn't always been that way. Luckily James' phone gave a little trill, and he quickly pulled it out of his pocket.

"Sorry. Just being told baseball practice is looking to be a late one."

"Oh, you've got kids." Gabe gave a mental sigh of relief. Kids always worked as a conversation starter.

"Just the one, Dylan. Bringing him up myself." There was blatant pride in James' words.

"That's great. He's in Little League?"

"Varsity actually. He's a senior."

Gabe took a hard, second look at the man sitting across the table from him and tried to figure out if it was healthy living, good genetics, or one hell of a plastic surgeon, because he didn't look even remotely old enough to have a son in senior year.

James gave a small laugh that ended with a closed-off expression. "I'll make the math easy. Dylan turned three the same week I graduated high school. And now you know how old I am as well."

"No judgment here. My two older sisters had their firsts before they were eighteen, though I can't say it was easy for them, or planned." If there was one rule of small talk Gabe had learned, it was to keep parents talking about their kids.

James shook his head. "No planning here either. Got caught kissing Benjamin Steven by the entire track team. Decided to prove I wasn't gay, despite overwhelming evidence to the contrary, by sleeping with the first girl I could. Nine months later, I'm a teenage parent statistic."

Gabe knew he should respond, but his brain got hung up on "gay." It always did, which spoke to the pathetic state of his love life and how amazingly out-of-whack his gaydar was.

"That must have been intense."

James sipped his coffee. "No regrets. I've got a great kid. He's going to Stanford on a baseball scholarship. Early admission."

"I went to Stanford." Something Gabe took no little amount of pride in.

James beamed with obvious pride of his own. "It's better than we ever hoped for. I was happy when the state schools started sniffing around."

"Tell him to avoid Dr. Moncrieff's freshman World History class. The man is a million years old and a hyperactive lunatic. But he teaches some obscure subject for the grad students, so they won't get rid of him."

"I'll pass that along." James' phone trilled again. He peeked at it. "Damn."

"What's wrong?"

"Oh, we're in competition with the tech support guys up the hill at Lawrence Livermore Labs. Every time a Nobel Prize winner forgets their login password, it's two points. One point if they leave the Caps Lock key on. They just had a particle physicist forget his password while the Caps Lock was on. It puts them ahead for the week."

Gabe laughed but knew full well he'd done it himself a time or two. "It's only Wednesday. I'm sure you can catch up."

"We're usually ahead. We've got more winners in different disciplines." Gabe took another sip of coffee. "Oh, I saw you on the cover of some glossy magazine the other day. Silicon Valley's most eligible?"

Gabe felt his cheeks burn. "If I could find some way of suing over that, I would. It's bad enough I'm on that list every damn year, but they always leave the word 'gay' out of the profile, so I spend a month chasing away women in short skirts and low-cut tops."

James looked briefly startled, then smoothed to neutral. Gabe was proud he'd gotten his sexual orientation into the conversation without an "Oh, by the way."

"Maybe you should write a letter to the editor."

"I'd be better off getting Tamyra to write it. She's much better at getting my rants to sound polite."

"Yes, I am." Gabe turned to find Tamyra standing behind him. "What exactly are you ranting about?"

"The most eligible list and the fact that they keep leaving out the most important bit in the 'looking for' section."

"I'll write something polite for you, but we need to get going."

"We also need to write *another* memo to the sixth floor. James here saved my bacon *again* today, because the patch meant to fix the projector instead nearly killed my laptop."

"I'm sure you can put the fear of God into them, but we need to get going."

He turned to James. "Sorry." He was honestly enjoying having coffee and a conversation with someone he wasn't working a business deal with.

"It's okay." James stood. "I have to get back too. Thanks for the coffee."

Tamyra wiggle her eyebrows at Gabe with a slight question on her face. "Oh, you think I could get your card in case I get an answer about the projector before next week?"

"Sure." He pulled a standard employee card from his wallet. Gabe recognized the number as the one that went to the Help Desk, but there was a personal university e-mail on it.

"Thanks, see you next week."

James gave a little smile and walked off.

"Awww." Tamyra grinned at him. "You are so cute when you're trying to flirt."

"I wasn't trying to flirt. I was making conversation."

"And that really pathetic attempt to get his number was...?"

"A really pathetic attempt to get a number. But," Gabe cut into Tamyra's next comment, "he's actually gay this time."

"I'm very impressed. Congratulations. We do need to get you back to the office, though."

"In four o'clock traffic?"

"In four o'clock traffic. It'll give you plenty of time to catch up on your messages."

3

A blood pressure cuff squeezed Gabe's arm while he was trying to text. It was not the best way to spend a Friday morning.

"Put it down and stop moving, or I'm going to start over."

Gabe put his phone down and leaned back in his chair. Dr. Gowda *tsk*ed. "Sorry, we'll have to try again."

"Are you sure?" Gabe hated getting poked by his doctor, even if it was in the comfort of his own office.

"I could just diagnose you as thirty seconds away from a stroke. Which you may very well be, but I'd like to double-check." Gabe closed his eyes and tried to quickly meditate his blood pressure lower. When the cuff loosened, his doctor made another *tsk*ing noise. "One-thirty over eighty-five. That's a bit high. If I keep seeing numbers like that, you are going on a low-sodium diet. You should be cutting down on your caffeine as it is."

"If you take away my caffeine, I will switch to hard drugs. I'm serious. It's either coffee or cocaine."

Dr. Gowda ignored him. "You also need to get more than six uninterrupted hours of sleep a night. I do not like the direction your last blood workup was pointing. You need more good sleep."

"I'd love to, but the funny thing is the world is round, and that means it's not daylight at the same time everywhere." Gabe knew he was short on sleep if he slipped into heavy sarcasm before noon.

"Do you want to try the Temazepam again?"

"God, no."

Dr. Gowda looked into his ears, then up his nose. "Have you been taking the vitamins I prescribed you?"

"Tamyra slips liquid vitamins into my morning latte and tries to cover the taste with sugar-free caramel syrup."

"You would be dead without that woman. Lift your shirt." Gabe pulled up his shirt and winced as the icy stethoscope was pressed to his chest. "And breathe."

Gabe used to get poked and prodded by a doctor maybe once a year. But once the company started netting eight figures, lawyers and insurance companies got curious about his health.

"Your lungs sound fine. Any more migraines?"

"No, but I haven't had to deal with my extended family lately."

Dr. Gowda scribbled some notes into his file. "Speaking of family. My nephew has just moved in from Bangalore. Very nice young man. Studying neurosurgery."

"If he's studying neurosurgery, then he has even less time to date than I do, but if I need a full brain transplant in a decade, I'll keep him in mind."

"I thought I'd give it a try. Now that he's out of the country, and out from under his parents, he's looking to date properly."

"I wish him luck on that front." Gabe's computer pinged as an e-mail notification popped up. He looked at the subject line and smiled. It was something he thought he might actually want to read.

JAMES WAS TRYING to phrase an e-mail to a department head in a way that wouldn't get him fired when the phone on his desk rang with a little light, saying a call was being put through to him. That meant Dave wasn't on the main desk.

He let it ring a couple of times. Most calls James *wanted* to hear went through to his cell phone. "Hello, James Maron, Technical Services."

"Hi, this is Gabe Juarez. I'm calling to tell you I got a message back about that projector locking up."

"Really?" James tried to push down a burst of excitement. That damn projector was a chronic irritation, and no one was willing to cough up the money to replace it since it *technically* still worked.

"Sorry it's not major news. I was told I needed to find out the exact make and model."

Of course, he thought with an internal sigh. "I guess I can get one of the maintenance guys up there with a ladder."

"Can you just check the documentation?"

James stared at the wall of manuals and documentation that had only been organized since his promotion. The relevant documents were probably balancing a desk somewhere in the English Department. "Finding a ladder would be easier than finding the documentation."

"Oh, well, I can give you my e-mail if you manage to get someone up there."

"Sure." James grabbed a pen. It was nice having someone actually trying to help.

"GabeJ at TechPrim dot com. That's my lower traffic e-mail, so it shouldn't get lost."

"Great, got it." James half wondered if lower traffic meant personal e-mails or more important ones. "I'll try to get those numbers for you."

"Thanks. Oh, how goes the password stupidity?"

James grinned. That had been the bright spot of his day. "We're trying to work out a whole new scoring system. We had an economist who turned the Number Lock off and couldn't figure out why the cursor kept jumping to other fields whenever he tried to type in his password, which is required to have a number in it. And he never bothered to try the numbers on the top row."

Gabe's laughter rolled down the line. "That has to be at least four points."

"At least."

GABE RUBBED his fork between his fingers and considered stabbing himself in the neck. His date, Marcel, was pretty enough, but that was about as far as the attraction went. He was nattering on about some reality star Gabe had never heard of getting married to some other reality star. He was pretty sure he was smiling and nodding at the right moments, but with every passing moment, the fork option was looking more and more appealing.

His phone chirped, and he quickly grabbed it. Being CFO of a giant, multinational organization with offices and clients all over the world made for great excuses when faced with nightmarish dates. He had used the line "Sorry, there's a crisis in the Chennai office I just have to deal with" on more than one occasion.

He'd received an e-mail but somewhat unusually, it was on his nonwork account. He apologized to his date as he tapped the message open. It was from James and contained all the pertinent numbers for one of their projector systems. He apologized to his date again and quickly typed a reply.

It's 8 on a Friday night. Please tell me you didn't just climb off a ladder?

He hit send and motioned for his date to continue, then realized his date hadn't actually stopped talking.

A minute later there was another chirp.

No, but am working late. Sorry if I'm interrupting anything.

Gabe smiled. *Just the date from hell. Or at least purgatory. Don't worry about it.*

Gabe looked up. His date was still talking, but now he was speaking to the waiter. He slowly plotted his revenge against Frank for this one.

THE WHOLE APARTMENT rattled as James slammed the door on the worst Saturday night in recent memory, his ears still ringing. He pulled off the nice jacket he'd been stupid enough to put on. He'd known picking up that phone and making that call had been a bad idea. Every date he'd ever been on in his entire life had been some level of bad idea, and it wasn't as if there had been many.

Dylan came out of his room.

"Things not go well?"

James tried not to grind his teeth. "If you even *think* to set me up with anyone ever again, I will ground you for the rest of your life, I swear to God. I will remove all your car privileges. I will send you to live with your mother!"

James knew that last one was a threat he'd never actually carry out, but the last time it had been used was when he'd found a dried-out joint in Dylan's room.

Dylan raised his hands. "Okay. I promise I will not try to set you up with anyone else but—"

"No." It came out as a full shout. "No. There are no buts in there. No buts. As long as I put the roof over our heads, my word is final!"

GABE BARELY GLANCED over the group of students he was supposed to be inspiring. The truth was he could sum up the secret to his success in three sentences: work your ass off, have no social life, and manage to get two genius übernerds with no business savvy as roommates.

Gabe continued his talk on the importance of face-time networking, especially when considering work in emerging markets.

He finished up, fielded some simple questions, took a few resumes, and waited for the room to clear. He looked up at the ceiling-mounted projector, then at James.

The second attempt at a software patch had frozen everything as quickly as the first. Gabe wasn't entirely surprised. The memo that had come with the patch explained they hadn't supported that particular bit of hardware in years, and it wasn't designed to talk to the newer systems. And Gabe always had the newest. The whole incident was becoming a little humiliating.

"I am going to write another memo. It will be to PR, explaining why it would be a very good thing if TechPrim kindly donated a new digital projection system to the UCB English Department."

"I'm sure it will be most welcome." James bit his lower lip. It looked like he was trying not to laugh. There was a bit of comedy in the whole situation even if Gabe felt like he was the punchline.

"If you've got time, I think I owe you another cup of coffee."

"I can squeeze out a few minutes for that."

GABE ACCEPTED the latte and black coffee from the same girl who now had neon pink-and-orange spikes in her hair. He took a sip. "So, where did you study?"

James snorted into his drink. "Study? I studied at good ol' Contra Costa College, where I got a two-year computer science certificate on government money. Dylan was five by then, and I really needed a job. Started entry level here."

"That's it?"

"That's it."

Gabe was surprised. He was familiar with CCC, having taken a few classes there himself during high school, and while it was a perfectly fine community college, he had certainly not expected it as James' place of higher education. "I asked because you seem to know your way around a half-dead computer pretty well."

"Really smart people are really good at screwing up their computers. I get a lot of practice fixing them on the fly." James looked down into his coffee, obviously uncomfortable with the turn in the conversation.

Gabe was still impressed. The people responsible for the recent fuck-ups were making well into six figures and had master's degrees. He didn't know how much the Tech Support guys were making, but considering how often UC employees were at the front of budget-cut protests, he'd be willing to guess not nearly as much.

"So…. How'd the date from purgatory go?"

Gabe rolled with the blatant subject change, even if the pain of that date was still fresh. "Not my worst date ever but certainly nowhere near the top ten. It was with my friend's second ex-wife's second cousin."

James was kind enough to cringe.

"I mean, he was pretty, but dear God, he was dumb. I don't

consider myself an intellectual snob, but I think that man was the reason blond jokes were invented."

"Could not have been worse than my Saturday night."

"Try me."

"Well, to start with, my son set it up. Not the first time he's done this. He found a guy. Set up a date for me. Should have said no and just grounded him, but the profile seemed reasonable. Said he liked music, wanted to take me to a gig. I like music, so I figure 'how bad can it be?'"

It was Gabe's turn to cringe. "Famous last words."

"Indeed. He seemed normal enough, but I do not consider death metal to be music. It took three days for the ringing in my ears to go away."

"I think you win on the crappy date front. Did you at least get dinner out of it?"

"Not a good one."

Gabe quickly looked around for Tamyra. She had a habit of popping up just when he was starting to relax or enjoy himself, and he was enjoying talking with James, who so far seemed to be intelligent, pleasant, nice looking without being overprimped pretty, and not angling for anything involving money, as far as he could tell. Basically the type of person he had not had a conversation with in a long time.

"What kind of music do you like, if not death metal?"

"I'm more into acoustic, for one. Folk, world, a little bluegrass, I have to confess. Just about anything they play down at the Freight."

"Where?"

"The Freight? Freight and Salvage?"

Gabe looked blank. He'd never heard of it.

"It's been around since the '60s."

Gabe shrugged.

"How long have you lived in the Bay Area?"

"Born and raised."

"Okay, no, that will not stand." James waved a finger at him. "Next Tuesday, 8:00 p.m. Open-mic night. Always good acts. I can get an extra ticket, and you are going to have your musical horizons expanded."

For a moment Gabe wondered if he'd just been asked on a date. It didn't really feel like it. Not that he thought he would have said no to a date. James seemed nice enough—maybe not his usual type, possibly even falling into Frank's definition of nice—but again, it didn't feel like a date request, just an offer to go to a concert with a friend. It was a nice feeling.

Gabe smiled and tried not to laugh.

"The last time someone offered to expand my horizons, wax and chocolate sauce were involved." James blushed. It was adorable. Gabe pulled out his phone. "Usually Tamyra doesn't let me make my own appointments, but I'm feeling naughty. Eight o'clock, someplace called the Freight and Salvage, and I'll add horizon expansion."

4

Gabe checked the time. It was nearly an hour to Berkeley in good traffic, which on 880 was never a given. He'd been looking forward to the evening and did not want to be late. The idea of sitting in a theater with someone normal, listening to acoustic music, had settled into his mind as possibly the best idea ever. Certainly infinitely better than most of his meetings and far better than listening to a pretty airhead talk about reality TV. He even had plans to put his phone on silent.

He was reaching for his jacket when Tamyra came in, dropping a bunch of files on his desk.

"Have fun on your date."

"It's not a date." They'd been arguing about it since she'd seen the event in his calendar.

"Then why are you wearing your first-date shirt?"

Gabe looked at the comfortable dark blue shirt he was wearing. "I do not have a first-date shirt."

"You have two, that one and the dark red one, which you wear on first dates."

"It's not a date. It's an open-mic night. He wants to expand my musical horizons."

"Yeah, that's the only thing he wants to expand."

Gabe's jaw dropped. Tamyra was sarcastic, snarky, and generally ruled his life with an iron fist, but she was rarely flat-out crude. "I can't believe you just said that."

"I saw the way he was looking you over in that lecture hall. If he invites you back to his place for a cup of coffee, don't be surprised."

"It's not a date, and even it was, it would be the first 'coffee' I've gotten in a while."

"I won't wait up, then."

Gabe headed for the door with plans to make a grand exit before a thought pulled him up short. "Do I have a second date shirt?"

"If you do, I've never seen it."

JAMES PULLED on his sweater since the fog was already rolling in thick over the bay.

"You are not wearing that sweater on a date." Dylan had been commenting on every aspect of his wardrobe as he got ready.

"It's cold outside, and it's not a date."

"No, you're just taking a guy you've had coffee with a few times to the place you have described as your one indulgence, and by extension, your sanity."

"It's just open-mic night, and it's not a date." James didn't ask people on dates. He had surprised himself to no end blurting out the offer. He wasn't even entirely sure what he'd been thinking at the time. He just knew that a seemingly nice person, who happened to be attractive, was acting like they cared about James' musical tastes, and had bent over backward trying to fix a piece of equipment they would never have to use again. People like that didn't stumble into his life often and usually not for very long.

"Is he hot?"

He decided not to grace Dylan's question with an answer. Yes, Gabe was hot, but it did not matter in the slightest, because it wasn't a date and there would be no activities where the hotness of people had anything to do with it. And it wasn't as if James could get someone that hot anyway, so it really didn't matter.

"I'm leaving now. Do your homework, don't burn the place down, don't have girls over, and it's not a date."

GABE STOOD in front of the theater waiting for James while watching an eclectic mix of people enter. There seemed to be a mix of quite young and late-middle-aged. Some had dreadlocks and hemp bracelets while others looked like part of the khaki-and-Prius set. It was ten to eight when he finally saw James hop off a bus.

"Hey, wasn't sure if you'd make it."

"I'd never miss this, but I do live at the whim of AC Transit."

Gabe couldn't remember the last time he'd been on a bus that wasn't showing him around a factory. He followed James into the large, airy lobby that looked brand-new. "I thought you said this place has been around since the '60s?"

"That was their old space, eighty folding chairs in a brick building, one bathroom, and no parking. It took them thirty years to scrape up the money for this." James gestured at the recessed lighting and fresh carpet. "Come on, let's get some seats."

As the show started, Gabe could honestly say he'd never given two thoughts to bluegrass music, except for some possible associations with *Deliverance*, but the kid on the fiddle who was part of the first act had the fastest fingers Gabe had ever seen. They were practically a blur. Next up were multicultural drummers, followed by a young woman singing folk tunes that sounded three times older than she was. In between numbers James would lean close to whisper some comment about other acts he'd seen or share some general knowledge of the genre.

As intermission neared, Gabe started wondering if maybe he was on a date. James' whispered breath in his ear was quite pleasant, but he couldn't tell for sure. He'd never been good with these moments. He could negotiate million-dollar deals in three languages, but he couldn't tell if he was actually on a date, if a date was intended, or if he'd simply made a friend who was horrified at his musical ignorance.

The houselights went up, and people started milling toward the coffee bar at the back of the theatre. "So, are you enjoying it?" James asked.

"Yeah, some of those acts are pretty impressive."

"Good. Coffee?"

Gabe told himself the offer was for actual coffee and not *coffee*. "Love some."

James collected their coffees and found a quiet corner. "So…. Tamyra spent the afternoon telling me I must be going on a date because according to her, this is my first-date shirt." Gabe was sure that sounded smooth and humorous in his head. A nervous chuckle spilled out even as the awkwardness of the whole situation skyrocketed. He knew he should have kept his mouth shut. "Not that I would mind if this was a date or not. I'm having a good time."

James flushed as he fiddled with the little straw in his coffee.

"Dylan kept saying the same thing. Not the shirt bit, but the date bit. Of course most of my dates are pretty disastrous, and I think I'm enjoying myself a little too much."

"I know what you mean." Gabe scrambled for something that would get the evening back on steady ground. "How about if this is a not-date? Like an un-birthday."

"Not-date. I like that."

Gabe relaxed as the awkwardness faded. The lights blinked, and there was a little chime. Everyone made for their seats.

The first kid out—he looked about fifteen—had his arms wrapped around a *guitarra huapanguera* that dwarfed him. But his fingers danced across the strings in the same *son huasteco* rhythms Gabe remembered coming from his grandmother's small radio when they would visit her in the Central Valley. She would place it in the window and turn it facing the garden so she could listen while picking peppers and tomatoes in the heat. Gabe would sit in the shade under the window, trying to catch a breeze with a glass of cold lemon-mint tea sweating in his hands.

The boy finished and took a small bow. Gabe clapped hard, suddenly craving cold mint tea despite the chill outside. He must have had an odd look on his face because James leaned in close.

"Are you all right?" he whispered.

"I'm fine. Just a bit of sense memory."

James touched his arm for a second before turning back to the stage.

For the rest of the show, Gabe's mind was three decades and a hundred miles away, deep in childhood summers. He managed to applaud the last act as the houselights came up, and the audience started filing out.

The fog had come in thick and damp, putting a sheen in the air.

"Well, what did you think?" asked James, breaking Gabe from his reverie.

"I liked it. You can count my musical horizons as having been expanded."

"You should come back some other time and see the pros."

"I'd like that." James averted his eyes. He looked happy but a bit bashful too. "I don't suppose you know anywhere around here that serves mint tea?" Gabe asked.

"Mint tea? Um…. There are some Moroccan places around here, but I'm not sure if they're open at this hour. Why?"

"Had a sudden craving." Gabe checked the time. The surrounding storefronts were mostly dark and the city was slowing down. "It is late, though."

"Yeah, I have to catch my bus."

"I can give you a lift."

"You don't have to."

"I'd be a very crappy not-date if I didn't. Just point the way."

JAMES DIRECTED them down from the first rolling hills of Berkeley into the flatlands of Albany and across San Pablo Avenue until they got to a stand of apartments. They weren't exactly project housing, but not the kind of place someone would live if they had an option for better.

"Here's me."

"You know, I had a nice time tonight."

"Me too."

The silence stretched. Gabe was hoping for an invite up for coffee. He'd spent the night taking a closer look at James. He had a nice smile that caused the corners of his eyes to crinkle in a particularly sweet way. His hair was a little shaggy but in an attractive instead of unkempt way. A nice body. And there was something pleasant about him that gave Gabe a desire to prolong the evening. Frank's definition of "nice" floated through his head.

"I better get going. Dylan's going to send out the dogs if I'm out too late."

Gabe swallowed his disappointment, though he had been the one protesting all afternoon it wasn't a date. "Yeah, I've got a long drive back. Can I get your number, though? Maybe we can do this again sometime."

"I thought you had my number?"

"I've got the number of a guy who slurps over the phone and is bad at taking messages." James smiled, his eyes crinkling. He pulled a pen from a pocket and wrote a number on the back of the program from the evening. "Old-school. I like it."

"Old-school is sort of me all over." James hopped out of the car. "Thank you for the lift. I'll talk to you later?"

"Absolutely."

Gabe waited until James was past the security gate of his building. It wasn't that it seemed to be a particularly bad neighborhood, just not exactly a great one.

"I'M HOME," James called as he dumped his keys in the bowl by the door.

"With company?" Dylan shouted from his room, sounding a little too eager.

"No." James leaned against the doorframe in Dylan's room. A pile of socks kicked into one corner reminded him he needed to get more laundry powder.

"How'd it go?"

"It was nice. A lot of good acts."

Dylan rolled his eyes. "I mean the date."

"It wasn't a date. It was a not-date. Like an un-birthday."

And it was far nicer than most of the dates I've been on, James thought.

"So how did the not-date go?"

"It was nice to be out with an adult."

"Nice enough that you might go out on a not-date again?"

"I have no idea, but he has my number." James wasn't going to admit to the pleasant feeling that had swelled when Gabe asked for his number.

"I suppose it's a start, but next time I'm going to pick what you wear, because that sweater is not going to get you any play."

"Dylan! And I'll have you know you gave me this sweater."

"When I was eleven, and Grandma helped me pick it out. If you want to snag a real boyfriend, you're going to have to step things up a notch."

GABE WAS HUMMING some half-remembered tune in half-remembered Spanish as he sorted through the overnight e-mails. Despite the late night and long drive back, he'd made it a point to get into the office early. He had done a lot of thinking on the drive home. Not much of it formed into anything conclusive, but he did realize, with no little embarrassment, that these days he used his Japanese more than his Spanish.

He'd also made sure to put the handwritten number into his phone before even getting out of the car. The program pamphlet from the Freight ended up on his pristine modern fridge, although he did have to hunt around for a magnet.

Tamyra put a bottle of sweetened iced tea on his desk. "I'm told that's all they have down in the cafeteria." Gabe was half-tempted to send it back, but he wasn't that much of a diva even on his worst days. "And since when do you drink iced tea?"

"Had a craving last night."

"Speaking of last night?"

"It was an enjoyable evening. Lots of good music."

"Any coffee?"

"Yes, the kind you get in a cup, which is fine because it wasn't a date." Gabe kept the disappointment out of his voice, having no desire to give Tamyra the satisfaction.

"Sure, it wasn't. You planning on another 'it's not a date'?"

"Maybe, but right now I have a bunch of sales figures from last month I need to look over."

"No, you don't."

"I don't?"

"No. You have a date with a camera."

Gabe looked at his schedule and suddenly remembered SMPS meant Sales/Marketing Photoshoot. "No. No. God no!"

"Hope you brushed your teeth."

FLASHBULBS WENT OFF. Gabe did his best not to squint or blink. It seemed like Sales and Marketing wanted photos with him, Frank, and Nate every other month, somehow believing if they tried enough times, they'd change the three of them into models. It was a Sisyphean task.

Gabe knew he was reasonably okay looking. An early article had described him as tall, dark, and handsome, but that had been several years ago. Gabe figured he now fell under the category of tall, dark, and "not bad looking for his age." He spent enough time in the gym to be healthy and always brushed his teeth. But then there were Frank and Nate. As much as he truly loved his business partners and cofounders of TechPrim, their photos would slip in nicely alongside the word 'nerd' in any dictionary. Frank was six foot six and in the right light looked like a redheaded praying mantis. Nate was five foot six with thinning dishwater-blond hair, and in spite of the best personal trainers money could buy, had an extra twenty pounds that refused to go away.

Gabe's face was starting to ache from smiling.

"You were wearing your first-date shirt yesterday," Frank mumbled from behind his forced smile.

"Gabe had a date?" Nate asked.

"It wasn't a date," Gabe mumbled back. Even if it was, he wasn't about to tell Nate and Frank. They had way too much interest in his love life for a couple of straight guys, and he had no desire to encourage them. Especially Frank.

"Then what was it?" Frank asked.

"It was a world music open-mic night with a guy I met in Berkeley."

The bulbs stopped flashing, and a woman rushed up to dab bits of powder on their faces.

Nate rolled his eyes. "Oh God, tell me it wasn't with some guy who wears Birkenstocks and smells like sandalwood?"

"That's rich, coming from a guy who regularly forgets deodorant and has to be horse-whipped into shoes."

"He's having a moment," Frank told the makeup girl in an exaggerated lisp. Gabe turned around and flicked Frank's ear, hard.

"Hey! What was that for?"

"Being an ass and having way too much interest in my love life." Gabe suddenly had a powder brush applied to his nose. He shooed it away. "Okay, you know what? We're done. No amount of lights, filters, gels, or makeup are going to make us look like anything other than what we are. And if the pictures are that bad, you can Photoshop them." From behind him, Frank cleared his throat. "Oh, I'm sorry, *Techpix* them." He swung around to his business partners, who had outvoted him on the idea of going up against the Adobe Creative Suite. "And really, of all the bits of software we could go head-to-head on, you pick that one? It's become a verb, for Christ's sake!"

"He's having a moment," Nate said to the photo crew with far less lisp.

"Nate, I know where you live."

"That's not a threat."

"I know where your PA lives."

"That is a threat."

"I am going back upstairs, washing this crap off my face, then trying to get some real work done."

———

GABE WAS nose-deep in financials when there was a knock on his door. "What?" The photoshoot had completely killed the afterglow of his un-date.

Frank leaned in. "Got a moment?"

"No." He was still annoyed at Frank.

Frank let himself in anyway. "Hey, look, sorry for being an ass down there."

"Yeah," Gabe grumbled, not looking up from the paperwork.

"Okay, maybe it wasn't a date, but if it was, that would be cool."

Gabe sighed. The argument was an old one that had been rehashed a dozen different ways.

"I mean, never mind getting off that stupid list, you need someone. Someone nice. Someone who will not let you live in this office."

"I have lots of work to do."

Frank reached across the desk, putting one of his freakishly large hands over the paperwork, forcing Gabe to look up. "We're not a start-up anymore. You have an army of bright people working under you just waiting for your orders. A third of the world uses something we or one of our subsidiaries makes. We're one of the only companies left in the Western world that can still afford to give out holiday bonuses. And yes, I know your business voodoo is one of the main things keeping us up, but we don't want to see you burn out. Nate and I know damn well that without you, we would just be a couple of code monkeys with thirty-year mortgages, and we are very grateful for that. And we also know that as things stand now, if you have a stroke or a breakdown or something, we are fucked. You need to delegate, and you need to relax."

"I'm not going to have a breakdown, but I do have a lot of work to do." Gabe wasn't lying. The stupid photoshoot had him behind schedule for the day. He tried to put his head back down into the paperwork as a sign that Frank should leave. He didn't take the hint, but then he never did.

"Okay, this 'it wasn't a date' date that you went on, did you have a nice time?"

"Yes." Gabe admitted after letting out a long sigh.

"Is the guy single?"

"Yes."

"Sane?"

"I think so."

"Not flaky?"

"Not so far."

"Decent looking?"

"Yes."

"Then why the hell don't you ask him on a real date so I don't have to set you up with brain-dead ex-cousins?"

"I will think about it if you go away."

"That is all that I ask."

IT WAS past six when Gabe scrolled through the next few days in his calendar. It was full, but that was always the case. As much as Frank and Nate had him grinding his teeth some days, Frank's words about finding a nice guy were stuck in his head like an irritating song. He was hardly paying attention by the time he thumbed through Saturday, then suddenly backed up. There was a good four-hour block in the afternoon highlighted in bright blue and labeled with the word "Mimir." He grinned, grabbed his phone, and dialed. James picked up.

"Hey, it's Gabe. Have you got a second?"

"Hi. Sure." James sounded reasonably cheerful, so Gabe pushed on.

"I was wondering if you had any plans for Saturday afternoon?"

"Um…. No."

Gabe looked at the blue block on his calendar. "Would you like to go to a charity garden party?"

"A what?"

"I have to do this charity garden party thing on Saturday. It'll involve champagne and nibbling things off trays. But I've gotten pretty good at sneaking out of those things early, so maybe we could get a proper late lunch and maybe catch a movie?" As Gabe's words sank into his head, he cringed, realizing how unappealing he'd made a date sound. He was sure he'd once had social skills that allowed him to ask someone normal on a date without sounding like a loser.

"You want to take me to a garden party, then sneak out of it?" James sounded incredulous.

"If nothing else it would be doing me a favor. If I show up with a guy on my arm, maybe the divorcées and ladder climbers will back off."

James laughed. "So you want an anti-beard?"

"It's a 'brave new world' out there, we've already been on a not-date, and I would like to see you again." There was mostly silence and some harsh whispering in the background.

"I'm being told if I don't say yes, I'm a moron." Gabe would have been offended if he hadn't heard the chuckle in James' voice.

"Great. I'll e-mail you the information, and I'll see you on Saturday."

"Saturday it is."

5

The crack in the bathroom mirror bent James' nose to a strange angle. He'd called the night before to ask Gabe what to wear and had been told it was khaki-and-polo-shirt casual. James dug out his one polo shirt. He still couldn't exactly believe he was going to a charity garden party at a country club. He flipped his hair to one side and then the other. He'd never put a lot of thought into his hair before. There were a lot of things he'd never put thought into before; he'd simply had other priorities.

"You look fine, Dad," Dylan critiqued from the doorway. "Just stop messing with it."

"Are you sure?"

"I'm sure. Now go snag yourself a rich, executive sugar daddy."

"Dylan!"

Dylan had become half-obsessed with the fact that it was a garden party, which meant Gabe almost certainly had a comfortable income. "I'm saying it wouldn't be a bad thing. Being a kept man and all, you could go back to school, cut loose a little."

"Enough."

"Okay, okay. But you have to promise to let him pay. He invited you, he picks up the check if you go out somewhere."

James was about to argue that he could handle himself, but he had no idea what Gabe had planned, and the monthly budget was getting tight. He took a deep calming breath and counted to five. It was something he'd done on an almost daily basis since Dylan turned twelve and became a smartass.

"Fine. I am leaving now. I love you. Be good, don't sneak in any girls, and I'll send you a text when I'm heading home."

"I love you too, Dad. Try not to be too good today. And if you want the place to yourself, send me a text and I'll be out of here."

James took a deep breath and counted to five again.

JAMES DOUBLE-CHECKED THE MAP. There was a vine-covered gate with a small guardhouse and high brick walls. An exceedingly discreet brass plaque read Oakbow Country Club. He pulled up to the guardhouse tucked beside high, heavy wood gates.

"Hi. I'm here for the garden party?"

"Help parks around the back, and you're late." The guard didn't even look at him.

James bristled. He spent his days fixing the stupid mistakes of people with doctorates who didn't give him a second look. He was not about to spend his weekend dealing with the little snot in the guardhouse.

"I was invited. By Gabe... Juarez."

That got the guard's attention, but he still squinted at James with suspicion. "Your name please?"

"James Maron."

The guard flipped through a few papers. "Ah, yes. Here you

are." The gates swung open. "If you turn your... vehicle to the left, a valet will park it for you. Sir."

The "sir" sounded so painful to get out that James didn't try to argue that his yellow '95 Volvo 850, aka the Lemon Drop Wonder, was a perfectly good car. He did grin at the valet as he handed over the keys. "She makes an odd squeaking sound when you go from neutral to drive. Don't worry about that, but you can't go from drive right into reverse. You need to go back to neutral first, or she'll just seize up."

The valet forced a smile. "I'll remember that, sir."

The valet indicated the correct path to follow, telling him the garden was to the left of the main clubhouse, a sprawling, elegant building of tall windows and dark wood that almost certainly wasn't as old as it was trying to look. The path twisted ahead and disappeared between high geometric hedges. As he neared he could make out the chatter of voices and the tinkling sound of glasses, and he began to get nervous. He was not, and never had been, a country club kind of guy. He'd worked for a few country-club-type people, but he'd never gotten near a real country club in his life, never thought he would, and was starting to feel a little strange about it.

He slid up to the edge of the gathering, trying not to be noticed. There were a couple dozen people there. Waiters were wandering around with trays of nibbles and glasses of champagne. The women were in summer dresses that looked far too flimsy for the weather. The men were in khakis and polo shirts, but the shirts had little things embroidered on the breast, which meant they cost a hundred bucks at a men's store instead of five bucks at Thrift Town.

James was about to pull a runner when a hand touched his arm. He spun around, more than half expecting to get thrown out, except Gabe was standing there, smiling.

"Hi. I was starting to worry you'd changed your mind."

"Yeah, sorry. I drove past the entrance about five times, then had to convince the guy at the gate I was on the guest list. I guess they don't get a lot of '95 Volvos through the front door."

"Probably not." Gabe put a quick kiss on his cheek, barely touching it, in a way that made James think of old Italian movies. "But I'm glad you made it." James didn't respond, as he was trying frantically to process the most intimate encounter he'd had in far too many years. A waiter passed with champagne before the silence could become uncomfortable. Gabe grabbed two glasses. "Champagne?"

"No, thank you," James stuttered. "I've never really liked it."

Gabe handed a glass over anyway. "It's a Veuve Clicquot. Give it a try."

James took a sip. It was light and sweet without being sugary and went down without an instant headache. "Okay." James took another sip. "It's apparently cheap pink champagne I've never liked."

Gabe was still smiling when a woman wrapped in a deep pink dress, with artificially dark curls and a regal bearing, sauntered over. James couldn't guess her age. He only noted that her face looked younger than her hands.

"Gabriel, you're neglecting the party."

James didn't particularly like the way the woman rolled Gabe's name around her mouth while leaning forward, showing off cleavage that also looked younger than her hands.

Gabe smiled and slid one arm around James' shoulders. "Marie, I'd like you to meet James Maron. James, Marie Callahan of the San Francisco Callahans."

Marie's smile became brittle as she held out her hand. He was pretty sure he'd be getting a hard squint if the woman in front of him was capable of squinting, but so far he hadn't seen her eyebrows move once.

"A pleasure, I'm sure." She gave James another look over. "And what business are you in?"

"Academia. UC Berkeley."

"Oh, how delightful." She turned away, the social minimum of polite conversation apparently over. "Gabriel, I'm going to see if Jonathan has arrived yet."

"You do that."

She gave the two of them what was almost a hard look before slinking off.

"Did you invite me just so you could do that to that woman?"

"No, I invited you because I wanted the pleasure of your company. But that was a huge bonus. She's been on the hunt since her husband dropped dead three years ago. Officially heart attack, unofficially suicide after looking at the family's taxes. Pure hateful rumor says she offed him."

"Definitely someone to avoid, then." James looked across the rest of the garden party, suddenly wondering if someone was about to drop dead under mysterious circumstances.

"Have you eaten?" Gabe asked.

"Not really."

"Let's find some hors d'oeuvres, then, while I smile at people who hate me. I'll be able to get us out of here in less than an hour."

James wondered if he'd stepped into a mystery novel and should risk eating the food.

Gabe stopped a waiter with a tray of canapés that looked like miniature works of modern art. He handed one that looked like a red-and-white striped brick to James. He took a bite and found it was a mini cucumber and tomato sandwich with sugar-sweet tomatoes and a bite of black pepper. A second exquisite bite finished it off.

"So," James asked quietly. "Who here hates you, and why? Just so I know when to duck."

Gabe laughed. It was a warm, open sound that wrapped itself around James in a pleasant fashion. "Look around. What do you notice?"

James scanned the four dozen or so people.

"Lots of Botox and hair plugs?"

"There is that." Gabe laughed again. "I'm the only Latino in this place that isn't mowing lawns or washing dishes, and I'm almost certainly the only one who's a native-born citizen. The young money are neocons or dripping with White Liberal Guilt, and the old money just sees me as some grotesque upstart who doesn't know his station. However, I'm also the only person here who isn't hearing the words 'austerity measures' or 'investment reallocation' from their financial advisor. And for that alone, I am an object of hate. Half of them are going broke but they're desperately trying to keep up appearances, and part of keeping up appearances is giving money to charitable organizations."

James looked at the small sea of diamond jewelry and expensive watches. "I sometimes give spare change to the kids that busk outside the BART station."

Gabe smiled at him. "And I can guarantee you do it with far more grace and integrity than this lot."

James felt himself blush and dipped his head, unsure what to say. He didn't exactly go through his days getting a lot of compliments, and grace and integrity certainly weren't on the list.

Gabe leaned close, lips nearly brushing his ear. "You're cute when you blush," he whispered.

"You're not helping."

"I know."

An older gentleman approached them, and there was a second round of introductions and light conversation, which turned into another and another as people stopped to talk with Gabe. James shook hands politely each time, trying to ignore looks that ranged from dismissive to confused, and one from a young woman that was openly hostile. In between he tried to pick nibbles off trays as they went by and not make embarrassing noises over how good everything was. For as hard as he'd worked at being a good parent, cooking was not a skill he'd ever mastered.

There was the *tink*ing sound of a fork against crystal. "Excuse me, everyone." The gathering turned toward a young man standing on the lower steps of a gazebo. "If I could have your attention for just a moment? I want to thank all of you for coming out today in support of the Mimir Foundation for Conflict-Zone Education. And I'd like to thank our host and founder, Gabriel Juarez, for throwing this little gathering." James swallowed a canapé whole and tried not to choke on it. "Gabe, if you'd like to come up here for a moment, say a few words."

Gabe traded places with the young man, and James gulped the last mouthful of champagne in his glass, trying to wash down the canapé.

"Thank you, Rob. Good afternoon, everyone." Gabe smiled. "I know many of you here call me the Accountant of the Damned, among other things, but I do believe in putting all that money in good places, which is why I founded the Mimir Foundation for Conflict Zone Education. It has been shown time and time again, across the world, over centuries, that one of the best ways of bringing long-term stability to a region is through education, but that can be easier said than done. Forget dodging gangs and bullets to get to school; try dodging RPGs. This is why the Mimir Foundation has made it its mission to build safe, secure, and integrated schools in some of the most dangerous corners of the globe. A child who receives a good education, along with at least one filling meal a day, is far less likely to fall into cycles of violence and extremism, which is something we can all appreciate. It will take time, but within a few generations we may be able to get on a plane without the overly friendly government pat-down." That got a polite chuckle from the crowd. "And I'd like to add that it doesn't cost much to do a lot of good. Today's champagne bill could feed hundreds of children for months. So ask yourself what the safety of future generations is worth, and if that new set of clubs you've been eyeing is *really* going to help your game, then dig deep into your pockets and do something to help bring a little peace and prosperity to the world. And remember, it's all tax deductible."

There was some polite applause, and Gabe slid back into the crowd, making a little light conversation and patting shoulders as he went. He finally got back to James.

"You didn't tell me this was *your* charity." James kept his voice low.

"Didn't I?" Gabe had an innocent look on his face that James didn't buy for one second.

"No. No, I think I would have remembered that."

"Would you have come if I had told you?"

James couldn't honestly say yes. The party was well out of his comfort zone. Being the host's date was not something he had planned for and, in truth, had not been the most comfortable experience of his life. Though the food was good.

"I'm not sure."

"Well, then I'm glad I didn't. Let me shake a few more hands, then I can mumble something about an international call, and we can get out of here."

"You'd ditch your own charity event?" James was wondering if he'd completely misjudged Gabe's character.

"I've done what I need to do already. They'll cough up more money if I'm not here making them angry with my existence, and the guy who introduced me could have gotten fifty bucks off Ebenezer Scrooge. He's a charity savant. I poached him off the Boy Scouts."

"Why do I think there's a dirty joke in there somewhere?"

"Because there probably is. Give me fifteen minutes, and we can find some real food that isn't served on a stick."

THE BROWNED CHEESE on top of his French onion soup gave a satisfying little crunch as Gabe broke through it. As soon as James had accepted his invitation, Gabe made reservations at a little place up the road from the country club. It was small and semiexclusive, but it was into the whole regional, seasonal, don't-fiddle-with-it-if-it-already-tastes-good ethos. He did have a brief panicky thought while entering the restaurant that James might be a vegetarian. He hadn't really taken note of what James had been eating off the trays, but James ordered the warm chicken salad.

Gabe pretended not to notice it was the cheapest item on the menu. James looked up into the antique redwood rafters of the converted barn. "This used to be part of a winery." Gabe was desperate to avoid any awkward silences. James already seemed off after finding out it was Gabe's charity. "Some idiot tried to put in vineyards here a hundred years ago, but he put in the wrong kinds of grapes. The vines rotted from the fog."

"I take it you come here often?"

"Every few months, usually when I'm trying to hide from social functions with people I don't like."

"Do you do that a lot? Hide?"

Gabe tried not to react like he was being judged, that instead James was feeling him out. "It goes in phases. There are months when I can't afford to have a free second to myself. I'm on conference calls at 2:00 a.m. and have to schedule afternoon naps so I don't pass out. After months like that, I become a bit antisocial for a while."

"I guess there's something to be said for my job. If no one notices you, then you don't have to deal with people."

"I noticed you."

James focused on his soup, trying to force away a smile. "You did."

"So how about you, James Maron? Aside from acoustic music and keeping geniuses from looking like idiots, who are you? What's your life?"

"I...." James looked up into the rafters again. "I'm a parent. Dylan is pretty much my life. Making sure he grows up into the best man he can be. Strong, healthy, happy, educated. Yeah."

"That's amazingly admirable." James gave a dismissive snort, and Gabe felt himself misstep again. "I'm serious. There are a lot of parents in far easier circumstances who don't put as much thought into the whole thing."

James stirred his soup. "Honestly, there wasn't much of a choice as far as I was concerned."

"How...? I'm sorry, I shouldn't pry." The question had been nagging him almost since that first cup of coffee with James. "I'm familiar with the whole single teen mother situation, but how do you end up a single teenaged father?"

James took a sip of his water. "I sued."

"You.... You sued?"

"I got caught kissing Benjamin Steven at the start of freshman year, which meant my life went right to hell. Or so I thought. A week later I got to go to my first high school party. Met a girl called Cindy Loo—I'm not making that up, her parents were weird. She was drunk, so was I, she swore she was on the pill. She didn't mention she'd only been on it for two days, not that I would have known any better."

"I see where that's going."

"Pretty standard. She told me she was having an abortion, and I was okay with that. Then she told me she wasn't, and I was... I was okay with that too. She said she had talked to her parents and they were going to raise the baby, and... she said I could be around if I wanted. And I was." James took a deep breath. "My folks were always big on personal responsibility, so I got books, and I went to appointments with her, and talked with her parents. Then when Cindy was about seven months in, I found out through a friend of a friend, who heard her talking with someone in the bathroom, that her parents had organized an out-of-state adoption. I wasn't even going to be told when she went into labor. So I did what any self-respecting, expectant, teenaged Californian father does."

"You sued."

"I sued. I found the sleaziest ambulance chaser of a lawyer willing to work pro bono. He got a cease and desist on the adoption, a prenatal restraining order so Cindy's parents couldn't be at the birth due to a risk of noncustodial kidnapping and child trafficking, and once everything shook out, Dylan came home with me. Never mind the fact that I wasn't old enough to drive and both my parents worked full-time and then some. The judge granted custody, but until I was eighteen, I had child services crawling all over me every three months."

"Really?" That surprised Gabe, but it shouldn't have. "When my sisters had their kids, child services never darkened our door."

James shrugged. "The squeaky wheel gets noticed. And I squeaked. And after everything, I wasn't going to risk losing him to some strangers."

Gabe's steak and James' chicken salad arrived before he could come up with a reply to express how impressed he was without sounding sarcastic or trite.

"What happens when he goes to college?"

James twisted the napkin around in his hands before letting out a long sigh. "That's what he keeps asking, and the answer is, I have no idea. Get a hobby, maybe? Besides, we haven't reached the finish line yet. He's not eighteen until June. That's still plenty of time for him to develop a drug problem, eating disorder, pyromaniac tendencies...."

Gabe laughed.

"Don't laugh. You don't have kids. Believe me, when you've

got a kid, you quickly realize there is no worry too outrageous to not spend a little time dwelling on it."

———————

JAMES SHIVERED in the late afternoon breeze. It was early in the season to be out in just a polo shirt, but he could handle the chill if it meant a little more time strolling along the grass. He was worried about what was supposed to happen next. He was sure there was some code of etiquette for getting invited to a country club, taken to a nice lunch, then invited back to the country club to take a walk in a secluded corner of it, but he was damned if he knew what it was.

They got to a small bridge that arched over an ornamental stream. Gabe stopped and leaned over the railing, looking into the water. There were a few golf balls sporting a thin layer of moss and tiny silver fish darting about.

"When I was just starting out, I knew this business manager, Gregory. He had jumped around a lot of the dot-coms. This was in the middle of the tech bubble, when venture capital —'stupid money'—was flowing. He was psychic or something. He told me that 90 percent of the Valley would be out of business by the millennium because it was being run by children with shiny new toys. He also told me I'd be okay as long as I started networking with the right people. Then he dragged me into this place kicking and screaming. I'm really not a country club kind of guy."

"You seem pretty comfortable."

Gabe chuckled. "You've never seen my golf game. Can't putt to save my soul." A wide oak leaf fluttered down from the canopy and into the stream, where it was whisked away. "That first year, when he would drag me here, I spent a lot of time hiding out, wandering around. Found this spot—I don't think most of the members even know they have this little corner."

There was a decent gust of cold air, and James couldn't control the chill that went through him.

"Oh, I'm sorry," Gabe said, noticing the sudden shiver.

"It's okay."

"We should go back up to the clubhouse, where it's warmer."

"I'm okay. Really. It's pretty here, relaxing."

"It is."

There was a flutter of wings, and James watched a little brown bird take to the sky. Gabe moved closer.

"James, would you mind horribly if I tried to kiss you now?"

"No." James' voice squeaked like a teenager's.

Gabe smiled and pressed their lips together. James gripped the railing of the bridge. He opened his lips to try to breathe. Gabe's tongue darted in, then he pulled back. James tried to look calm, but his heart was pounding hard enough that some part of him was worrying about a heart attack.

"Was that okay?"

"Yep." James' voice squeaked again, and he gave a little cough. He was amazed he could speak at all.

"Good." Gabe looped an arm around his waist. Gabe was a couple inches taller, and James had to tilt his head back a bit, but it still felt nice. He shivered again but not from the cold. There could have been a blizzard raging, and he wouldn't have felt anything but the warmth Gabe was putting out. He pried his fingers off the bridge and wrapped his arms around Gabe. He was trying to avoid coming across as desperate, but eight years was a long time to go between kisses.

Gabe laced his fingers into James' hair, then kissed him again, twisting his tongue around James', taking full control of the kiss. James felt his knees start to go, and he was sure he was very close to embarrassing himself. Gabe pulled away. James tried to catch his breath. He wasn't sure how he looked, but he felt like he'd just done a hundred-meter dash against the wind.

"I don't suppose you'd like to come back to my place for a cup of coffee?" Gabe asked, managing to sound a little uncertain.

"Yes." James' libido answered before his brain could kick in. "No." His brain contradicted. "I can't. Dylan has an early game tomorrow way up in Vallejo. I'm keeping all the team stats this year, and I haven't even gotten the ones from the last game into the system yet."

"That's okay." He saw the flash of disappointment on Gabe's face and wondered if he'd just lost himself a chance at another date. Gabe pressed his lips to James' jaw, just below his ear. "Rain check?"

The relief flooded through. "Oh God, yes."

Gabe chuckled, a warm sound James wanted to wrap himself in to keep out the cold. "If you need to get going, at least let me walk you back up to your car."

"I think you'll have to. I'd probably get lost trying to find my own way."

"Then I shall be your loyal guide."

They didn't move with any hurry, taking the time to kick at stray leaves. James didn't mind. The afternoon was the nicest he'd had in a long time, not totally by choice, but pleasure had always come second to responsibility.

They got up to the clubhouse. The valet brought around the car without being told which one. Gabe looked it over.

"It's called the Lemon Drop Wonder."

Gabe looked like he was flipping through possible comments. James had heard them all. "And it runs?"

"It rattles a bit between thirty and thirty-five, but that just makes getting on the freeway a little more exciting."

"Well, drive carefully." Gabe gave him a quick peck on the lips. "Give me a text when you get home?"

James rolled his eyes but felt an odd little thrill at Gabe's concern. "You're as bad as Dylan. I'll be fine. I'll talk to you later?"

"I look forward to it."

GABE WATCHED the Lemon Drop Wonder drive off. The left rear wheel wiggled, obviously out of alignment. He was tempted to hop in his own car and follow James all the way back to Albany.

Instead he stood there and licked at his lips. He wondered if he had gone too fast. He'd been able to feel James' heart pounding when he pulled their bodies together. He was pretty sure he was a decent kisser, but he wasn't sure if he was that good. Still, it had felt unbelievably nice.

It wasn't that his life was totally devoid of company. He had the occasional one-night stand, and up until a year earlier, he'd had at least one good friend with benefits, but there had never been a lot of kissing. Not the slow lingering kisses that started a relationship.

That he was even thinking the word "relationship" already was unexpected, but James was ticking the boxes. Intelligent, pleasant, decent looking, and there was the extra bonus of having probably more strength and integrity than the vast majority of people he associated with. He knew plenty of guys who sent out their child support payments with the water bill and paid more attention to the water.

He was sure there was not a single one who would have been willing to step up at age fourteen and toss away the rest of their childhood to be a father. He knew the fathers of his sisters' kids had had damn near nothing to do with their offspring.

He pulled out his phone, ignored the seventeen messages,

opened his calendar, and began desperately looking for a spot to put that rain check in.

———————

"DYLAN," James called as he let himself into the apartment. He'd hit traffic, and it was nearly seven. "Dylan," he called again while wandering into the kitchen. There was a note on the fridge.

STAYING with Stephen tonight (in case you need the place to yourself). Will come home early before leaving for the game. There's some leftover corned beef hash in the fridge.–Dylan
    P.S. Your phone isn't picking up again.

JAMES TOOK his phone from a pocket to find three missed calls, even though he hadn't heard it ring once. He skipped over the two from Dylan, partly because he didn't need to hear that much innuendo coming from his son. The next call was from Gabe.

"Hi there. It's me. I know you said you'd text when you got home, but it's getting kind of late, and I noticed your rear wheel was looking kinda wobbly. I just want to make sure you're not stuck by the side of the road somewhere. And since this is going right to voice mail, I'll take a guess that if you are stuck somewhere, it's someplace you don't have coverage so... um... I hope you make it home safe and, yeah. I'll talk to you later."

James quickly called back and gave half a chuckle when he got voice mail as well. "Hi. It's me, James. I'm home in one piece. Hit traffic. My phone's going through one of its antisocial phases where it just doesn't like to ring and hangs up on calls for me, so don't take it personally. I had a nice time too and... yeah, I guess I'll talk to you later."

James closed his eyes and listened to the quiet of the apartment. He usually used nights when Dylan was out to catch up on some reading, or cleaning, or watching some TV. The desire or even the idea of going out had vanished years earlier. Tonight, though, he knew where he'd rather be, and it was not the tiny apartment he'd called home since Dylan was five.

He'd only had part-time work that first year, and the rent chewed up most of every paycheck. Money had been so tight, he'd gotten Dylan on the free lunch program at his school, then sucked up his pride and applied for food stamps. Even with that, James had needed to stretch every cent as far as he could. He'd caught a glimpse of the lunch bill that afternoon, and it was easily a month of grocery money in those days. Six weeks if he could find some good deals.

He stepped into the bathroom and turned on the light, staring at his reflection in the mirror. He looked his age, and it was always a surprise. The moment Dylan was born, he'd looked up and caught a glimpse of himself in the mirror that was in the birthing room for some reason. He'd had a zit high on his nose and was still six months away from his last major growth spurt, so still had the last drops of baby fat on his cheeks. His mental image of himself had frozen in that moment. The lines starting to etch their way between his eyebrows and around the corners of his eyes looked like they belonged to someone else.

He didn't need anyone from the Psych Department to tell him that a large part of himself had frozen in that moment, that there were important developmental steps he'd missed and experiences he'd never had.

He put his fingers to his jaw, right where Gabe had pressed his lips. His toes had curled, and everything had felt so alive in that moment. He wondered if he should try calling Gabe again.

Dylan would probably tell him not to, that it would make him sound desperate, even if he was. A not-date and a date were sadly the closest thing to a relationship with a man he'd ever had. Gabe was nice, damn good-looking, and for some weird reason seemed to actually enjoy his company.

He put his hands to either side of the bathroom mirror and leaned close. "James Maron, do not fuck this up."

THE RICKETY WOOD stand shook under James and the other parents as they leapt to their feet. The ball Dylan had just hit dropped to earth in far right field. Dylan sprinted around to third, sending two of his teammates home ahead of him, wrapping up the game neatly.

James checked the stands for scouts. It had become a compulsive habit since Dylan started showing real talent. Between academics and baseball, Dylan had gotten an early offer from Stanford, but that was no reason not to keep an eye out for pro scouts. He knew, logically, Dylan wasn't playing at that level and possibly never would, but a father could dream.

As the rest of the spectators departed, James waited by the locker rooms with some of the other parents. He knew them all well, but he'd always had a slightly odd relationship with them, being only a handful of years older than some of their eldest children. He wasn't sure how much breath he'd wasted over the years, starting at Little League, explaining he was Dylan's father and not an older half brother or something.

While the other fathers chatted, he checked his phone for the fifth time in eight minutes, but that was only because it was still buggy and didn't always put through his calls.

Coach Frasier came out before any of the team, his broad shoulders and massive stride dwarfing every parent there. He'd coached Dylan's summer Little League back in the day and was the first to say that Dylan could use baseball to get someplace in life. He'd even been good enough to turn a blind eye to missed dues and secondhand shoes. James had a slightly strange relationship with Coach Frasier, seeing as how he hadn't been that many years out of high school himself when they'd first met. He always had a funny feeling that the coach saw them as some sort of double mentoring project.

"James, how's it going?" He delivered a bone-rattling slap to James' back. "Your boy did good today."

"I don't know. It looked like he was favoring his ankle a bit in the seventh."

"He'll be fine. And I got those stats you sent last night. They're always a help."

"No problem. Sorry I got them out a bit late."

"That's understandable." He gave James a bit of an elbow to the side. "I hear you had a date last night?"

From the corner of his eye, James could see the other parents listening in. "Dylan told you?"

"Boys do gossip. They're worse than girls at the end of the day. And Dylan's damn happy about it. He worries about you."

"No one should be worrying about me, especially him." It was a phrase he was sure he'd been repeating daily for months now.

"That's not going to happen. I remember when you turned twenty-five, he worried himself sick. Thought you were going to have some sort of early midlife crisis."

"What did he think I was going to do?"

"I don't know, but it got him all worked up."

It was getting James worked up. "Well, for the record, yes, I had a date, yes, it was nice. Am I having another one? I don't know. And he needs to not worry about me and keep focused on his game. If he gets sloppy and twists his ankle again, that's his scholarship gone."

"I know, James." Coach Frasier gave him a careful pat on the shoulder this time. "We're all keeping an eye on him. I've put more than a few years of work into him myself. I want to be able to put his baseball card up on the wall of my office and say 'I coached that boy.'"

"I just want to get him to eighteen alive and with minimal damage. Then I'll start worrying about his Major League career."

GABE LOOKED AT HIS PHONE, then at his papers, then back at his phone. He checked the time, picked up the receiver, then put it back down.

Tamyra brought in his morning coffee. He didn't grab for it; he was too busy staring at the phone and internally growling at it. He'd spent all of Sunday practically sitting on his hands to keep from calling James. That wasn't the way his dates went. If a guy was worth calling back, he'd get to it within a few days, if the guy didn't call first. He did not spend his weekend obsessing. That wasn't how it was supposed to work.

Tamyra put her hands on her hips. "Okay, what is it?"

"How long do I have to wait to call someone about another date without sounding desperate and needy?"

"You are desperate and needy."

"Thank you. Answer the question."

There was a quick knock, and the door opened. Frank and Nate let themselves in, wearing matching grins. Nate lifted his phone to read off it. "According to today's weekend gossip roundup, Most Eligible Bachelor, Gabriel Juarez, CFO of TechPrim Industries, came out over the weekend by arriving at his own charity event on the arm of a UCB academic named James Mazon."

Gabe grabbed the Tux stress penguin on his desk. It had taken him through acquisitions, million-dollar deals, and relationship meltdowns. He squeezed, hard. "First, his name is James Maron, he's with UCB Tech Support, and what the fuck do they mean, I came out? I came out when I was sixteen and my mom found my Playgirls. My cousins kicked my ass, and my mother still says the rosary twice a day for my soul. I haven't been *in* in years!"

Nate raised his arms. "Don't kill the messenger. At least this way you'll stop getting resumes with photo accompaniments."

Gabe squeezed Tux a few more times.

"Aside from it being your big coming out, how'd your date go?" Nate asked.

"He's trying to figure out how long he needs to wait to call him so he doesn't sound desperate and needy," Tamyra supplied.

"Dude, just call him" was Frank's instant advice.

"I don't want to scare him off."

Frank and Nate shared a surprised look, then perched on either end of his desk like lopsided bookends. Gabe glared at them, and they hopped off the desk. It was an antique Art Nouveau piece that clashed with every other piece of furniture in the organization. There were standing death threats toward the first person dumb enough to break it, his partners included. Frank and Nate slouched into the guest chairs instead.

"Is this serious?" Frank asked. "I mean, do you want it to be serious?"

Gabe knew a straight-out yes would bring too much baggage, but he could not answer with a no. "Would I be stressing over a phone call if I wasn't thinking about this seriously?"

Nate shrugged. "I don't know. There was that phase when you had a habit of falling in and out of love every other week."

"A phase that finished when I was twenty-four, and you know it."

"Just pick up the phone and call him" was Frank's advice.

Gabe looked at Nate. As much as he usually trusted Frank's opinion, the fact was he was on Wife Number Three. Nate, on the other hand, was married to the same girl who had force-fed him a worm in the first grade.

"Before we let you get back into a cycle of being lovesick, for the sake of the company, tell us about this guy. What's he like?"

Gabe mentally pulled up short. He'd been expecting Nate to tell him to pick up the phone as well. "He's…. He's nice?"

"I'm a nice guy, and you're not mooning over me."

"Damn straight I'm not. Um…." Gabe tried to think of how to describe James in a way that didn't make him sound dishwater dull. "He's… intelligent, but not in an annoying way, like you two. He's—I want to say innocent, but that's really not the right word. I'm not sure there is a right word. He's got integrity, and he's really cute when he blushes. He still blushes."

"Okay." Nate drew out the word. "I don't think I've ever heard you describe anyone as having integrity, ever."

"He's a single parent. Guess how old the kid is."

"Eight, nine?" Frank guessed.

"Seventeen. About to go to Stanford on scholarship. He had a son at fifteen. Fought to keep him. I don't think he's done much of anything for himself in, oh, about eighteen years and… I don't know. This job has probably made me cynical as all fuck, but I don't think he's working an angle on anyone. I mean, he actually seems like a good person and…."

"Call him." Frank, Nate, and Tamyra said in unison.

"So I should call him, then?"

Tamyra reached over, lifted the phone out of its charger, and placed it in his hand. "You're already sweet on this guy. Just call him."

JAMES LOOKED at the stack of envelopes sitting on the table, the spiral-bound notebook, and his checkbook. He took a deep breath and tried to focus on the task at hand. It wasn't easy. He'd just been asked on a second date for the first time in his life and had said yes. Dylan would be so proud. He took another breath and opened the first bill. He was sure most people didn't use spiral-bound notebooks to keep track of their budgets anymore, but his first budget had been written in the back of his English notebook, and it was what he was used to.

Savings, power, water, phone, cell phone, and rent all happened neatly and almost without thought. His last promotion, such as it was, from Grade 4 technician to Team Leader had made those things, if not comfortable, then at least less panic-inducing than they'd once been.

James picked up the bill he had saved for last. It bore the name of Dylan's physical therapist. This was where the math came in. The number was larger than was comfortable, but with luck, wouldn't break the bank as long as he shifted things around.

He'd just decided he could put off getting the Lemon Drop realigned for another month when Dylan came into the kitchen and looked over his shoulder.

"Dad, just take it out of savings."

"No!" It was the millionth time they'd had this argument. "Savings are called savings for a reason."

"And a *full* scholarship is called a full scholarship for a reason."

"And what happens if your ankle goes out again for good? That scholarship goes right out with it, and those savings are going to come in handy."

"Our combined net worth will not cover a semester at Stanford."

"That doesn't mean you're not going to college."

"It's one therapy bill."

"And if we can justify dipping in for one bill, then we can justify it for another and another, and the next thing you know, you're picking up a two-year diploma at a community college and begging for a minimum-wage entry-level job somewhere."

Dylan put his hands up. "Okay. But the Lemon Drop really does need a realignment."

"So did your ankle."

GABE RUBBED his eyes after he hung up on the last of his international lawyers stationed in Prague. The day had started far too early for a Friday, but he wanted to clear up anything that might possibly interrupt his Saturday night. He noticed a light blinking on his phone.

"Tamyra, who's on hold on three, and can I tell them to call back later?"

Tamyra came in and put a glass of water and two pills on his desk. "It's Roy Edsworth."

"Who?"

"Your cousin Felipe's lawyer."

Those were four words Gabe dreaded hearing. He looked at the pills and recognized the prescription migraine medication he hadn't used in a year. Gabe took the pills, drank the water, and picked up the phone.

"Mr. Edsworth. What can I do for you?"

"I'm calling with some good news. Felipe's parole hearing has been moved up to next Thursday."

"That's good news?"

"Well... yes. It means he has a chance of getting out next week."

"He beat a man into a coma over eight ounces of coke, and the only reason his parole hearing is next week instead of in a decade is because I hired you. And the only reason I hired you is because my mother begged me because 'Felipe is a good boy, he's just misunderstood.' So I'll ask you again, how is this good news?"

There was some uncomfortable throat clearing. "Um.... Your cousin has a better chance of getting parole if his family is present."

"Then call his family."

"He is your cousin."

"He broke my jaw when I was sixteen."

"I do believe he is a changed man. From what I understand, he's found Jesus."

Gabe pressed his thumb to the corner of his eye as a spike of pain shot from there to the back of his skull and down his neck. "Of course he's found Jesus!" Gabe shouted. "We're fucking Catholics! I was at his fucking confirmation." There was silence at the other end of the line. "Look, I'm sure my mother and Auntie Loreen and all my other cousins will show up and sob and wring their hands. But frankly, even if I did give a tiny rat's ass about my cousin, which I don't, next Thursday I'm going to be in Prague, attempting to make a deal that might actually lead to some high-tech manufacturing jobs here in America. American jobs are good things, aren't they?"

"Yes, yes, of course. I won't take any more of your time, Mr. Juarez."

"Thank you." Gabe hung up before another word could be said. Tamyra came back in with another cup of water.

"I just cleared a half hour in your schedule. I also blew off the *Advocate* again, but PR wants you to do an interview."

"No."

"That's what I told them. Lie down on the couch while those drugs kick in."

Gabe still had his thumb in the corner of his eye. "Tam, how long have you been my PA?"

"Damn near a decade."

He cracked open his eyes and looked up at her. "You do know if I was a woman, I'd marry you?"

"What the hell makes you think I'd even have you? You'd probably have a flat chest and no ass."

Gabe managed a grin. "Put 'Buy Tamyra something really nice' on my to-do list."

"I'll put it right at the top."

6

The late-season rain was coming down in fast, heavy drops, creating a dull hum that filled the inside of Gabe's car. It was the kind of rain that was rare in California any time of year, though always desperately needed. Gabe checked his teeth in the rearview mirror, then closed his eyes for a moment, trying to push away thoughts of work.

It was still early in the evening, and he and James had made plans to go out. Nothing fancy this time, no concerts or country clubs, just a nice quiet dinner. He had been hoping to beat the weather so they weren't out and about in the wet. He finally took a deep breath and dashed through the rain to the security gate. The wind managed to whip its way under his umbrella and land a particularly large drop on the back of his neck, right where it could roll down under his shirt. He hissed and punched in the code James had given to him, since the intercom at the gate wasn't working.

Once inside he found the elevator also out of order. As he climbed the stairs to the fourth floor, he noted the building didn't look that bad. The industrial carpet in the halls was threadbare, but it didn't look as if anyone had died on it. There was a bit of peeling paint but no graffiti. It had the feeling of a place for people who were reaching for something better but couldn't quite manage it.

He knocked on a door that looked like it could be broken down with no more effort than a firm kick.

James opened it, a smile on his face. "Hey there, come on in."

Gabe gave James a peck on the cheek before stepping into the small apartment. He took it all in with a glance. It was spartan and lived-in, but also tidy with warmth to it. A set of shelves against one wall, made of bricks and boards, was filled with baseball trophies. Various school awards were taped to the wall around it. There were family photos, plenty of books that all looked third- or fourth-hand, a sofa draped with a knitted blanket about the same color as the Lemon Drop Wonder, and a TV that looked like it still needed rabbit ears.

James took Gabe's umbrella and leaned it by the door. "I wasn't sure if you'd make it. I thought I saw a rowboat going down the street earlier."

"It's a little wild out there. I saw three accidents on my way up."

"Second it rains everyone forgets how to drive. I told Dylan if he wanted to take the car tonight, he had to stay off the freeways."

Gabe didn't comment that James' car didn't look like it should be on the road in any weather. "I was thinking, I know this little Italian place. Really quiet, laid-back, great tiramisu, if you're still up for going out?"

James grinned despite the rain crashing against the windows. "Absolutely. Let me get my coat."

As they sprinted to the car, Gabe did his best to keep his umbrella between James and the driving rain, since James' coat was little more than a windbreaker. Once in the car, James ran his hand through his damp hair, causing it to shimmer in the streetlight and stick out at weird angles. The urge to skip dinner and jump right to making out in the car was a strong one. He wanted to get his fingers into James' hair and mess it up even more.

"Where's this place?"

Gabe dragged his focus back to the date part of the date. "Berkeley, right off Bancroft."

THE WINDOWS of La Barillette were lit with a warm glow, and the heavy smell of tomatoes and spices permeated the wet night. There were a few other couples scattered among the fake Roman vases and Italian travel posters, but mostly it seemed quiet as they were shown to their table.

"Don't let the décor fool you, most of the menu is pretty traditional."

James took a deep breath. "Smells good already."

Gabe flipped through the menu, trying to decide if he should have the risotto again or be more adventurous. He was about to ask James what he was considering when the doors banged open and people streamed in out of the rain. It looked like a family, possibly two or three, and at least fifteen people all talking at the top of their lungs, drowning out the *Il Divo* playing over the speakers.

Gabe watched with a sinking feeling as the waitstaff quickly shoved a bunch of tables together and brought out bottles of wine that were ordered before the families even got seated.

Gabe leaned over the table. "I'm sorry." He had to raise his voice a bit. "This is usually a really quiet place."

"It's okay. I don't mind."

A woman's particularly shrill laugh cut through the restaurant, followed by the whine of a small child. Gabe saw a little twitch at the corner of James' eyes. There was a flash of light and a clap of thunder overhead that caused the whole place to jump, then the family started talking even louder.

"You know this place does meals to go?" Gabe all but shouted. "I'm really so sorry."

James chuckled and lowered his head. "It's okay. Really not your fault." There was the sound of a glass breaking. "Do they do the tiramisu to go?"

"I'm sure of it."

———

THE FOOD WAS STILL warm when they unwrapped it at James' small kitchen table.

Gabe managed to keep most of the conversation off himself, because he knew he had little to talk about outside his job. James, fortunately, seemed to have no interest in reality TV but did have great stories of people with genius-level IQs forgetting which office was theirs, hitting "reply all" and sending bitchy responses to the entire university, and one divorce that resulted in the husband having to move his research lab to the other side of campus.

They took their dessert to the couch. The tiramisu was rich and ever-so-mildly alcoholic. A bit of cream was at the corner of James' mouth. Gabe reached out with his thumb to wipe it away. James quickly reached for a napkin, but Gabe stopped that with a kiss.

James squeaked, and Gabe felt him tremble a little. He pulled away.

"I'm sorry. Are you okay? I mean—"

"I'm fine." James cut in. "You just startled me."

"It's startling that I want to kiss you?"

"A little, yeah."

Gabe started to wonder how long a dry spell James was on, he looked so shy and nervous. He mentally reworked his plans for a bit of hot and heavy action to something a little slower. Not that he had any problem with slow. It all got them to the same place in the end.

He stroked James' cheek. "Would you mind if I try to kiss you again?"

"No."

Gabe brushed his lips across James'. James started to kiss back, but Gabe pulled away to ghost his lips across James' jaw and then down his neck. James rolled his head back and moaned softly. He pressed his lips against James' pulse and felt the blood racing under his skin.

He wrapped his arms gently around James' slim frame, which was trembling, and nuzzled his throat. "It's okay," he whispered. "It's okay." He kissed James' throat.

James clenched Gabe's arms tight enough to bruise. He gave a tiny whimper that sounded as if he were in pain.

Gabe was sure the last time he'd had a partner react like that, it was his second college boyfriend who'd been—

Gabe's brain skidded to a halt. He carefully removed his lips from James' throat. He unwrapped his arms, but held James' hands in his.

"James?"

"Yes?" James' pupils were already blown wide open, his face was flushed, and he was nearly gasping for breath.

"I swear the answer to this question won't change anything at all but... um... I mean... and it's fine really... um... are you... I mean, have you done this... it before?"

James' face burned bright red in barely a second, and he whipped his hands away. "I have a child, you know."

"I don't mean in that way."

James squeezed his eyes shut, sucking in hard breaths through his teeth. "I've been a little busy," he hissed. "I've had other priorities. Responsibilities. More pressing concerns than—"

"It's okay, it's okay," Gabe said, quickly gathering up James' hands and putting his lips to a burning cheek. "It's okay. I just... I don't want to scare you by moving too fast. Or hurt you or something." James pried his eyes open. "I'm starting too really kinda like you, and I don't want to screw this up."

James pulled back again, curling in on himself. "I'm sorry. I should have said something...."

"No. No. It's fine. It's actually been a really long time since I've been with someone and not hopped into bed on the second date. And it's also been a really long time since I've made it much past a third date. And frankly anything past a fourth date counts as a relationship these days. So... yeah." Gabe felt shame, the confession burning his own cheeks.

James turned his still flushed face from Gabe. "I haven't had a relationship in... ever. There was one kiss at fourteen, then Cindy Loo, then this other father at a father/son weekend camping thing, but he was still married and there's only so far you can get surrounded by nine-year-olds. I get set up on dates a few times a year, but say the words 'single parent' and watch the guy head for the hills and not call back."

Gabe's heart broke. James was, as far as he could tell, a not-bad-looking, intelligent, sweet, stand-up guy. Even in the reasonably large Bay Area dating pool, guys like that were rare. And no one should spend their life that alone.

He stroked his thumb along the back of James' neck. "Come here." James leaned in, and Gabe kissed him again. He kept his kisses soft and careful, letting James be the one to deepen them. It didn't take long before James began to dart his tongue out, flicking it along the edges of Gabe's teeth. Gabe held him tight; he was warm but had stopped trembling.

Gabe leaned back, stretching out on the sofa, guiding James until he was stretched out on top of him.

"Am I too heavy?"

"Not at all." He drew James in for a kiss, and James kissed

back, hot and deep. He slid a hand under James' shirt and rested it on his lower back. James wriggled at the touch, and Gabe raised his hips in response.

James let a deep moan slip into the kiss, and soon they were in a gentle rhythm, rolling against each other. Gabe started to lose himself in the peace of it all. It had been years since he'd just made out or even had a decent date that didn't turn into a frantic rush to the bedroom. Not that he wasn't planning on making it to the bedroom eventually. The part of his mind usually thinking about fifty-year market trends and political stability in emerging economies was being reprioritized. It was thinking about a candlelit dinner for two, massage oils, and high-thread-count sheets. It was debating champagne versus a good wine. It was thinking about all the wonderful things Gabe wished his own first time had been, instead of something done quickly and shamefully in a cold back bedroom while patrol cars slid slowly through the neighborhood.

He squeezed James a little tighter. Then he heard the front door open. James bolted to his feet, managing to knee Gabe in the groin in the process. Gabe curled in on himself and rolled to the floor, choking back some very unmanly noises. Someone shouted "Dad!" and there was a high female shriek.

Gabe managed to get to his feet in time for the extreme awkwardness to kick in.

Standing in front of the open door was a young man. Tall, built, blond, and blue-eyed, but Gabe spotted a bit of James around the eyes and nose. Next to him was a young, buxom blonde young woman, trying to straighten her clothing, her cheeks bright red. Gabe had a feeling his were a similar color.

"What are you doing here?" Dylan was the first to ask. "You were going out!"

"We got dinner to go instead. What are you doing here? I thought you were out at some club."

"The band sucked and we... I mean, I...." Dylan was quickly

wilting under a very impressive parental glare. James' eyes flicked to the girl. "Oh yeah, this is Gemma. Gemma, my dad."

"Hi, Mr. Maron." Gemma held out her hand for the world's quickest handshake.

"And this is Gabe, I guess?" Dylan's tone didn't sound unfriendly, but it was a blatant attempt at a subject change.

"Um... yes. Gabe, my son, Dylan."

"Hi." Gabe held out his hand for an even quicker shake. There was silence.

Dylan broke it. "You know, Dad, warm-up acts always suck. I'm sure the good band is up by now. We can just—" He gestured randomly in the direction of the door.

"No," Gemma piped up, her cheeks still burning. "Um... It's getting late, and I really have a test I need to study for."

"Yeah... I've got a test... uh, conference call I've got to get ready for." As much as Gabe wanted to pick up where they'd left off, the mood had been officially killed, buried, and the earth over it salted. He gave James a quick peck on the cheek to prove he had some balls. "I'll call you tomorrow?"

"Sure." James was still glaring at Dylan.

"Yeah." Gemma sidled toward the door as well. "I'll see you in class."

"Okay." Dylan only managed to give his girlfriend's hand a quick squeeze before she bolted, with Gabe right behind. The door closed, and Gabe leaned against the hallway wall. He looked at Gemma, who was doing the same.

"Was that the singularly most embarrassing moment of your life?" she asked.

"No, but it makes the top five. Of course I'm older."

"Crap," she suddenly said.

"What?"

"Dylan was my ride."

"I can give you a lift."

She looked him over. "Normally I don't take rides from

strange men, but I'm going to take a guess that you don't have any real desire to get in my pants?"

"Not really, no."

JAMES STARED AT HIS SON, the embarrassment choking any voice from him. Dylan's phone bleeped, and he quickly checked it. "Gemma's grabbing a ride with your boyfriend." That was the point when James remembered he was the adult and parent in this situation.

"So you thought I was out and decided to sneak a girl into the apartment despite my very reasonable and understandable rules on the issue?"

Dylan's shoulders hunched. "I...." James put his hands on his hips. "I mean...." James glared. The embarrassment had shifted to anger mixed with disappointment. "I'm really grounded, aren't I?"

"Oh yes."

"How bad are we talking?"

"Here, school, practice. One month."

"A month! But—"

James gave a sharp wave of his hand. He was not going to put up with any argument on this one. He gave Dylan a lot of freedom, but there were some hard, permanent lines that were not to be crossed, and this was one of them.

"Stay on my good side, and we'll talk about early parole."

Dylan shut his mouth and lowered his head. "I'm sorry," he said quietly. "It was really stupid of me, and I totally get why you have the rules you do."

"Good. Now look me in the eye and tell me you're still a virgin. Feel free to lie."

"Yes, Dad. Virgin. Absolutely saving myself for my wedding day."

"Don't push it. And you better be using protection, and the pill doesn't count."

"Yes, Dad, I use—"

"Nope!" James cut in quickly. "Don't need details."

"Okay, no details."

"Good."

There was silence again, and they could hear the rain still banging against the kitchen window. "So, Dad, speaking of no details, next time put a rubber band on the doorknob or something. I mean, I am all for you having some grown-up alone time."

James felt the embarrassment from earlier creep back. "I assure you any other grown-up alone time that may or may not happen will not be any of your concern."

"May or may not? Come on, Dad, that guy totally falls under the tall, dark, and handsome category, and if that ride out front is his, he's totally loaded."

"Yes, he may be those things, but I am not, and he…." James ran out of argument. He was still more than a little confused by the whole turn of events. He, James Maron, single father of the twenty-first century, technology-sector servant class, did not attract rich, handsome executives. The more he thought about it, the more the unpleasant but understandable idea that Gabe was simply slumming crept into his mind, and if the whole teenaged-son-in-the-abstract situation hadn't chased him off, coming face-to-face with the issue certainly would.

"Dad." Dylan rested his hands on James' shoulders. "You are, like, the nicest guy on the planet. If that guy isn't into you, then he's a moron. And frankly he looked pretty into you."

"We'll see how long that lasts."

"Dad, you know why I want you to get a boyfriend?"

"So I don't turn into a crazy old lady with lots of cats?"

"Yes, but it's mainly because you've earned someone. You have landed father of the year eighteen years running—it's time to do something for yourself. Time to catch up on all those things you missed, and don't give me that 'you regret nothing' line. Just because you don't regret missing something doesn't mean you didn't miss it."

James didn't quite know what to say. It was true. No matter how hard it was, he had no regrets about keeping Dylan, but that didn't mean there hadn't been some damn lonely days he had forced himself to ignore.

James sighed, suddenly feeling tired, and gave Dylan a pat on the arm. "I'll see what I can manage."

7

James was typing on autopilot, dwelling on his interrupted date and trying to focus on the better parts, when a sensation that he was being stared at began to creep over him.

"Hey, boss, can I ask you something?"

He curled his back as if making himself smaller would somehow make Dave, and whatever his almost certainly stupid question was, disappear.

"Boss?"

James turned to face Dave. It was never a pleasant thing. He knew he sounded like a cranky old man, but whenever he looked at Dave, all he could see was a man-child with no future or skills that didn't involve riding other people's hard work.

"Yes?"

"So, um, you've got a kid, right?"

"Yes, I do." James wondered if he was about to be hit up for Ritalin or something.

"Are they hard?"

"Are what hard? Kids?"

"Yeah, are kids hard?"

A rock of dread and depression sank into his stomach.

"They're exhausting. Why do you ask?"

Dave pulled over a chair. "It's just, my girlfriend's pregnant."

"Are you sure it's yours?" He couldn't picture anyone wanting to sleep with Dave. The chronic Cheetos stains should have been reasonably effective birth control.

Dave looked thoughtful. "Yeah, I'm pretty sure it's mine."

"Okay, what are you going to do?"

"I don't know, man. That's why I'm asking you."

James looked over this prospective father. When he'd been Dave's age, Dylan was already ten. He'd been five years out of his parents' house and in the workforce. He'd faced down lawyers, social workers, judgmental teachers, PTA mothers, and survived potty training, temper tantrums, teething, and that hellish seven-year-old testosterone boost no one had warned him about. He looked Dave over again. He felt a little twitch in the corner of his eye.

"First things first," he said, working to keep his voice calm and soothing. "Is your girlfriend planning on going through with the pregnancy?"

"She hasn't decided yet."

"If the answer is no, then what you are going to do is be there for her. You go to the appointments, hold her hand, tell her it's okay, because it takes two to tango and you are number two."

Dave started looking green. "And if she decides to keep it? I think she will. I mean, it seems like she's leaning that way, but I'm not sure I'm ready to do the whole dad thing yet, you know?"

James didn't even try to stop himself. He whacked Dave on the side of the head. The sound reverberated through the room. Everyone looked up from their stations. In seventeen years, he'd never laid a hand on Dylan and he never would, but as far as he was concerned, physically knocking a bit of sense into Dave counted as a social good.

"I had my son at *fifteen*! You're what, twenty-five? If a life is coming into this world containing your DNA, then what you do is grow the fuck up! You move out of your parents' place. You start working at this job so you don't get fired, because you have offspring to support. You accept the fact that for the next three years, you will not sleep. You will become completely immune to piss, shit, drool, snot, and vomit because infants produce all of those things pretty much nonstop the first two years, and in there is also teething, and if you're really unlucky, colic, croup, and ear infections. And just when you're managing to handle all that, they learn to talk and become smart-alecky little shits, and it is your job to love them unconditionally and turn them into good, kind, moral, caring, contributing members of society."

Dave's normal pallor had shifted to chalky blue. The room had gone silent. James became aware of the rest of the staff staring at them.

"What if I can't do it?" Dave's voice cracked.

James leaned forward. "Failure is not an option."

"But—"

"No." James got up and grabbed a blank notebook and pen from the stationery shelf. He thrust them into Dave's hands, looming over him the best he could. "Put the date at the top of the first page and write what I say." Dave scribbled the date and looked up. "On this date, I, Dave Melinick, did accept the fact that I will become a parent. That a life will be brought into this world containing my genetic material, and I will be responsible for it. I understand I will do whatever must be done to secure the health and well-being of my child, no matter the cost to myself, and I will have no regrets."

Dave looked down at the words and back up to James. His eyes were filled with terror.

"Sign it."

"What?"

"Sign your name below those words. Use the rest of the notebook to document everything that's about to happen, but the first thing you do every day is you read those words and look at your signature below them."

Dave swallowed a few times, then signed his name.

"Can I get some advice as I go along?"

James clenched his teeth and forced his lips into a smile. "It would be my pleasure."

EXHAUSTION AND GABE WERE OLD, if unwilling, friends. He'd given James a quick call on Sunday, but he was a few days out from a big acquisition trip to Prague, and that meant everything was go.

He had a small army of lawyers, accountants, and sales people backing him up, but he'd had his hand on every major TechPrim deal since day one, and the idea of not being face-to-face with a major client or future partner made his palms itch. He'd been told the CFOs of other companies spent their time trying to balance the company budget and justify executive bonuses, but other companies had their backs against the wall and congress breathing down their necks, whereas TechPrim didn't. Fairly simple logic told him he must be doing something right.

He looked out the car window at gridlocked San Francisco traffic. He checked his schedule on his phone. There was a free space, but Tamyra had a habit of scheduling for traffic. He looked at the cars going the other direction onto the Bay Bridge. It was flowing smoothly in the direction of Berkeley. A bit of stress melted away. Gabe dialed a number he'd quickly committed to memory.

"Hello. James Maron." James sounded reasonably perky.

"Hey, it's me. Sorry I haven't called. I got kinda bogged

down in work."

"That's okay. It happens." He sounded a little too understanding, leaving Gabe to wonder at the truth of it.

"I was wondering when you're planning to take lunch today?" Tamyra looked over at him, her lips a little pinched.

"I was going to take a break in about ten minutes."

"Could you hold off on that for about half an hour and let me take you somewhere?"

"Sure. I mean, are you in the area?"

A little more stress vanished. "I will be."

"See you soon, then."

James hung up.

"Jared. Spin us around."

"You know you have six more meetings today?" Tamyra reminded him.

"Yes, and I'm leaving for Prague tomorrow night, and I want to see James before I go."

Tamyra was still scowling, but he spotted the twitch at the corner of her lips and decided he wasn't in that much trouble. She had certainly been approving of James so far.

———

THERE WAS a bit of musical chairs as Tamyra climbed into the front seat and James was pulled into the back. Gabe gave him a kiss before anything else and watched him blush. "James, this is my driver, Jared."

Jared waved from the front.

"Hi." James waved back, looking awkward. "You have a driver?" he asked quietly.

"Only during work hours, so I can dial into conference calls on the freeway." He gave James another kiss. "Lunch?"

"Sure, where?"

"I know a place."

GABE HAD CALLED AHEAD to a place off University Ave. that was used to doing the half-hour power lunch. It would be the first time he'd ever gone without it being some sort of business meeting.

They were quickly shown to a table, the maître d' scanning James' worn jeans and generic shoes, but Gabe was in a business where CEOs went about in bare feet, so no comment was made.

"Do you have time for this?" James asked, looking over the menu.

"These guys are pros. They could do up a Thanksgiving turkey in ten minutes if they needed to."

"That would be impressive to see, but I think I'll just go with the pasta."

A waiter was over in minutes to take their order, then bustled off to another table. "So, sorry I haven't called. I'm flying to Prague tomorrow night, and it's been a mad scramble to get everything sorted out."

"It's okay. Work happens."

Gabe looked closely at James. In the past when Gabe had told a boyfriend he didn't call because of work, the "it's okay" was a blatant and obvious lie. Looking at James, he could see no lie.

"Anything interesting going on in the wild world of academia?"

James gave an epic eye roll. "Dave, Mr. Can't Take a Phone Message?"

"Yeah?"

"Knocked up his girlfriend. Came sniffling to me for advice because he wasn't sure if he was ready to be a parent."

Gabe barked out a laugh. "I've got to ask, what did you do?"

"Oh, just completely flipped out at him. I whacked him on

the side of the head, and told him to grow the fuck up and get his act together. As a result he spent all morning asking me the most inane questions about pregnancy. Seriously, all stuff he could have gotten off the net in about two seconds."

"I'm sure he's looking to you as some sort of role model or father figure." Gabe was trying to hold back more laughter.

"God help me."

"Speaking of, how much trouble is Dylan in?"

"Lots and lots. I know he's snuck in girls in the past, but I've never managed to catch him. I mean, he's basically a good kid, but he is, I am sad to say, a bit of a player, and it is far too easy for me to picture him showing up with his Flavor of the Week and saying 'Dad, we have something to tell you.'"

"I can understand how that would be a reasonable worry." Dylan had certainly looked like he would never have trouble getting company, and even the smartest of teenagers could be a bit dumb about certain things.

"I'm sure it would qualify as some sort of sick galactic karmic joke, but it also qualifies as a nightmare."

"You'd probably handle it better than your parents did."

"My parents looked at me and actually said 'But, honey, we were sure you were gay.'" The drinks arrived while Gabe was choking with laughter. "That was how I came out. I'm gay, and you're going to be grandparents. Surprise." James gave a camp flip of the wrist.

"Better than my coming out."

"Do tell."

Gabe seldom talked about how he'd come out, but conversation with James came so easily. "When I was sixteen, my mother found my Playgirls, and as eldest and only son in a big Mexican Catholic family, that just didn't work. She spent ten minutes screaming and crying in two different languages and still thinks I'm going to hell."

"I'm sorry."

"Could have been worse, I guess. They didn't throw me out. My cousins kicked my ass when word got around." Gabe lifted the glass of white wine he'd ordered and took a moment to look at the world through its light golden hue. "But I suppose there's something to be said for living exceedingly well as a form of petty, petty revenge."

THE JET WAS HUMMING and waiting to taxi when an e-mail from Frank popped up on Gabe's phone.

"GABRIEL JUAREZ, CFO of TechPrim Industries, was seen lunching with his partner, James Mazon, a UCB professor, at the exclusive Les Papilles dining room." :D —F&N

GABE HIT REPLY.

I HATE YOU ALL. —G

JAMES YANKED the phone out of his pocket, ready to hit the ignore button on whomever it was. He was running late to set up for an evening symposium, though he didn't see how it was his fault when someone else filled out the wrong paperwork and then submitted it at the absolute last second.

Gabe's name was on the little screen, and James' thumb hovered over ignore for only half a second before he answered it while still power walking across campus as quickly as possible.

"Hello?"

"Hey there." Gabe's words were bright, loud, and slurred.

James held the phone away from his ear. "Gabe?"

"Yep!"

"Are you still in Prague?"

"Yes, I am!"

"What time is it?"

"I don't know." There was the sound of a dull *thump*. "This clock says two."

"In the morning?"

"I don't know. It's dark out." Gabe's giggle was high and strained.

"Are you drunk?" James knew it was an obvious question. Gabe sounded absolutely wasted, but he wanted to hear Gabe's reply.

"No…. Maybe. I missed you. I wanted to hear your voice."

A warm feeling filled James at the idea that he was missed, but it didn't change the fact that he was running late. "That's very sweet, but I was supposed to be up the hill five minutes ago."

Gabe hummed. "I'd like to see you up." His voice was suddenly low and smooth.

James froze, nearly tripping over his feet. "Could you please repeat that?"

"I want to see you up, and hard, and naked." Gabe started to mumble on the last few words.

"Wow." James wasn't sure how to reply. His brain seemed to be attempting a forced shutdown. He fought it. "Okay. That's nice for the ego and all, but I have a funny feeling you are completely wasted."

"You don't want to be naked for me?" There was a sad little whine in Gabe's voice.

"Only if you're naked too." A student rushing past gave him a double take but kept moving.

"That would be nice. On a beach. I've never been naked on a beach."

"Neither have I."

"We could go swimming on the beach. No, you can't swim on a beach. There's all that sand."

James bit his lip, trying not to laugh. "We can go swimming in the water."

"You'd look cute wet."

"I'd probably look like a drowned rat, but I'll let your drunken imagination wallow in whatever fantasy it wants since I'm thinking you're not going to remember this in the morning."

"I have a nice soft bed. I could lay you out on it and...."

There was silence, then James heard soft snoring. "Gabe!" he snapped.

"I'm up," Gabe said, probably reflexively.

"Gabe, turn off your phone so you don't run up your long distance bill and go to sleep." James used his most polite tech support voice, hoping it would cut through the alcohol.

"I'm awake," he mumbled.

"No, you're not," James said very gently. "Now hang up your phone, try to get a drink of water, then crawl into bed. I'll talk with you when you get back."

"Next time I come to Prague, you have to come with me. Save me from the Prague people." Gabe giggled at something that was apparently funny in his own mind.

"Promise. Now hang up and go to sleep."

"Miss you," Gabe mumbled one more time, then hung up.

James looked at his phone for a long time while the little voices in his head argued. Gabe missed him. Gabe had also been drunk. Gabe wanted to have sex with him. Gabe had been shitfaced wasted.

James sighed and filed it all away for later; he was already running late.

8

The large soup bowl in James' hand was filled with a thick mix of beef, tomatoes, garlic, Italian spices, and about half a dozen different vegetables, drowning a few anemic strands of spaghetti, the necessary excuse for his mother to make her sauce. He passed the bowl to Dylan before grabbing his own.

It had been over a month since he'd gotten around to visiting his parents, despite them still living barely twenty minutes away. His mother had sent him an e-mail, informing him she was making spaghetti, knowing full well it was a culinary bribe to see her son and grandson. He took his seat at the far end of the fake-wood Formica-and-aluminum table his parents had gotten when they were married. His mother had always sworn that when they had the money, she'd get herself a proper wood dining room set, but something else always took priority.

Once everyone had their food in front of them, there was a moment of quiet. Not that any of the Marons were particularly religious; it was more a family punctuation mark separating predinner discussion from dinner conversation.

"How have you boys been?" his mother asked.

"Dad's got a boyfriend," Dylan blurted out.

"About time," James' father stated from the other end of the table.

James felt like he was fourteen again and about to die of embarrassment. "He's not…. We've…. We've just been out a couple times. That's it. We are still a long way from 'boyfriend.'"

"Anywhere close to boyfriend is a good thing."

"Mom," James whined. The embarrassment was not subsiding.

"Who is this not-yet boyfriend?" his father asked.

James knew there was no way he was getting out of this grilling. "He's just this guy I met."

"His name's Gabe. He's an executive with a tech company, he's a bit older than Dad, I think, he's hot, and he's got to have money."

"Dylan!" James snapped.

"Am I wrong on any of those points?"

"No, but—"

"Executive?" his father repeated.

"He took Dad to a charity garden party at a country club."

"Which is completely beside the point," James cut in. "He's a nice guy, we get on well, I don't know how far or how long it's going to go, but for now it's quite nice, and I'm going with the flow. Is everyone okay with that?"

His mother patted his hand. "It's just fine, dear. It's nice to know you're seeing someone. Your father and I still worry about you out there on your own."

GABE KNEW he was somewhere over a bunch of flat states, the sun was up, and his body couldn't figure out if it was supposed to be asleep, awake, or flat-out dead. Tamyra was asleep, and

Gabe figured he should follow suit, but his brain wouldn't settle down. According to his phone, he had called James around 2:00 a.m. Prague time. He had no real memory of this and was frantically hoping he hadn't said anything too stupid. He'd lost one relationship over a drunk dial, but he hadn't gotten a "fuck off and die" text from James yet, so he was hoping he was okay.

His thoughts settled on James and slid into the gutter. He wanted to scoop James up and drag him off to bed as soon as they landed, but that was out of the question because James was a goddamned virgin. That thought both excited and terrified him no end.

The idea that he could be James' first was an exciting one. Gabe had been around the block a couple of times and knew some interesting things he was sure James would like. But there was also the fear he could screw up, scare James, put him off sex. He didn't want James to think he was just looking for something physical or that it was some sort of requirement.

He sighed. There was no point in planning ahead until he found out how bad the drunk dial had been, so he closed his eyes and tried to catch some sleep.

———

JAMES WAS bored half to death, scraping some really nasty virus-infected porn out of the temp files of a university-issued laptop, when his phone rang. He didn't even bother to look at caller ID. He was glad for the distraction.

"Hello?"

"Hey, it's me. I just landed. Catch you at a bad time?"

James perked up. He'd been hoping for any distraction but hearing Gabe's apparently sober voice was a perfect one.

"No, it's a great time. Just deleting images of women doing weird things with asparagus from a university-issued laptop."

There was silence for a long moment. "Are you joking?"

"Wish I was. And if I wasn't gay before, I sure am now." James deleted another image. This one involved some sort of root vegetable.

"Okay. Um.... To completely change the subject, would you like to go out this Friday night?"

"Sure. Yes." James started up the virus scan for a third pass. He'd been hoping that Gabe might call within a few days of getting back from his trip; he certainly hadn't expected one the minute he landed. "Do you have anything in mind?" He hoped it wasn't anything too fancy. Despite Dylan badgering him on dating rules, he felt guilty every time he didn't pick up his half of the check. Never mind the fact that Gabe's picks were usually well out of James' budget.

"I was thinking I could come up there. Pick you up after work. We could make a second attempt at a dinner out, then maybe a movie, make out in the car?" Gabe's voice heated up.

James heated up too. "I can get behind all those ideas."

"Good. Friday it is."

"Friday."

As Gabe hung up, James wondered if he should have mentioned the drunk dial. It could very well be that Gabe didn't even remember doing it, let alone what he'd said. He decided he was going to let it slide. Embarrassing Gabe wouldn't serve any purpose, especially if it interfered with getting to the making-out part of a date.

GABE'S CAR purred as he weaved through street traffic. He understood the practicalities behind having a personal driver during work hours, but he still loved getting behind the wheel; always had. That didn't mean he had a huge garage with a hundred cars, though he could afford it. He had four: a six-year-old Prius in storage, a new Tesla for the commute, and when he was playing Uncle Gabe, an Audi R8 Frank had talked him into getting after a particularly difficult product launch, coupled with an equally difficult breakup. He kept meaning to sell it. And then he had his Mustang. Vintage 1968, she was a deep green and ran better than when she'd been new. He wasn't sure if James was a car guy. Possibly not, considering the Lemon Drop, but he'd yet to meet anyone who hadn't enjoyed the Mustang. On the open highway, it felt like driving sex.

He saw James standing on the sidewalk and quickly double-parked. "Hop in," he shouted through the passenger window. James looked startled and quickly got in.

"Hi." James looked around as if he wasn't quite sure where he was. "Nice car." Gabe pulled back into traffic, but he still took a second to turn and grin.

"Thanks. It's Friday evening, and I thought it would be as good a time as any to take the Mustang out for a drive." Gabe pulled onto the freeway going against rush-hour traffic and opened her up a little. If James was any other date, he would skip the dinner and movie and instead just take him for a fast drive, then move on to other potentially car-based activities.

"So. Dinner and a movie? Anything in particular you want to see?" James asked.

Gabe had plans for something a little cooler than a multiplex and put more pressure on the accelerator. "I've got some ideas. Trust me?"

James was pressed back in the seat but was also grinning. "Sure."

He had made reservations for two at a modern Mexican restaurant that specialized in dishes from the state of Veracruz. He had no recollection of exactly which of a million lunch and dinner meetings had introduced him to the place, but it was a favorite. Though he was pretty sure he'd never used it for a date.

They were shown to a romantic booth for two, with candlelight dancing on the table. James took a deep breath. "It smells good."

"You have to try the *arroz a la tumbada*."

"Okay." James picked up the menu. "What is it?"

"It's, um, it's Mexican paella."

James scanned rapidly down the menu. "You seem to know a lot of good restaurants."

"I don't think there's a restaurant in the Bay I haven't had at least one business meeting in."

"You should write a guidebook."

"Tempting." Gabe was sure he could do it. He could name three other really good restaurants and a half-dozen other nice places within a ten-minute walk of where they were.

The waiter came and took their order. Gabe was a little embarrassed that James had a better accent than he did as he read off the menu. He consoled himself by pointing out he was spending a lot of time with a Russian/English dictionary, whereas James…. Actually he wasn't sure where James might have learned Spanish, though he wouldn't be surprised if it was just around his neighborhood.

Before the conversation went any further, Gabe took a sip of his water and decided it was time to ask the big question. "I don't suppose I called you the other night? Say at about 2:00 a.m. Prague time?"

James looked into his glass, but Gabe could see him trying to suppress a smile. "A call may have occurred."

He closed his eyes and mentally braced himself for the coming humiliation. "Okay, what did I say?"

"You giggled a lot. Mumbled something about me saving you from the Prague people. Briefly talked about how you can't swim on sand, then passed out."

Gabe opened his eyes, the relief almost jarring. He figured it couldn't have been too bad if James had said yes to a date, but it could have been so much worse. "Oh thank God. I've completely screwed up relationships by drunk dialing from foreign countries. If all I did was giggle and babble, I think I'll live."

"So you drunk dial a lot?"

Oops, Gabe thought. *Way to make yourself sound like an alcoholic.*

"I try not to. I'm really not much of a drinker, but there are lots of places on Earth where major and minor deals are finalized with a ceremonial drink or fifty. I'm working on this deal in Russia right now. I want it to go through, but my liver is already dreading the final negotiations."

James nodded, but Gabe couldn't quite read his face. "That's why you were hungover at that first lecture."

"Very large deal, very large quantities of sake. And crying for mercy would only have dishonored myself, my family, my company, and my nation."

"I can count on one hand the number of times I've been truly drunk."

"I never drank to excess. I seldom drank at all until the first big international deal I was part of. It was in London, the paperwork got signed, and then it was all 'let's go to the pub, here have a whiskey, have a pint, have another whiskey,' and the eight hours after that are all a bit of a blur. I'm told I ate a curry, a deep-fried Mars Bar, hit on the Minister for Economic Development, then got sick in the Thames. But that's all hearsay."

James' expression finally broke, and he chuckled into his hand. "You're going to have a lot of fun in Russia."

"Tell me about it." Their drinks arrived with perfect timing. Gabe was slightly regretting not ordering water. He watched as James took a sip of his wine and seemed to enjoy it. "So... asparagus?"

James dropped his face into his hands. "People borrow

university computers, ignore policy on their use, or leave them laying around for other people to use, then forget to clean out the temp files."

"That's stupid."

"Yeah."

"And you can't just hit Select All, then Delete?"

"We don't go through all the computers by default, but if it's picked up a virus, or it's obviously been used for something outside the borrowing agreement, then we do."

"That is really disgusting."

"We get those disinfectant wipes for electronics in bulk."

Gabe couldn't help making a face. "You have my sympathies."

James waved. "Someone's got to do it."

Gabe decided he needed to shift the small talk quickly, as the spicy crab-stuffed chilies he'd ordered arrived.

"How's Dylan doing?"

"Still grounded, and needs to bring up his science grade. I'm not sure if he's not focusing in chemistry or if he's just not good at it."

"I was okay with it, but my Auntie Loreen made me help out in the kitchen, so I could fudge the practical results."

"I'm a terrible cook, and I know Dylan can't cook either." James took a bite of a chili. "I do wish I could cook these."

"Told you this place was good."

"You really need to write a book."

They chatted about memorable culinary mishaps, which somehow turned into Gabe telling stories of international travel disasters and half-remembered drunken humiliations. By the time the cinnamon-banana ice cream was set in front of them, James' face was flushed with laughter, and his smile was bright in the candlelight.

The phone in Gabe's pocket had buzzed three times, but he'd ignored it. He was on a date. He was on a date with someone who didn't make him want to stab himself with a fork. For a few hours, everything else could wait.

He did take a quick glance at his phone to check the time.

"Are we late for the movie?"

"Nope, and the theater is just around the corner."

Gabe paid the bill and led them outside, not to a Cineplex but to the grand art deco Paramount Theatre.

James looked up at the intricate gilding of the ninety-year-old building. "They still show movies here?"

"Classic films, in between the symphony, opera, and ballet. They're showing *Casablanca* tonight."

"I've never seen it on the big screen."

"Well, this is a really big screen."

An old friend had dragged him to see *Gone with the Wind* years earlier on the three-story-high screen. Their seats were in the balcony, and he took James' hand as the theater went dark. Gabe couldn't recall the last time he'd gone to a movie with a date, which said something sad about the time he put into most dates. It seemed like such a high school thing to do, but James was grinning as the opening credits bathed the theater in soft silver light. He had a feeling James hadn't seen many movies in high school that weren't produced by Disney.

It had been ages since Gabe had seen *Casablanca*, and he was soon caught up in how gorgeous it all was.

Only once did he break focus enough to lean over and whisper in James' ear. "You know Louie wants Rick for himself."

James snickered.

And after three thousand people whispered along to the last lines and the credits rolled, Gabe led them back out into the night.

"So, nice dinner and a nice movie." James grinned. "Now as far as I've been told, the next step in all this is making out in the car?"

"I know just the spot."

Gabe was thankful for the clear night as he weaved his way up into the hills and parked off a dirt access road under some electric pylons. In front of them was a panoramic view of San Francisco, lit up in her glory. He knew he was biased, but he did believe San Francisco was one of the prettier cityscapes you could get.

"When I was a teenager, I would park up here to make out. I never did appreciate the view at the time, but now I get why people pay a million dollars for homes in these hills."

"I have no idea where kids in my school might have gone to make out."

"Me neither. I never dated guys from my own high school. Too complicated."

"Yeah, Dylan's mother transferred just after he was born. I can't even begin to imagine how weird that would have been."

"Probably very."

Gabe trailed his fingers along James' arms. "There's no need to worry about things like that now, and I hate to say it, but you have some catching up to do on the making-out front."

"Well, then. We better not dawdle."

Gabe slid over as far as he could and kissed James. James tentatively returned the kiss but soon relaxed into it, twisting so he could kiss Gabe deeper. He skimmed his hands across James' body, then laced them in his hair. James moaned and his strokes along Gabe's body became bolder.

Gabe tried to pull James as close as possible, quietly cursing the little voices of his better graces that had talked him out of getting a hotel room to ravish James in. He guided one of James' hands south until it was warming Gabe's thigh, each touch getting closer to the important area.

There was a sudden tap on the window. Gabe jumped, knowing exactly what the sound of a flashlight on fogged-up glass sounded like and meant.

He very slowly rolled down the window in case it wasn't a cop. He shielded his eyes from the flashlight until he could see the uniform. "Evening, Officer."

The cop flashed his light around the inside of the Mustang. "Aren't you boys a little old to be making out in cars?"

"I have a teenager at home," James blurted out.

"And I live in San Jose."

"And you couldn't just get a hotel room?"

"We're taking it slow." The interruption had Gabe on the defensive. "And... this is a sort of traditional spot for certain activities. At least it was?"

The cop laughed. "Hate to break it to you, but most of what goes on here these days are small-change drug deals."

Gabe leaned his head on the steering wheel. "Thank you, Officer." Gabe looked at James, who was shaking with silent laughter.

"It's okay. I had a nice evening."

Gabe sighed. He should have gotten a hotel room. "Thank you, Officer. I believe we'll be calling it a night."

The cop looked like he was trying not to laugh as well. "Drive carefully."

9

James rolled another tamale to add to the growing pile in the middle of Mrs. Meza's kitchen table. Around him the room was filled with the gossip of the women of the Hill View Estates as they added their own tamales to the pile.

James had been in the building almost a year before the women invited him to the monthly tamale marathons with promises he could take a couple dozen home. It was another year before he tuned in to the flowing Spanish accented in a dozen different ways. It had been two years before his tamales met with consistent approval.

The low rumble of boiling water heated the apartment and firmed up the tamales. After so many years, it was a comforting way to spend a Saturday afternoon. It was a *little* strange to reflect that the night before he'd been making out with Gabe in a classic car after a fancy date, when now he was back rolling tamales with the women like it was any other weekend.

"The Estrada boy down on second is the father," Mrs. Maldonado stated with absolute certainty, the gossip of the day being an obvious, if unannounced, pregnancy. It was something James had a bit of sympathy for.

"Actually, he's not." Everyone turned to James. It wasn't often he got the jump on gossip, but Dylan had a line to the other teenagers in the building and had let him in on the identity of the father of Maria Perez's baby.

"Of course it is. Who else would it be?" There was a slight accusation in Mrs. Fernandez's voice. Dylan had developed an unfortunate reputation.

"Ahmed Hami on first. Dylan told me." James grinned as the women all started talking at once. He also had it on good authority—Dylan—the Estrada boy was gay, and Maria had somehow talked him into taking the blame once she started showing.

"But what kind of wedding would they have?" Mrs. Avila asked at full voice.

"Ahmed is fifteen, Maria is sixteen. I don't think any wedding is going to be happening."

That set off another flurry of debate. James knew there'd once been a time when the idea of sitting around a kitchen table, gossiping on a Sunday afternoon with a bunch of older women, would have filled him with a certain amount of embarrassment, but those years were long gone. Instead he'd spent the week itching for the right moment to share that one little piece of intel.

He knew Dylan would say this was why he needed to date and why he was on the road to crazy-old-cat-lady-dom, but these women were his friends, his support group, and really, some gossip was just way too good not to share.

GABE LEANED down and gave Margaret a kiss on the cheek and passed her a bottle of wine as she let him into the cozy, blond-wooded foyer of her and Nate's home. Unlike a lot of the '90s tech-bubble guys, neither he, nor Frank, nor Nate had gone *completely* overboard on their living situations. Not that Nate didn't have an exquisite custom-built home on a large plot of land, but it wasn't a gilded, fifty-room mansion.

The smell of a pork roast came from the kitchen and Gabe's stomach rumbled. "Your roasts always smell so good."

"Everything should be ready in about fifteen minutes. Nate's in the living room with the kids."

He followed the sounds of things getting hacked to pieces until he found his godchildren, Sarah and Harry, along with their father, plunked down in front of a large TV with game controllers in their hands.

He wasn't sure what the game was, but there were a lot of swords and blood splatter. "Hey, guys."

"Hey, Uncle Gabe," the kids answered in unison, not taking their eyes from the screen.

"Hey, Uncle Gabe," Nate parroted.

Gabe didn't say anything else, as the game seemed to be coming to some sort of climax. There was a sudden splatter of digital blood across the screen. Nate and Harry threw down their controllers as Sarah jumped up and began an inspired victory dance. Nate reached for the controller again.

"You don't have time for another round," Margaret called from nearly the other side of the house.

There were some groans. "Okay, you heard your mother. Go help in the kitchen." Nate shooed his kids from the room.

Gabe shook his head as they passed. "I swear to God, they keep getting taller."

"They are at that age. Fourteen, and they will not stop eating. Especially Harry."

"I guess we were all there once." Gabe had turned to follow the kids to the kitchen when Nate grabbed his arm.

"Actually—" Nate's voice was low. "—I was wondering if maybe you could talk to Harry at some point."

"About?"

Nate cringed as if in pain, a deep red flush crawling across his pasty complexion. "Well, you see, his mother found some, um, photographic material in his room the other day."

"You can say the word 'porn,' and I'm pretty sure giving that talk is your job."

"Yeah, I would. Except it wasn't quite the type of porn we were expecting, and I think he needs a slightly different flavor of talk." Nate's voice was still low, and he looked very close to "death by raw embarrassment."

"Oh." Gabe looked over his shoulder. "Really?" He'd never gotten any gay vibe off his godson, but then it wasn't like he'd been looking.

"I don't know, maybe he's just curious or thinking experimentally, but every time I even think about bringing it up, my brain stutters and I have no clue where to start. I'd get Margaret to do it, but we made a deal a long time ago: she'd give Sarah the talk, and I'd give Harry the talk."

Gabe was tempted to tell him to man up and go talk to his son, but his whole demeanor was one of pleading. "Look, I will tell him I'm here if he wants to talk about anything, but you're his father, and you'll have to talk to him at some point, and if he is heading in that direction, he's going to need to know you love him no matter what."

"Of course I do." That seemed to snap Nate out of the embarrassment.

"He's going to need to hear that at least once, and I will talk to him as long as I can ask you and Margaret for some advice later."

"About?"

"Just... later."

"Boys!" Margaret's voice rang across the house again. "Come eat."

GABE LEANED back in his chair, feeling overly full. He always did when Margaret decided to embrace the English half of her heritage by roasting large pieces of meat and root vegetables. There was little mystery as to why Nate never lost that last twenty pounds, but he never seemed too worried about it, especially when there was pork crackling on his plate.

"That was amazing, Margaret, as always."

"Thank you. I think the pork might have been a little dry, though."

Nate leaned over and gave his wife a kiss on the cheek. "It was perfect. I promise." Gabe smiled. He always liked the time he spent with Nate's family. He had good kids and a good marriage to a woman who could give him a hug and a kick in the ass simultaneously. "Okay, kids, help clear the table, then go finish your homework."

Gabe pitched in as well. He'd moved from guest to family about two days after Nate and Margaret moved in together. The kitchen still smelled like roast pork, and Gabe's stomach tried to talk him into picking a little more meat off the bone.

Margaret lightly smacked his hand. "That's for soup tomorrow." Gabe tried his puppy-dog face. "Okay, just a little."

He picked off a bit, pleased that after all these years that face still worked on Margaret. She was immune when it came from her husband and kids.

As the last dish was loaded into the washer, the twins were shooed upstairs to tackle homework.

Nate gestured with his head after them.

"Now?" Gabe said.

Nate put on his version of a puppy-dog face. "Please? I don't want this to drag out."

Gabe let out a long sigh. Unfortunately he *wasn't* completely immune to Nate's puppy face. "Fine. But you're going to have to talk to him at some point. Both of you."

"Thank you, Gabe."

Gabe made a random grumbling noise and marched up the stairs. He'd always thought one of the good things about not getting around to having kids was he got to avoid things like having uncomfortable talks with teenagers.

He knocked on Harry's door.

"Yeah?"

Gabe let himself in, then closed the door behind him.

"Hey, Uncle Gabe."

"Hey."

"What's up?"

Gabe opened his mouth, then realized he had no more ideas as to how to start the conversation than Nate had. "Okay, I'm going to be blunt, and maybe this will be quick and painless, but I somehow doubt it. Your mom found gay porn in your room, and your dad wants me to talk to you in case you need to talk."

Harry turned bright red. It was not a good color on him. "Oh. My. God." He buried his face in his hands. "Fuck, fuckfuckfuckfuck."

He gave Harry a minute to use every swear word he knew several times over. "So…?"

"Maybe. I don't know. Probably. I'm still figuring it out."

"That's fine. You're young. Plenty of time to work out what you want, what you're interested in."

"I guess." Harry slumped in his chair.

"Tell you what. I'll give you a quick version of the talk. That way you can save your dad some pain when it's his turn. Don't have unprotected sex. Don't have anonymous sex. Don't go to see anyone you meet on the Internet. Respect yourself. Respect your partner. Don't do drugs. And if someone ever hurts you, come talk to me, because I still have some cousins in the neighborhood who are only on their first strike and are proficient in those sacred ancient weapons, the switchblade and bike chain. And you can pass that last one on to your sister."

Harry gave a small laugh, looking a little less embarrassed. "I'll keep that in mind. Is Dad really going to try to talk to me?"

"Yes."

"That's going to be so embarrassing."

Gabe sat on the edge of Harry's bed, which was still draped in an *X-Men* blanket.

"Look, when you're the eldest and only son in a Mexican Catholic family, you don't get to be gay. It's not an option. When my mother found out, she threw a fit. Screamed at me, cried for three days, sent me to our priest. If embarrassment is your biggest worry, you're doing it the easy way. Your parents love you no matter what. My mother says a rosary twice a day for my soul."

Harry stared at him. Gabe didn't talk much about his family or childhood with Harry and Sarah. There didn't seem much point to it.

"What about your dad?" he asked quietly.

"My dad?" Gabe rubbed at his face. "My dad was... odd. My mother was standing there in my room, screaming at me, and he just stood there and looked at me for the longest time. And I was bracing myself. I'd convinced myself he was going to throw me out, yell, maybe even take a swing at me. Then my mother stopped for breath, and he touched my face and gave me a hug. He said *hijo mío*, my son. Then told me to make sure my homework was done before dinner."

"That was it?"

"That was it. We've never talked about it, but I figure maybe it's best to leave some things alone."

They both fell silent. Gabe did his best not to dwell on those times. He knew he should thank his father for not living down to expectation, for acting as a buffer between him and his mother all these years, but his father had never been much for talking.

Gabe slapped his thighs. "So…. Okay… I'm here if you need to talk. Don't do anything stupid. And… don't underestimate people. A lot of times they are what they are, but every once in a while, they can step up and really surprise you."

GABE FLOPPED onto the living room couch and stared at Margaret and Nate. They were on the love seat cuddled together. Gabe was envious. As the guys liked to point out, he wasn't getting any younger, and bed-hopping was a game for the young. Not that he was even doing much of that anymore. He tried to recall the last time he'd had someone he could cuddle with on a love seat without there being pressure for it to become something more by the end of the night. The memory he came across was old and sour, and he quickly shoved it away.

"First off, we are square for the Comic-Con incident. Okay? That debt is paid in full."

"Okay. What did Harry say?"

"That he's not sure yet but probably. I gave him the standard 'don't have unsafe sex and avoid Internet weirdos' speech. He'll be fine. And I told him he could call me whenever."

Margaret turned to her husband. "I told you." She turned back to Gabe. "Now, what did you want advice on?"

It was Gabe's turn to be uncomfortable. "Um…. You two…. You still have a good relationship, romantic, I mean?"

They looked at each other. "On the odd occasion when we can get rid of the children, my dear husband has been known to provide flowers."

"Flowers, right."

"Gabriel." Margaret drew out his name, giving it a hint of British trill. "Are you asking us for romantic advice?"

Gabe closed his eyes. He wasn't sure if he was blushing, but he could feel the overall embarrassment level creep up. He couldn't believe he was even asking, but he'd gone over his plans so many times, he couldn't tell if they were good anymore.

"Well, I'm not going to ask Frank."

"I'm guessing you haven't sealed the deal with this James guy yet?" Nate asked.

Now Gabe knew he was blushing. "Oh, shut up."

"Oh no, I'm amused. There's someone out there who hasn't fallen for your 'I'm a filthy rich, hot Latin lover, want to shag?' line."

"First off, I have never used that line. Secondly, shag? Hanging out with your in-laws again?"

"Nate, leave him be." Margaret peered at Gabe, giving him the type of scrutiny that only a mother could really manage. "Have you tried and failed, or just haven't tried?"

"I... I haven't tried. He's the best thing to come my way in a while, and he deserves better than my usual flaky 'Hey, want to shag?' lines."

Nate made a cutesy face. "That's so sweet."

"Okay, you know what—"

Gabe started to stand.

"Gabriel, sit down."

Gabe sat back down but perched on the edge of the sofa.

"I guess the first question is what is he used to so you can do something different?"

"Nothing. He's thirty-two, and he's never had an adult relationship because he's been too busy raising his son solo." He didn't mention that James was basically a virgin.

Margaret made the kind of face she usually reserved for puppies.

Nate grinned. "In that case, it doesn't matter what you do. He won't know the difference." That comment earned him a solid shove from his wife.

"Ignore my husband. If he hasn't had a relationship, he's probably nervous and unsure about the whole thing. You want to keep it romantic but relaxed. You don't need a live string quartet and a catered meal. You've got a perfectly nice place. Some candles, some flowers, something relaxing on the sound system. Cook him dinner, but you don't have to go overboard with it. Not too much alcohol. You don't want him to regret anything in the morning."

"I can't cook."

"You cook just fine, you just don't. Get some recipes off your sister. You want to show him who you are at home, what it is he might really be getting, but mostly keep it relaxed."

"Relaxed." Gabe took a deep breath. "I can do relaxed." He was pretty sure he could do relaxed. He had some vague memories of what relaxed was.

"You'll be fine. If nothing else you're a filthy rich, hot Latin lover. That should get you halfway right there."

JAMES WAS WEDGED under a desk trying to untangle about twenty different cables when his phone rang. He managed to fish it out of his pocket and shove it between his shoulder and ear without looking at the screen.

"Hello." He cringed at his own voice, which sounded more than a little cranky.

"Hey, it's me. Is this a bad time?"

Gabe's voice gave James a little happy flash, but it wasn't enough to overwhelm the pre-existing bad mood. "No. I'm just wedged under a desk, desperately wishing there was some universal standard of color coding for different kinds of cables.

I mean, why in the hell do they all have to be black, white, or gray? What's wrong with red, or green, or fuchsia?" James pulled on a cord and looked at the end of it. "And why in the hell does everything have to be USB now? Remember when a monitor plug looked like a monitor plug and a printer cable looked like a fucking printer cable?"

"Maybe I should call back later."

James sighed. "No, no. I'm sorry. It's just turning into a Monday. How's your day going?"

"From the sound of it, better than yours. Actually, I was wondering if you're doing anything Friday night?"

James pulled on another cable and heard something rattle on the desk above him. "Friday? Unless the server room catches on fire, I'm free."

"I was wondering if you'd like to come down to my place? I could make dinner."

James let go of the cables and tried to shift into a comfortable position. Gabe sounded a bit uncertain, and despite a distinct lack of experience, James could think of reasons other than dinner why Gabe might be inviting him over. That sent a knot of nerves twisting around his stomach.

"Sure, that sounds nice."

"Great." Gabe already sounded more relaxed. "Um... maybe eightish, or really whenever is good for you. Or Saturday if that would be easier? Or I could come up and get you?"

"I can get there. Friday is fine and eightish sounds good."

"I'll e-mail you my address, and let you get back to your cables."

"Thanks. I'll see you Friday."

"Okay. Bye."

James swallowed hard, suddenly very aroused at the thought of what Friday might bring, though he knew he shouldn't make assumptions. It could just be dinner.

"Hey, boss?"

James gritted his teeth as the sound of Dave's voice shot his arousal dead. "I'm down here."

Dave's head came into view. "Hey, um, people in the English Department are saying their mail has been bouncing for the last hour, and are you doing anything for lunch? 'Cause I've been reading, and I've got some questions."

James really wanted it to be Friday.

10

It had already been a painfully slow week when Tamyra dropped three large binders onto Gabe's desk, nearly sending him out of his skin with fright. He'd spent half the morning on the phone with his sister, trying to work out a dinner he wouldn't fail at, and his mind was still on salad options.

"Here."

"What am I looking at?"

"Your weekend reading. Mostly Russian property law. Also lists and backgrounds for issues that might come up in the next phase of the *Buduŝie tehnologii* negotiations."

"I've got plans for the weekend." Plans that would hopefully involve getting James into bed and have nothing to do with Russian property law.

"So do I. That's why I read it all already."

Gabe looked at the six inches worth of binders. He flipped open the top one. The first page was in photocopied and in Cyrillic with handwritten translations under each line.

"And when does this need to be done by?"

"Monday morning, if you know what's good for you."

"Monday." He flipped a page to find more Cyrillic. "Don't I have people who are supposed to read these for me?"

"Yes, you do, and they already have, but you always say you want to be 100 percent in the loop. Well, here's the loop."

JAMES LOOKED at himself in the mirror and tried to flip his hair around again. He'd thought about getting a cut and maybe a shirt that was less than three years old, but it was nearly the end of the month, and there wasn't room in the budget. He'd tried on half his wardrobe, trying to find something that didn't make him look drab.

There was a knock on his bedroom door.

"Yeah?"

Dylan let himself in. He held out a Sears bag. "Happy birthday."

James took the bag. "My birthday isn't for months."

"I know. It's early." He opened the bag and pulled out a shirt. It was a deep green button-down of some sort of light material. "Try it on."

He pulled off the light blue work shirt he'd settled on and put on the green one. He was pretty sure the fabric wasn't silk, but it still felt nice. He began to button it up, but Dylan stopped his hands before they got to the top.

"Nope, top two stay undone."

James looked in the mirror again, feeling rather exposed. Dylan reached out and brushed his hair around to the side. It suddenly went from messy to stylish.

"There. Green looks good on you."

James didn't know what to say. "Thank you, but—"

"No buts. Go out tonight, enjoy dinner, and I don't want to see you back here until sometime tomorrow."

"Dylan." It seemed like they were having this discussion every other day.

"No, Dad," Dylan snapped. "No. I know every adult in your life. I know every relationship you've ever had, which is none. I know every date you've ever been on, and you've always been home before ten, usually before nine. I know about that guy at the camping thing, and you couldn't have gotten far there. And by the way, gross. He was like twenty years older than you." James felt a flash of shame. "This Gabe guy seems to like you and makes you happy, so please, Dad, please, go have some adult alone time. Lots of it."

James squinted at his son. "If I stay out, you do not get to bring girls over."

Dylan put one hand over his heart and raised the other. "I swear on the grave of Joe DiMaggio, if you go out and try to be unvirtuous, I will stay in and be as virtuous as humanly possible."

James peered at the shirt and the strip of bare chest he was showing, and wondered at what kind of message it was sending. "Are you sure two buttons aren't too many?"

"They're perfect. I promise."

THE ELEVATOR QUIETLY PINGED, telling James he'd reached the penthouse level before the doors whisked open. The first thing he saw was Gabe smiling at him. Then there was a rush of scent and sound. Light jazz and the aroma of tomatoes and peppers surrounded him. Gabe gave him a peck on the cheek, smelling of spices himself, and pulled him out of the elevator.

"Come on in."

Gabe stepped aside, and James stepped directly into a living room that was easily larger than his entire apartment but still managed to feel warm and cozy. An open-plan kitchen was half-visible from his vantage point, and through every window to the outside he could see a patio with benches and a few potted plants. James had been expecting sleek and modern for the penthouse of a fancy building, but instead there was warm wood, leather, and woven fabrics. The paintings on the walls were of seascapes with vast skies and rolling waves.

"Dinner is almost ready." Gabe helped slip his jacket from his shoulders before hanging it on some thick pegs by the elevator door. "Kick off your shoes if you like." James reached into his jacket pocket and pulled out a CD. His heart was already going too fast, and he felt a small tremble in his hands.

"Before I forget, I have something for you." He handed over the CD. "That kid you liked at open-mic night, the one with the guitar, I looked him up. Turns out he did a self-recorded CD."

Gabe grinned and gave him another quick kiss. "Thank you so much. I'll put it on." Gabe headed for what James thought was an empty wall, until a portion of it rolled aside to reveal an impressive sound system. The jazz was quickly switched out. At the first few notes of the Mexican guitar, Gabe closed his eyes and smiled to himself. "That's really sweet. Thank you. Would you like a glass of wine?"

"Sure." He hoped a little wine would help him calm down. If tonight was going where he hoped it was going, he didn't want to be a frantic mess.

"I'll go get it."

"I really like this place," James said, looking closely at a nearby painting. "It's not what I expected."

"What were you expecting?" Gabe called from the kitchen.

"I don't know, modern, glass, chrome, high-tech everything."

"I get enough of that at work. On the rare occasions I manage to drag my ass home, I want it to be somewhere that feels comfortable." Gabe returned with two glasses of white wine. "Just after this place was finished up, I was dating this guy who was an ornithologist. He told me I was a bowerbird. That I'd gone and built myself a fancy feathered nest and was hopping around outside trying to lure someone into it."

"A bowerbird?"

"He was a little odd." Gabe took a sip of his wine. "By the way, you look really nice tonight. Green is a good color on you."

James looked down at himself. He'd lost a bit of confidence in the car and had done up an extra button. "Thank you. It was a gift from Dylan. You look nice too." Nice wasn't exactly the word James was thinking. Gabe was in jeans and a tight V-necked T-shirt that showed a good bit of chest and gave him the urge to run his tongue along Gabe's collarbone. That was an urge he could honestly say he'd never had before with anyone, and despite some nerves, he had a growing desire to skip dinner. He took a first taste of his wine, trying to steady himself.

There was a chime from the kitchen. "And that would be dinner."

"It smells nice." James followed Gabe into the kitchen that was sleek and modern, and looked big enough to cater a small army.

"I shook down my sister for a recipe or two." Gabe reached into a vast oven and pulled out a foil-covered baking pan.

"Do you need a hand?"

"Nope, in fact—" James was quickly led from the kitchen to a beautifully set table for two with votives already lit and floating in a cut-glass bowl. "You sit right here." Gabe pulled out a chair. "I'll be just a second."

James set down his glass of wine and sat while Gabe slipped back into the kitchen. He watched the candles float gently in their bowl, their flickering light blending sharply in the angled glass. He tried to focus on them instead of the places his mind wanted to wander. While on the surface Gabe had simply extended a dinner invitation, James had not been raised in a convent. He was well aware when someone invited you to their lavish penthouse condo, plied you with wine, and cooked a romantic meal, they were not planning on ending the night playing checkers. And he was okay with that. He was tired of his almost-virginity hanging over his head, and Gabe was certainly handsome.

Gabe emerged from the kitchen with a plate in each hand and a bottle of wine tucked under his arm. "Here we are." Gabe set the plates down carefully. "Spanish rice, cucumber and avocado salad, and chicken braised with tomatillos, cilantro, and poblanos. My sister's recipes, and if I've ruined it, you're supposed to call and tell her."

"I'm sure it'll be great. And it can't be any worse than my famous ketchup-and-hot-dog spaghetti sauce."

Gabe froze with his glass halfway to his mouth. "I'd ask if you were joking…."

"It was what we had in the fridge."

"Well, here's hoping this is better."

It was better, and James took his time, trying to savor every bite. He also decided he was going to have to get hold of the recipe, for Dylan's sake if nothing else. Unfortunately, ketchup-and-hot-dog spaghetti had not been a one-time meal.

The music switched to another song, and Gabe closed his eyes for a moment.

"Everything okay?"

"Yes. My grandmother used to listen to this kind of music. She had this place out on the far edge of Modesto, and we'd drive out there a few times a summer when we were kids. I hadn't heard it in years until the other night. I always liked it out there. She had this tiny house on a big plot of land. It was full of fruit trees and her garden. It was peaceful." Gabe looked beyond James into some point in his past.

"It sounds nice."

"It was."

"We used to drive through Modesto once a summer. My parents could never afford to go anywhere fancy for vacation but once a year, we'd wake up early, pile into the car, then drive about a million miles to the other side of the Sierras. We'd set up camp near Mono Lake, stay for about a week, then drive all the way back. We did that every year until I left home."

Gabe's brows pulled together. "You know, I can honestly say I've never been camping."

"Really?" Camping had been the only kind of vacation his parents could regularly afford.

"Really."

James hadn't been camping in ages. Despite the long drive, it had always been a highlight of his childhood summers. "Well, if you're willing to drive about five hours, I know a great spot for it."

Gabe grinned. "If I can get three days in a row off anytime in the next year, I will absolutely let you take me camping."

"Don't you get vacation time?" He'd wondered about Gabe's work schedule. Even on weekends he seemed to always be calling from his office or his car.

"I've got stacks of it. The trick is wedging it in somewhere. These days it feels like, if you take your eye off the ball for more than two seconds, the ball is going to get stolen or simply disintegrate."

"I think they have cell coverage around the lake now. I'm sure you'd be fine."

Gabe poured them both another glass of wine. James found himself relaxing, but then he often did around Gabe. He wasn't one for energies or chakras or any of that, but Gabe's presence always seemed to make some little knot between his shoulders unravel, and it felt like he could breathe easier.

He scraped his plate clean as they talked, hoping he didn't look like a glutton.

"Did you like it?" Gabe asked with a smile that glowed bright in the candlelight.

"You can tell your sister I fully approve."

"Good. I hope you saved room for dessert."

"I think I can manage a little something."

Gabe whisked away the plates and returned with two glasses of chocolate pudding. "I'm afraid I used what cooking mojo I have on dinner."

"That's okay. I love pudding."

"Would you like to take dessert outside?" Gabe gestured to the balcony that wrapped all the way around the entire penthouse.

"Sure."

Gabe led him to an old-fashioned swing for two that let them look out over the South Bay.

James leaned back into the cushions and took a couple bites of pudding. He wasn't kidding when he'd said he loved chocolate pudding. Dessert was a rare treat in his house. A box of pudding and some milk was about all his budget and culinary skills could handle. There was something comforting about it. He let the swing rock and enjoyed the warmth of Gabe's body just touching his. In the distance, lines of traffic snaked north and south.

"When I get my house built, it's going to have a proper view instead of just the South Bay." Gabe's voice was wistful.

"You're building a house?"

"No. I wish. It's on my to-do list for when I have time, which at this rate will be when I'm three days dead."

"I'd like to build a house one day," James said mostly to

himself. He could feel Gabe looking at him. He took another few bites of pudding in the silence.

"If you could go anywhere or do anything right now, where would you like to be?" Gabe suddenly asked.

James tried to picture the whole world spread out before him. It was too much. The very thought scared him, and he pulled away from it. "I think... I think I'd like to be eating chocolate pudding on a balcony in San Jose with a very attractive man, who for reasons I'm not quite sure of seems to like me."

Gabe set aside his pudding and leaned in for a kiss. It was slow and soft. James melted and wrapped his arms around Gabe before completely dissolving into a puddle. He wasn't exactly submissive by nature, but there was something about Gabe's strength and gentle warmth that made him relax.

Gabe pulled away from the kiss. "Would you like to move this back inside?" he whispered.

James' heart slammed against his ribs, and he understood what Gabe was really asking. "Yes, I think I would." He was proud at the steadiness of his voice.

Gabe stood and took James by the hand, leading him around the balcony, through another set of french doors, into a bedroom. It was done in dark woods and rich blues and greens. The mattress was thick and looked warm and soft. James could picture himself sinking into it and sleeping for a decade.

He turned around to mention that, but the comment stopped in his throat. Gabe was standing inches from him, looking suddenly taller than his two extra inches. His eyes were dark and focused. A few butterflies returned to James' stomach and started fighting with the strongest arousal he'd ever experienced.

Gabe settled his hands lightly on James' hips, and put his lips to his cheek, right by his ear.

"Nothing has to happen that you don't want," Gabe whispered. "Just say so, anytime."

James nodded, not trusting his voice not to crack.

Gabe kissed him again. It was too soft, and James pressed himself into it. He wasn't made of glass, and no one had ever treated him like he was. Gabe got the hint, slipping his tongue between James' lips and pulling them together. He moaned. He could feel how hard Gabe was even though his jeans. The next wave of lust brought with it a sudden desperate need to get Gabe naked. He slipped his hands under Gabe's T-shirt, sliding them along the smooth, hot skin.

Gabe stepped back and pulled off his T-shirt, flinging it across the room. He was tan, with a broad, well-muscled chest and small, hard nipples.

James swallowed hard. "How much time do you spend at the gym?" He didn't care if his voice squeaked.

"Not as much as my personal trainer would like."

James reached out tentatively, like Gabe might not be entirely real, and ran a single finger across Gabe's chest, then down his centerline.

"Is this okay?"

"Yeah."

"Good."

Gabe undid the top button of James' shirt. James hunched his shoulders, suddenly feeling shy. He knew he was pale and on the thin side. Gabe's hands froze.

He stepped in close and cupped James' cheek. "There's nothing under there I don't want to see."

James took a breath and pulled his shirt up and over his head. The fabric was cool and smooth across his face. He dropped the shirt and tried not to hunch his shoulders again.

Gabe settled his hands onto James' waist. "There. That wasn't so bad, was it?" Gabe didn't give him a chance to answer, bringing their lips together. He was okay with that. Gabe's warm, full kisses were familiar ground and still comfortable, even as their bare chests pressed against each other.

He ran his hands along the smooth skin of Gabe's back, tracing the muscles until he found a patch of rough skin over the left shoulder blade. "Old injury. I'll tell you about it some time." James frowned and stroked the spot.

Like a dance partner, Gabe guided them both to the bed, James easily following his lead.

"If this is too much for you…?"

"No."

Gabe kissed him while easing them down. The duvet was a deep green, almost black. The mattress molded under James' body but wasn't too soft. The little knot of stress that lived at the base of his skull loosened. He closed his eyes, unable to do anything but sigh.

"I take it you like my bed?"

"I could learn to live with it."

"Good, because I'd very much like to keep you in it for a while." Gabe rolled James onto his back and started kissing his way down James' body. James had to grip Gabe's shoulders as each kiss sent a wave of some new kind of pleasure through him. By the time Gabe was nuzzling at the thin line of hair below his navel, it was too much.

"Wait," James gasped.

Gabe froze, then pulled back. "What's wrong?"

"Nothing. I just… I just need to catch my breath."

Gabe smiled and climbed back up the bed, lying next to James.

"Sorry," James breathed.

"Don't be. I'm in no rush. I even left my cell phone in the other room."

"Wow." James felt honored. Gabe seemed like the type

who'd be the first to have his phone surgically implanted. "Are you jonesing for a hit yet?"

"Starting to." He ran his fingers across James' lips. "But I have something I can distract myself with."

James kissed the tips of Gabe's fingers. They still tasted of sweet peppers. "I think I've caught my breath now."

"Good." Gabe slid his hands down and cupped James' backside. "Did you know you have a great ass?"

"No one has ever mentioned it."

Gabe nuzzled at his neck, causing James' toes to curl. "Well, you do. That second lecture, every time you leaned over to unlock my computer, I was checking you out." Then he slid his hand around to the front of James' body. James nearly jumped out of his skin as Gabe teased at his erection through his jeans. "And then there's this. I fully intend to get this into my mouth before the night is up."

"Jesus." His head swam with the very idea. He pressed his hips into Gabe's hand without conscious thought, simply craving more touch. Gabe nipped at his throat, then popped the button of James' jeans with one hand and slowly drew down the zipper.

He buried his face into Gabe's shoulder. He felt an overload building again, but he didn't want things to stop.

"Just keep breathing and let me make you feel good," Gabe said softly.

Then Gabe slipped his hand under the waistband of James' underwear and closed it around his cock. It was the first hand other than James' own to be there. It was too much. With a shout and a shudder and a single wild thrust, he came.

"Fuck," he cursed.

"It's okay."

"No, it's not," James snapped, the humiliation crushing down on him, his face burning with shame. He couldn't imagine what Gabe must think of such a pathetic and juvenile display. He tried to roll off the bed, but Gabe held him tight. He tried to cover his face.

"Yes, it is. You've been on edge your entire adult life. That was going to happen." Gabe kissed the back of his neck. "Now we can really take our time."

James still couldn't show his face. He felt Gabe get off the bed, then heard fabric hitting the floor. He looked over his shoulder. Gabe was naked, and James felt that little bit more inferior. It wasn't as if Gabe was abnormally huge or anything, but he had nothing to be ashamed of and was sporting at least twice what James was.

Gabe crawled back onto the bed and curled himself around James. "I'm sorry, but it really is okay. And if you shimmy out of those jeans, I'd love the chance to pull you right back to that edge."

James squeezed his eyes shut while Gabe rubbed circles on his chest. He could feel semen sticking to himself and knew there was no way he could wear that underwear home, so he might as well get out of it now. He pulled off his jeans and pushed them to the floor, then tried to cover himself, but Gabe gently grabbed his wrists.

"Nope."

Despite lingering embarrassment, he let Gabe guide him onto his back. Gabe kissed James' chest, right over his heart, then began simply stroking him. No one had ever touched him like that. No one had ever touched him. Gabe stroked places James had always thought were of no consequence, but they were suddenly sending messages of arousal rushing across his body in waves. Gabe interspersed his touches with soft, sucking kisses along James' throat and chest. His tongue curled around James' ear, and with a shudder and a moan, the last of the embarrassed tension left James.

Gabe headed south, teasing around his hips and belly but

halting for a moment at the scars across the top of James' left thigh.

"It was when Dylan was a week old. I was exhausted and trying to sterilize bottles. I knocked the pot off the stove somehow."

Gabe didn't say anything, just caressed the spot as if trying to sooth a wound long since healed. He kissed James again, then threw his leg up and over so he was straddling James' hips. James felt himself, fully swollen again, twitch against Gabe's ass. He dragged the tips of his fingers across James' torso, causing him to giggle.

"Ticklish?"

"A little, I guess."

"What would you like to do? Right now?" Gabe's voice had dropped, and it vibrated through James' frame.

James' mind, already slowed in a lust-filled haze, simply stopped. "I don't know. I've never…." He raised a hand slightly, then let it drop.

Gabe laced his fingers in with James'. "I've touched you. Would you like to give it a try?"

James nodded. Gabe leaned forward, guiding their hands to his chest. He felt Gabe's heart beating in a steady rhythm, so different from his own, which wouldn't slow down. He slowly explored Gabe's broad hairless chest, almost analytically noting the heat and smoothness. He barely touched a small hard nipple, and Gabe softly hummed. James froze.

"It's okay. No need to stop."

James carefully stroked his hand across the nipple again. The skin of it was a little smoother than the rest of Gabe's chest. He ran a fingertip around it, and Gabe gave that same little hum. He tried a slightly bolder touch, and Gabe smiled and shifted his hips.

James jumped at the quick tickle of pleasure, but the smile on Gabe's face made him feel brave. He abandoned the nipple and slid his fingertips down Gabe's body until he managed to find a ticklish spot to the left of his navel. He touched all around the area but only got a giggle when he touched maybe two square inches of skin. James spent some time on it, as every time Gabe giggled, it caused vibrations to slide across his own cock.

"That's so weird."

"I'm sure you've got weird bits on you too." Gabe grabbed his hand and kissed his fingertips. "And I intend to find all of them."

He let James' fingers go, and James knew his next move. It was staring him in the face, quite literally. He slid his hand down, then slowly touched Gabe's cock.

Gabe moaned soft and low. "Feel free to linger in that area."

He used the tips of his fingers to start. He was honestly as curious as he was aroused. The skin was soft and gave a little as it slid over the hard flesh under it. He traced a thick vein, even pressing on it for half a second. He squeezed the glans at the tip ever so gently and watched the way Gabe's tip opened. All the while, Gabe gave little sighs and moans and the occasional gasp. Finally he grasped James' hand, and set it over his cock. James took the hint and squeezed. This time Gabe's groan was deep and filled with relief.

"Oh Lord, James, you are a tease."

"I'm sorry—"

"No. It's fine. Just keep…."

James squeezed again, and Gabe rolled into his hand, pressing his ass against James' cock in the process. It was James' turn to moan and stutter, but he tried to work out some sort of rhythm.

"Wait." This time it was Gabe who said the word.

James yanked his hand away, wondering what he'd done wrong. Gabe climbed off James and James sat up.

"What's wrong?"

"Absolutely nothing." Gabe sat loosely cross-legged in the center of the large bed and beckoned James over. "Here, wrap your legs around my waist."

It took a bit of wriggling, but James settled himself on Gabe's lap. Gabe wrapped his arms around James and pulled him close, trapping their cocks between their bodies. A shock went through him as he felt Gabe's cock against his for the first time. He pressed his face into Gabe's shoulder. He smelled of clean sweat and a little of peppers.

"There," Gabe whispered in his ear. "Now I can hold you."

Gabe pressed his hips forward. That small movement of Gabe's cock shifting against James' sent his whole body twitching. Gabe held him tighter. "I've got you," he whispered even as he began rolling his hips in a slow, easy rhythm. He kissed James' ear. "Just relax. Let yourself feel. No plans, no worries. Just our bodies pressed against each other."

Gabe cupped James' ass, pulling him just that tiny bit closer. James whimpered as every place their bodies touched began to burn. He squeezed his eyes shut as his vision began to go hazy.

"Let yourself go. This is just a first experience. There are so many things I want to show you."

James began to drive his hips against Gabe. He could feel that edge creeping up already.

"I want to kiss every part of you. I want to suck you down."

James moaned at the image, his lungs beginning to ache as they struggled for more air.

"I want to be inside you."

James gasped as an extra wave of arousal slammed in hard and fast.

"I want you to be inside of me."

Gabe's voice kept washing over James as if it was a physical presence, but he was beginning to lose track of the words.

"I want to find every bit of your body that turns you on."

Gabe sucked on his neck. "I want to find out if you have any kinks or fetishes and try them all."

James couldn't begin to answer. His body was no longer taking his brain's commands as he thrust his hips against Gabe's without control, his arms locked around Gabe's body as if releasing him would mean death. Gabe caught his mouth in a deep kiss and slid a hand between them, squeezing their cocks together, and gave a stroke.

It was enough. A shout ripped its way from James' lungs as he spasmed against Gabe, pleasure squeezing his eyes closed tight and sending lightning across his nerves. But Gabe didn't stop. He kept stroking, sending aftershocks across James' body until Gabe growled low. With a couple of bruising thrusts, Gabe spilled between their bellies.

James tried to catch his breath. His eyes were still squeezed shut, and his heart was racing hard and fast. He pressed his face into the curve of Gabe's neck. Gabe slowly leaned forward until James was lying on his back, his limbs limp, refusing to respond to his will.

He opened his eyes, but it took a moment for them to focus. Gabe was smiling down at him. James smiled back, then closed his eyes and felt the world begin to fade.

GABE WATCHED JAMES' face until he was sure James had slipped into sleep. He quietly pulled some soft cloths from his bedside table. James stirred the smallest amount as he was quickly cleaned. He pulled the blanket of spun silk that was folded neatly at the foot of the bed up over both of them. Then he closed his eyes and, enjoying the rare comfort of someone warm beside him, slept.

GABE WOKE as James kicked and jerked his head to the side. He mumbled something Gabe couldn't make out, his face crumpling. Gabe stroked his hair, easing James out of the dream he was having. His eyes fluttered open.

"You okay? I think you were having a nightmare."

James yawned and rubbed his eyes. "Sorry for falling asleep."

Gabe glanced at the bedside clock. "It was only about half an hour. Are you okay?"

"Yeah." James yawned again. "Stress dream. Late for work, the bus breaks down, have to walk, but the streets keep shifting."

"I get those. I'm in some important meeting, but I can't remember what it's for, and when I go to look at my notes, they've been photocopied so many times I can't read them."

"I used to have dreams like that in high school."

"Me too." He leaned in and gave James a soft, lingering kiss, which James returned without hesitation. "How are you feeling?"

James smiled. He seemed sleepy still and a bit dazed. "I am feeling bizarrely good."

"Bizarrely?"

"How about relaxed and content, which is a very odd and rare state for me to be in."

"Maybe with a bit of work, we can make it more common."

"I think I'd like that."

"Good." Gabe went back to kissing him. It was a nice comfortable place for the both of them. James skimmed his fingers along Gabe's back until he found the patch of scar tissue again.

"It feels like road rash, just worse," James commented.

"It basically is."

James stroked it lightly. "What happened?"

"Car accident. It was after the company shifted from being a start-up to something more solid. I had to go all the way up to Napa one day to get some paperwork signed for this big deal. I was driving back, and there was traffic on the bridge and all the way down 101, and I was supposed to be in on a conference call. I got onto 280 instead, driving in the left lane doing close to ninety, trying to make up time. My phone rang because people wanted to know where I was."

"I think I can guess the rest."

Gabe could never remember what had happened after that phone rang but had been able to make a guess moments after waking up. "I'm told I rolled about eight times and tied up traffic for three hours. All I can remember is waking up in the ambulance with a bump on my head, a broken wrist, broken nose, cracked ribs, a broken collarbone, and a combination of road gravel and safety glass somehow ground into my shoulder blade. But it could have been worse."

"You could have died."

"I could have pulled a Wozniak and crashed a plane."

James chuckled.

"Anyway, after that the budget got fiddled around with so I could have a driver on company time. That way, if I needed to dial into conference calls on the freeway—"

"You'd be less likely to end up in a bloody heap by the side of the road?"

"Basically." James sat up and traced Gabe's collarbone until he came to the bump where it had snapped. He leaned in and kissed the spot, sending a soft warmth through Gabe. No one had ever done that, ever kissed one of his injuries. He stroked James' head. "Are you sure you've never done anything like this before? Because you're awfully good at it."

"I'm sure."

"Well, you're a natural. Give me a couple of days, and I'll make a total hedonist out of you."

James turned his head away. "Did you mean all those things you said? The things you want to do?"

"Every one of them, but there's no need to try for them all in one night." James craned his head around to look at the clock. "Do you need to be somewhere?" James hadn't mentioned other plans, but then Gabe hadn't asked. He kicked himself for that.

"No." James answered quickly. "I wasn't sure... um...."

James flushed. Gabe gave James a quick kiss he hoped was reassuring. "You better be spending the night. Breakfast is the one meal of the day I'm really good at, and I was hoping to impress you. Do you have to be anywhere tomorrow?"

"No. Dylan's got a game Sunday afternoon, and I need to do laundry."

Gabe wrestled James onto his back with a laugh and a kiss. "I don't suppose I could talk you into skipping laundry so I can keep you in this bed all day?"

"Well...." James stretched out the word. "I was looking forward to watching Ernesto discover that Gabriella is his illegitimate half sister."

Gabe groaned and pressed his forehead to James' chest. "Oh God, no, you watch telenovelas."

"They're always on at the laundromat. And *Siete Palomas* is really engrossing."

"I think my sister is watching that one."

"Everyone's watching that one. Ask her how far she thinks Catalina will go to seduce young Father Reynaldo."

Leave it to me to find a white boy who's into the novellas, Gabe mused to himself.

"You can ask her yourself," Gabe said without thinking.

James went still. "You want me to meet your sister?" His voice was full of confusion.

It took Gabe a moment to process what he had just said. He rarely introduced boyfriends to his family, and that was usually only after a lot of nagging on someone's part. Most of the time, he didn't even admit he had a family until it became unavoidable. But James didn't exactly fit into the same category as most of his boyfriends.

"Yeah, at some point. I mean if you want?"

"No, no, that's fine, I'm just…. I'm not totally sure how these relationship things work." James' brows pulled together. "This is a relationship?"

"No, it's an incredibly complicated one-night stand." Gabe put a kiss on the little crease between James' eyes. "I'm all for this being a relationship. I mean, we don't have to move any faster than you're comfortable with, but you already mean a lot to me. A lot more than any of my one-night stands. Hell, a lot more than some of my longer relationships. Is that okay?"

Gabe really hoped it was, because he wasn't blowing smoke. James was creeping under his skin at a scary rate. And even more terrifying was the realization that he didn't want to slow down. He knew he had to let James set the pace, but he was already planning ahead to more dates, and nights in, and sex. And even more telling, he hadn't crept out to check his messages.

"Sure." James' voice gave that endearing little squeak Gabe recognized as James being nervous and in unfamiliar waters but trying to put on a brave face.

"For what it's worth, I'd like to meet your family at some point. I'd like to meet Dylan under slightly less mortifying circumstances."

James chuckled. "Not the most embarrassing moment of my life, but I'd say it's in the top three."

"Top five for me."

James rolled on his side and squinted at Gabe. "Okay, most embarrassing?"

Gabe felt his cheeks begin to redden remembering it. "Only if you tell me yours."

"Deal."

Gabe took a deep breath. "I met my two best friends, Frank and Nate, when we were all in college together. Stanford. We were put together as roommates, and these guys are a couple of committed hetero übernerds. We weren't even meant to be in the same residence hall, but there was flooding in one and.... Anyway, after about six weeks, they tell me one Saturday afternoon they're off to play Dungeons and Dragons and they're starting a new campaign, and I had learned by this point not to expect them in until the next morning. Great. So I call up the guy I've been sort of seeing because I figured we had all the time in the world." James put a hand to his mouth, trying and failing to press down a smile. "Well, the DM's girlfriend got sick after a couple of hours, the game was called off, and by the time Frank and Nate came in, we had stripped naked, gotten a bit inventive with edible body paint, and were doing it hard and fast across my desk. This is also how they found out I was gay."

James lost it and started to laugh. "So getting walked in on is nothing new for you," James managed to gasp.

"At least we were still fully clothed, and I didn't have the words 'dirty little girl' painted across my chest."

James went into fresh peals of laughter. "Dirty little girl?"

"I'd painted 'insert here' with some arrows on him." After that, he, Frank, and Nate developed some very strict rules about what was allowed to go on in the rooms and when. It had also killed that relationship. James' giggles settled down. "Okay, your turn."

"Right. When Dylan was about five, he started asking questions about why his mommy wasn't around and why we didn't live with mommy and things like that. So I gave him a very sugarcoated version of what had happened. Then I had to explain what gay was. Not too long later, we're at Back to School night for the kindergarten. I'm trying to make small talk with one of the other parents about the fine intricacies of macaroni art, and I've got Dylan by the hand, but I'm not really paying attention to him. He's chatting away with one of his friends—to this day I don't know about what—but he suddenly pipes up in a voice just loud enough for everyone to hear, 'It's okay, my daddy only likes boys.'"

Gabe hissed in sympathetic pain.

"I could have died. The room went silent, and I could have just dropped dead and melted into the floor."

"I am so sorry."

"And the thing is, there is no way you can try to explain that, or make a joke of it, or anything else. Anything that comes out of your mouth after that just sounds bad. I prayed so hard for an earthquake or asteroid strike or fire alarm. Anything."

"I don't think I would have survived that," Gabe said. "I mean, when my goddaughter was seven, I went to some family fund-raising night at her school, and she tried to set me up with her teacher. That was embarrassing enough."

"Was the teacher at least male?"

"Yes. He was also straight."

James managed a cringe and laugh at the same time, which crinkled up the corners of his eyes. Gabe leaned in for a fresh kiss. James opened to him without hesitation and was soon driving the kiss himself, skimming his hands over Gabe's body.

He tossed a leg up over James' hip, pulling their bodies flush. James got his fingers into Gabe's hair. Gabe was sure the bit of hair-pulling was accidental, but it was one of his few kinks. His cock was working its way back to life quickly, and by the feel of things, so was James'.

James pulled back from the kiss, and Gabe took the opportunity to roll James on his back, then slide down his body.

He nuzzled his face high on James' thigh, which already smelled thickly of sex. James' hips bucked violently. He readjusted himself so he could pin James' thighs down before taking a long lick of his cock.

James let out a curse, arms flailing. Gabe took another lick. James' cock was a little thin but well-formed. Curving up beautifully from a patch of blond curls, it was a shade of deep pink. He kept up the licks, already tasting cum. With each lick James' entire body jerked. He twirled his tongue around the tip, causing James to let out that pained whimper. He kept up the teasing, positive James would come at the first full suck.

Gabe reached between his legs and started stroking himself slowly in time with each lick. James had stopped flopping and now had the duvet in a white-knuckled grip, his hips arching up with each touch to his cock.

Gabe stroked himself faster, imagining what could be ahead of them. There were still some parts of James he had yet to even touch, but the desire to flip James over and slide in was a strong one. He wanted to try sex in the shower or the bath, both of which could easily fit two. He wanted to abuse his position in the company and join the mile-high club in the corporate jet.

James' hips were beginning to buck erratically, and his eyes were squeezed shut. Gabe took pity and sucked James down as far as he could manage. James screamed but didn't cum. Gabe stroked himself hard and fast as James thrust into his mouth. Finally James' back arched, and he froze for a second before pumping himself dry into Gabe's mouth. He glanced up to see James' face, open and wild, full of nothing but passion. Gabe swelled with pride that he had been the first person to put that look on James' face.

He swallowed and sucked James through the aftershocks before releasing into his hand and collapsing against James' thighs.

JAMES' eyes fluttered open. The room was dim. He must have fallen asleep again. He tried to sit up, but Gabe pulled a blanket up over the both of them and pulled him back down.

Gabe pressed his lips to the side of James' head. "Get some rest," he whispered.

James closed his eyes, filled his nose with Gabe's scent, and slept.

The next time James awoke, there was light in the room. The clock told him it was after six, and from the other room, he could make out Gabe's voice. He couldn't hear a second voice so he figured Gabe had to be on his phone. Either that or he'd just spent the night having sex with a lunatic.

James smiled to himself. He'd spent the night having sex. A giggle spilled from his lips, then another. Bits of his body ached, and he could smell himself and Gabe, but he felt so good. His cock twitched, sending an ache into the surrounding muscles, but it was such a good ache!

He swung his legs off the bed and reached for his jeans, only to find them missing. He was pretty sure he'd dropped them right by the bed. He got up and wandered around the room, feeling exposed in his nakedness, but found nothing except a dark blue silk robe folded neatly on top of the dresser. He was pretty sure it hadn't been there the night before.

He wrapped the sensuous cloth around himself and stepped out of the bedroom. Fortunately it connected to the far side of the living room, where Gabe was on his phone, pacing about, a slightly grumpy look on his face. He was also naked. James' cock gave a twitch of interest.

Gabe turned in his pacing, noticed James, and smiled. He waved James over, then put his hand over the bottom half of his phone. James could still hear multiple voices talking. "I tossed your clothes in a quick rinse cycle," he said softly. "This shouldn't take more than a couple minutes, if you want to grab a shower. Then I'll make breakfast."

James mouthed okay and received a quick kiss.

Gabe took his hand off the phone. "Enough," he snapped. "This is a nonissue. This shouldn't even be on the table. I don't know what memo floated up from where or what ladder-climber is trying to drag this in on the bottom of his shoe, but this conversation should not even be happening." Whatever reply Gabe got didn't agree with him, and he rolled his eyes.

James went to take a shower. He found the bathroom and had to stop at the door to take it in. It was at least twice as large as his kitchen. The sun coming through a large skylight illuminated a half-sunken tub easily big enough for two. The shower looked like it could hold a dozen people and was large enough to qualify as its own separate room. There were also two sinks comprised of matching porcelain bowls. One was surrounded by bottles, combs, an electric razor, and a toothbrush sitting in a coffee cup. The other sink seemed to be unused except for an unwrapped toothbrush, but it was still there, waiting.

Bowerbird, James thought as he headed to the shower. In the distance he could still make out Gabe's voice.

He had to stop again at the entrance to the shower room, not so much to take in its size, though it was large, but to absorb its complexity. There were two stone benches, three shower hoses with different heads, and a large rain showerhead hanging from the ceiling. There was a whole collection of knobs, handles, and dials. He stepped in, peering at each one even before taking off his robe. He was looking at what he thought might be the rain showerhead control when he heard the bathroom door open.

"It's a little overengineered." James turned. Gabe was leaning against the shower entrance, still naked. "I can only assume I was *really* not paying attention when I signed off on it."

"Did you also sign off on it being big enough to hold a dozen people?"

"Oh, hell if I know. Though considering my designer, he may very well have been contemplating that." Gabe stepped close, gently tugging on the belt of James' robe. "I prefer just two, though." He stroked James' thigh. "That's a good color on you."

"You picked it. You seem to be good at that."

Gabe pressed his lips to James' neck. "A hard-fought-for skill."

"You fought for the ability to pick out colors?"

Gabe hummed against his throat, sending a pleasant wave down his body. "My old business manager, Gregory, didn't just drag me to the country club. Tailors, stylists, vineyards, anything he could think of." Gabe's voice took on a hint of darkness.

"Was he... I mean...?"

"Long in the past and long gone from my life." Gabe stripped the belt from James' robe, letting it fall open. James had been half-hard since seeing Gabe pacing naked around his living room. Feeling Gabe flush against him brought him to full mast. Gabe slipped the robe from his shoulders and tossed it toward the sinks.

"Do the people you're talking to know you take conference calls naked?"

"No. It could make negotiations more interesting."

Gabe went to the row of knobs and spun a few. The rain showerhead came to life. James stepped under it and decided he wanted to be nowhere else on earth. "Oh, God." The water was almost too hot and coming down on his head like a massage.

"Now that's something I don't regret signing off on."

Gabe joined him under the water and kissed him hard. It was a bruising kiss, almost possessive, but James melted into it, drinking it up. The idea that someone desired him, especially someone like Gabe, was still novel, and he wasn't quite sure it was real. But Gabe's arms wrapped around him felt real enough.

Gabe pulled back. James felt Gabe's erection against his stomach and his pupils were blown open. "There, that's how I wanted to start this morning. Not yelling at idiots."

James didn't answer. His brain was already in the process of shorting out. Gabe pressed a button on the wall. A small nozzle came out and soap fell into his hand.

James managed an amused look. "Yes, it's a bit overengineered."

Gabe ran his soapy hands across James' back. He leaned heavily against Gabe so he didn't collapse.

"You like that?"

James smiled and gave a happy little mumble. Words were too much trouble.

"Good." Gabe's hands slid a bit lower, then a soapy finger slid between James' cheeks. He leaped forward against Gabe as a shock of electricity went from the tip of Gabe's fingers up his spine and stopped somewhere behind his eyes.

"Oh, God!" James managed to breathe, his eyes squeezed tight.

Gabe chuckled and held him tight with his free arm. "Should I do that again?"

James nodded but kept his eyes closed.

Gabe's finger slid a little lower and was soon circling his hole. For James, something like that had always been an abstract concept. He'd never taken the time to do much more than wash back there, and it certainly had never felt anything like this. Now he felt like he was about to fly right out of his skin. His core was chilled and his skin felt like it was burning. Then just the tip of Gabe's finger slid in.

James was aware of his own cries echoing off the bathroom

wall as he ground himself against Gabe's leg, desperate for release as Gabe twisted his finger slowly. Then Gabe slid his hand down between James' legs and pressed a spot behind his balls.

James' legs nearly gave out under him as he poured onto Gabe, having no idea anything could feel any better than the night before. Gabe managed to guide him over to one of the benches. James leaned back against the wall.

"Liked that, did you?"

James nodded. Gabe turned the shower off before sitting down and pulling him close.

As James came back to earth, Gabe started slowly stroking himself. James shivered at the eroticism of it. It was something he had always considered secret and private, but here was Gabe doing it right in front of him like it was something to be shared. Maybe it was. He reached out and carefully placed a hand over Gabe's.

Gabe smiled and made a content humming noise. He slid his fingers between Gabe's but let Gabe set the pace. Gabe started to speed up, then suddenly slipped his hand out from under James'. James kept going as Gabe moaned and thrust up into his hand. He watched as Gabe's cock shifted to a darker red, darker than his own ever became, and as he stroked, he felt it twitch and jump in his hand.

"Little faster, please," Gabe asked, a high whine in his voice.

He sped up, but he only had to give a few strokes before Gabe's cock jerked violently. Suddenly semen was pouring out the top and over James' fingers. Gabe let out a long, low moan as it happened.

"Oh Jesus," Gabe gasped out. "You are really good at that."

James rubbed the semen between his fingers, then tentatively stuck out his tongue and took a taste.

"You are a tease, and you are trying to kill me."

In the distance James heard a cell phone ring. "Are you going to get that?"

"No. I have a very strict rule. No getting out of the shower to answer my phone."

"And how many times have you taken extra-long showers to avoid calls?"

Gabe grinned. "You already know me too well."

"No, I just have a teenager and lead a team of Olympic-level procrastinators."

"I see." Gabe gave him a quick kiss. "Then I will stop procrastinating, get us cleaned up, and cook breakfast. How does that sound?"

James' stomach gave a small rumble, throwing in its vote for breakfast. "I think that sounds fine."

James figured they'd just rinse off, but Gabe had other ideas, taking the time to wash James' hair with something that smelled faintly of green tea. If he could have come again, he probably would have, just from the sensation of Gabe massaging his scalp.

Then Gabe dried him with towels that were soft and warm and big enough to wear as togas.

James' stomach was positively grumbling by then. Gabe helped him back into the blue robe before pulling on a pair of maroon sleep pants that somehow made him look more indecent than when he'd been naked.

Only when they were in the kitchen did Gabe listen to the message on his phone. He groaned in what sounded like pain.

"Is everything okay?"

"Yeah." Gabe opened his eyes again, then pushed a button on a very complicated bit of machinery that in some distant future universe might be a coffeemaker. "We're at the panic phase of negotiations with this Russian company. It always happens. Things get agreed on, then before it goes down on paper, the other party starts listening to advice from random people, and they panic about things that aren't really a problem. It's like people who go to their doctor, then spend five hours online convincing themselves their doctor is wrong." Gabe placed a mug in the machine, and it quickly filled with coffee. "You take milk in yours?"

"Please."

Gabe grabbed a carton of 1 percent milk from the fridge.

"All that and it doesn't put the milk in for you?"

Gabe chuckled even while rolling his eyes. "It was a gift. When it finally breaks, I'm going back to my old stovetop percolator; I don't care how badly it clashes with the décor."

James took a seat on a tall chair on the other side of the kitchen counter; Gabe handed over the mug. James took a sip. The coffee wasn't burnt or bitter. It had a slightly nutty flavor and a smooth feel in his mouth.

"Okay, it does make a decent cup of coffee."

Gabe retrieved his own mug from the machine. "It does do that. Now, breakfast. I can do eggs about a dozen different ways. I've got bacon, chorizos, sausages, smoked salmon. My pancakes aren't bad, and I make a good omelet as well."

James' stomach grumbled loudly. His breakfast usually consisted of oatmeal, which was warm, filling, and cheap. "How about an omelet?"

"Omelet it is."

James sipped coffee and watched Gabe make breakfast. It was possibly the most erotic thing he had ever seen. Something about the way Gabe's sleep pants hung low on his hips was sexier than when he was pacing about naked. They curved around his ass, and when he moved certain ways, James could make out the outline of his cock, hanging low and waiting. James' cock was hard and protruding from his robe, and he was glad he was sitting on the other side of the kitchen counter.

"If you keep staring at me like that, I'm going to burn the eggs while I ravish you on the floor."

James blushed and started examining his coffee instead. Gabe gave a warm, rolling chuckle.

James did look back up and watched the way the muscles of Gabe's arms and chest flexed as he whisked the eggs. His arms weren't bulging and unnatural looking, but they were well defined. He could still feel the way they had held him the night before. For possibly the first time in his adult life, just for a second, he felt safe and free from his problems. He knew it wasn't a feeling he could afford to linger on, but it had still been nice.

The eggs sizzled in the pan, the smell combining with the slight tang of sourdough toast in the air.

Gabe slid the large omelet smoothly from the pan and sliced it in two. A few seconds later, an omelet, buttered toast, and orange juice were placed in front of him before Gabe joined him on the other side of the bench. He tried to cover his erection, which had only half subsided.

"Is that okay?"

James was salivating. "It looks wonderful." James took a bite. The eggs weren't dry or runny. The ham and cheese were nicely blended, and the peppers set the whole thing off. "You can definitely make breakfast."

"I learned a long time ago that charm might get you a first date, but breakfast gets you a second."

James thought about a second date, and his erection sprang back to life. Gabe teased his fingers over it. James almost choked on a bite of omelet. Then Gabe's phone started to ring with what sounded like a tinny version of "Dancing Queen."

"That's Tamyra." He grabbed the phone quickly. "What? And good morning…." He glanced at James. "Do you really have to? This can't wait? Okay, okay. I'll see you in a minute." James pulled his robe tight as Gabe hung up. "Tamyra is coming up for two minutes to drop off some papers. That's it, I promise."

James looked around for someplace to hide. "Should I go

find clothes?" James didn't worry about his erection, which had promptly curled up.

Gabe kissed him. "Don't worry about it. She's seen me in far less and much worse. Eat your breakfast before it gets cold."

The elevator dinged. James looked over his shoulder as Tamyra stepped out. James knew he had no interest in women, but even he could appreciate Tamyra on an aesthetic level. She was in a little black dress that showed off ample cleavage without being trashy. It accented curves ancient sculptors would have killed to get a glimpse of. The black spiked heels gave her already long, lean legs that extra oomph and made her at least as tall as Gabe. Her hair was perfect, but her makeup was definitely smeared.

Gabe was smirking. "Oh my. The Walk of Shame dress."

"Who said anything about shame?"

"It's before eight on a Saturday morning."

"And my date had an early shift at the hospital."

Gabe's face fell. "Oh God. You're not back with Ming Lee?"

"Like you care."

"I do care. She's looking for a housewife to bear her children, which isn't you, and if she somehow talks you into it, I, and possibly the entire company, am screwed."

"It was just a fun evening. And speaking of—good morning, James."

For some reason James turned bright red. "Morning."

"Ah, you're right, he does blush."

James felt his cheeks absolutely burn. She handed a stack of folders to Gabe.

"Aren't we meant to be living in a paperless society by now?"

"Tell that to the Russians."

Gabe flipped open the top folder. James caught a glimpse of a very large number with a dollar sign next to it. "That's a lot of zeros."

Gabe gave a random little wave. "That's a rough estimate. It'll change depending on the political stability of OPEC nations, where the euro stands, rates of violence in Afghanistan, and who wins the next Australian parliamentary elections."

"All that."

Gabe pulled his head from the file. "This kind of business is all about butterfly effect. An old lady in Grand Rapids can't figure out the grandson's Prius, crashes, claims it went out of control, it gets on the news, and the next day Toyota stocks are down two points, taking all other major car manufactures a half a point down with it. And you better believe twenty-four-hour news and social media has just made the whole thing worse."

James was still fixated on that number. "I fix computers for really smart people."

"And on a lot of levels, I envy you that."

There was the muffled sound of a phone ringing. Everyone looked around.

"Oh!" James jumped up. "It's mine." He fished it from the pocket of his coat, still hanging by the elevator door, before it went to voice mail.

"Hello?"

"Hey, Dad. How's it going?" Dylan's voice was bright and perky.

"Fine. Is something wrong?"

"Nope. Wanted to check on you. That's all."

James rolled his eyes even with no one there to see. "I'm fine. Thank you."

"Just fine?"

"Digging for details?"

"No, no. Just checking in. Any idea when you might be home?"

James looked over his shoulder. Gabe and Tamyra had their

heads bent over a folder again, and James saw the muscles of Gabe's back tense. "Actually I don't think I'll be staying that much later."

"Don't rush home on my account."

"It's fine. I'll talk to you later."

"Bye."

James went back to the kitchen. Gabe was already on his phone, and Tamyra was chewing on Gabe's toast while looking at her own phone. James' omelet had started to go cold, but he finished it anyway. He did not waste food.

He was draining his orange juice when Gabe finally got off the phone. "I'm really sorry about that."

"It's okay. You've got to do what has to be done." Gabe frowned as James swallowed a bit of disappointment. He had liked the idea of a weekend in bed, but with the amount of work Gabe had, he was surprised he'd been able to spend the night. And he was pretty sure getting clingy and demanding was not a good way to start off a relationship. "I really should be getting home, if for no other reason than to make sure Dylan didn't try to have an orgy while I was out."

Both Gabe and Tamyra laughed.

"Okay, but only if I get to make up for my neglect later?" Gabe stepped close, and James was once again aware he wasn't wearing anything but a thin robe.

"It's a deal if you point me toward my clothes."

Gabe gave him a kiss first, then pointed him toward a utility room where his clothes were still warm in the dryer. As he got dressed, his brain started to run ahead of him as it always did. Laundry, groceries, game on Sunday, work on Monday, fixing anything that had broken over the weekend.

Gabe was back on the phone by the time James returned to the kitchen.

"I should go," James mouthed silently.

"Just a second," Gabe told whomever he'd been talking to.

Then he grabbed James, pulling him into a deep, possessive kiss that left his head spinning. "I absolutely promise I'll make this up to you. I swear. Call me when you get home so I know you made it?"

"I will."

Gabe gave him another quick kiss before returning to his call.

11

When Gabe hung up his phone, the clock told him it was nearly ten. He'd known an ex-Soviet coder back in the start-up days who told him Russians liked having meetings late because they'd gotten in the habit during the revolution. He hadn't believed it at the time, but Moscow was exactly ten hours ahead, making it 8:00 p.m. on a Saturday night, and they seemed perfectly willing to talk for another two hours.

Five messages had come in while he talked to the Russians. He ignored them all except for the one from James. James assured him he'd gotten home okay. What's more, James didn't sound angry. Certainly if Gabe had been in James' position, he'd be a little peeved. He would have to think of something to make it up to James. There was another voice in the background of the message, and James talking with someone quickly and quietly. Gabe strained to hear what was being said before James cleared his throat.

"You're also invited to Dylan's baseball game tomorrow, if you can make it."

That startled Gabe, but he supposed it shouldn't. He'd done Meet the Parents before, but from James' offhand comments,

Dylan seemed like the kind to worry about his father, and inspecting the boyfriend was going to be part of that.

Gabe grinned at that thought. He and James were definitely at boyfriend level, which, while maybe a little fast, felt rather nice. He half listened to the other messages and wondered what he should wear to the game.

ON THE SMALL WALL-MOUNTED TELEVISION, Ernesto confronted his father over Gabriella's parentage. Normally the laundromat was aflutter with chatter and gossip at 1:00 p.m. on a Saturday, but Ernesto's great revelation had been building for weeks, and anyone who couldn't tune in daily was not about to miss the weekend catch-up.

There was a slight gasp from the women as Gabriella fainted, falling into Ernesto's strong arms.

James' attention slipped from the TV as he remembered how Gabe's arms had felt around him. Gabe had held him tight, and in those moments, James knew he'd breathed easier than ever before. The small panicky voice that commented on every aspect of his life was briefly drowned out by the memory of Gabe's warm, soothing words.

And he had slept. When Gabe told him to rest, he had melted into that soft bed, and he'd woke feeling better than he could ever remember.

That little panicky voice pointed out that now that Gabe had gotten what he wanted, there were good odds he'd move on. And he certainly had bigger priorities than romancing James. That number had had a *lot* of zeros. There was no way a person could juggle a number like that and also have a relationship. Certainly the wives of the successful businessmen in the telenovelas never seemed happy.

James frowned to himself as Gabriella emerged from her

faint in time to see Ernesto strike his father. Then the credits rolled.

The little voice pointed out that at least he wasn't a virgin anymore, and maybe he could go out and find a nice schoolteacher or something once Dylan started college in September.

GABE HIT THE REMOTE, shifting the music from his sound system to his bedroom. It was the CD James had given him; he'd listened to it five times so far.

He stripped off his shirt and pulled on another. He turned a little, getting a good look at himself in the full-length mirror. He hadn't put that much thought into what he'd worn to seduce James; he knew what made him look sexy. But meeting Dylan was a whole different ball of wax. He was going to a high school baseball game, so a suit was out. He didn't want to look too country club, because that wasn't really who he was. He didn't want to look like some rich twit who was trying to dress down, but he had a feeling he just might be a rich twit trying to dress down. And while he wanted to look good for James, he didn't want to look too slutty.

He sighed, picked up his phone, and pressed one on the speed dial. The phone on the other end only rang twice.

"Tam, I'm going to a high school baseball game to meet James' son. What do I wear?"

There was a moment of silence. "Gabe, you know the rules."

He sighed. "Are you taking raspberry syrup in your lattes?"

"Yes, I am. And make it a chocolate-cake donut tomorrow."

"Chocolate cake and raspberry latte. Now tell me how to do something I am *sure* I used to be able to do on my own."

"Your boot-cut jeans that are a little faded, the dark gray, long-sleeved polo shirt, and the dark blue, long wool windbreaker, because the fog should be rolling in tonight."

Gabe yanked a few things out of his closet and held them up to himself. "Thank you, Mother."

Tamyra snorted. "For that you also owe me lunch. Are you going to be ready to talk about next year's preliminary development goals Monday morning?"

"Do I have a choice?"

"No."

"Then I'll be ready."

THERE WAS a single free parking spot under a sign welcoming Gabe to the Home of the Fighting Cougars. He was running a little late and followed a few other stragglers toward the sports fields. Gabe was not one to get nostalgic for high school. High school was mainly an exercise in survival, but he did envy the youths he saw around him with their nearly boundless energy and ability to simply leap at things. He got to the stands and looked up at the crowd, scanning them, hoping to catch James' face.

He turned around quickly when he felt a hand touch his shoulder. James was standing behind him dressed in team colors and holding a little pennant flag.

"Hey, you made it."

Gabe couldn't control the grin that broke across his face "Got all my homework done early." He wanted to lean in for at least a kiss on the cheek but wasn't sure how public displays of affection would be received yet.

James covered the awkward moment by handing him the pennant. He pointed toward a small set of stands near the dugout. "Team families sit over there."

Gabe didn't comment on that as he followed James. He was

sure he didn't fall anywhere near the family category yet, but there were two spaces reserved in the front row. The visiting team was finishing their warm-up. He gave his pennant a practice wave as he looked around. There were a couple of glances his way, but they varied between curious and amused. No one seemed particularly hostile.

Dylan was taking practice swings with the bat, and Gabe understood why James was so terrified of him getting some girl knocked up. It looked like he was the team power hitter. In the front row of the stands, a group of girls were making eyes at him. If he was sixteen again, Gabe would have probably been right there with them. There was some cue, and the teams went back to their dugouts. An announcer read out the names of the players. The home crowd cheered at Dylan's name, and James smiled.

Gabe had never been much of a sports guy. He'd gotten pushed around by too many jocks, but James' focus was contagious. He was keeping statistics for the game, and with every swing of the bat, he put some odd notation into a column next to a name. Then Dylan came out to bat. There was cheering, and he waved at his groupies. James sighed.

There were a couple of balls, then a strike, then Dylan sent the ball out past second base in a clean arch. It hit the ground and bounced, letting Dylan get to second and one of his teammates get home.

Dylan didn't make it home himself, as the next batter swung three times and was out.

James started a new column of notation. The fog started to roll in thick and fast by the fifth inning, and Gabe was glad for his windbreaker. James seemed happy overall with the game until the sixth inning. Dylan slid feetfirst into third, and when he got up, even Gabe could see he was putting all his weight on his left foot.

"Shit," James hissed, leaning forward. "Shit, shit, shit."

The man sitting behind them leaned between them and put his hand on James' shoulder. "He'll be fine, James," the man said. "He's just being careful."

Dylan tapped his right toe on the ground a few times, as if testing it, then balanced out his weight. He turned and gave a nod to his dad. James nodded back before collapsing into himself.

"What's wrong?" Gabe asked, trying to figure out how a slide into third could warrant that kind of panicked reaction.

James shook his head tightly, not taking his eyes from Dylan. There was a bunt, and Dylan bolted for home but was cleanly tagged out. He hadn't really stood a chance, but he gave his dad another smile and nod as the teams changed positions.

James leaned closer. "When Dylan was thirteen, he took a bad fall and pretty much shredded his ankle. The doctors wanted to do surgery, but we couldn't even begin to afford it. We could barely afford the X-rays. Best we could do was wrap it up. He spent a month on crutches, and we did hydrotherapy in the bathtub, but it's always been a bit funny. If anything keeps him out of the majors, it won't be a bad day at bat, it'll be him rolling out of bed one morning and his ankle going out from under him."

"Is there any way it could be fixed now?" Gabe asked.

"If we could somehow scrape up the money for surgery, it would still mean six weeks in a cast and six months of physical therapy with no guarantee as to strength and mobility once it was all over, plus a risk of nerve damage. So short answer, no."

Gabe watched as Dylan took his position in the outfield. He'd always made sure that all TechPrim employees had full health coverage for their families. Even if something like reconstructive ankle surgery wasn't 100 percent covered, it shouldn't have been completely out of the question. Watching Dylan subtly shift his weight onto his good ankle reminded him that TechPrim was a bit of an odd duck as far as employee benefits went.

A crack drew Gabe's attention back to the game. A ball arched high into the air. Dylan took all of three steps to his left, put his arm up, and the ball dropped neatly into his glove. There were cheers, and Gabe waved his little flag.

It wasn't a close game at the end. The Cougars made three runs in the seventh, holding the other team at bay. Dylan got one more at-bat in the ninth, getting neatly struck out by the other team's relief pitcher, but the damage had been done already, and in the end the Cougars were victorious.

Dylan jogged over to the stands while the rest of the team headed toward the gym buildings. He stopped in front of Gabe and held out his hand. "Dylan."

"Gabe." Dylan had a good firm shake. "It's nice to meet you under not completely embarrassing circumstances."

"Same." Dylan turned to his father. "I'll get cleaned up quick, and we can head home."

"Sure."

Dylan turned back to Gabe, a slightly suspicious squint in his eyes. "Why don't you come around for dinner? Dad's making his famous pork shoulder in mushroom cream sauce over egg pasta."

Gabe knew he wasn't being invited to dinner as much as to an interrogation. "That sounds nice."

James gave an annoyed little huff. "It's Spam with cream of mushroom soup over noodles."

"It still sounds nice." Gabe knew even if it was dog food, the dinner invite was nonnegotiable. Dylan was going to give the guy dating his dad the once-over, one way or another.

A SPARE CHAIR had been commandeered from Dylan's room,

and three places had been set around the small kitchen table. Gabe watched as James cooked and Dylan helped. There was no clashing of movement and not much conversation. There wasn't the same underlying power struggle there seemed to be with every other teenager and parent he'd ever encountered. Maybe it was the unusual age difference or the fact that it was just the two of them, but they worked together more like good friends than anything else.

"Anything I can do to help?" Gabe asked as James scooped the noodles and Spam into a serving dish. It smelled fairly good for something that had come out of two cans and a box.

"No, thank you. I think we've got it."

Dylan moved the Spam to the table, placing it next to a bowl of peas. "Would you like something to drink?" he asked.

"Water is fine." Gabe actually wanted a shot of tequila for a bit of liquid courage. Dylan had been giving him sideways glances since he'd gotten there. Now that the embarrassment of their first encounter was over and done with, Dylan seemed determined to size up the man who was now sleeping with his father.

Dylan filled up two glasses with water. One he put in front of Gabe's plate, the other got a spoonful of sugar, a dash of salt, and a squeeze of lemon juice from a plastic lemon-shaped bottle. Dylan chugged it. Gabe tried not to cringe.

"It's basically Gatorade without the food coloring. Got to rehydrate."

The idea of needing to rehydrate led to a naughty little thought and a mental sigh. He was sure spending the night would be completely out of the question, but he still wanted to get James back into bed as soon as possible. A rather irritating part of his brain pointed out that his longest relationship had started without lots of sex. It was also the relationship that had ended in a nightmare.

Everyone took a seat, with Gabe across from Dylan and

James between them. That close, Gabe could smell James. He always smelled clean, with a hint of soap, and Gabe quite liked it. James dished up. There was no grace or any other ceremony. Dylan immediately started inhaling his food, but at his age and size, that wasn't surprising. He was a little curious as to what percentage of James' pay went for groceries.

Gabe dug into his meal as well. It was surprisingly good, especially once he'd mixed his peas in the way Dylan had. Dylan took a sip of water and opened his mouth, almost certainly to start the first volley of questions.

Gabe quickly turned to James. "Oh, Frank and Nate are going to want to meet you at some point soon."

"Really?"

"They like to meet anyone I've seen more than three times. They say it's to protect me from bad relationships, but really, they just like any excuse to give me shit."

James smiled. "I'm sure I can pencil it in somewhere."

"Oh, there's no rush. They're my best friends, but they are people you can't unmeet, and they both take great pleasure in sticking their noses into my love life. For a couple of straight guys, they have way too much interest."

James flashed a quick look at Dylan. "I do know that feeling."

Dylan took another sip of water and started again. "Dad says you're an executive down in the Valley. Which company?"

"TechPrim, right?" James answered for him.

Dylan froze solid, his fork hanging in front of him. "Your name is Gabe, right?" Dylan finally said.

"Last I checked."

"That would be short for Gabriel, wouldn't it?"

James gave his son a hard look. "Dylan, don't be rude."

Gabe nodded, even as his stomach dropped. "Yes." He realized that James might not actually be aware of what his position in TechPrim was. He was pretty sure they'd never discussed it. Maybe James didn't care what he did. That was a nice thought. Or maybe he knew and hadn't told Dylan.

Dylan ignored his father. "Gabriel Juarez?"

"Yes."

"I'm guessing Nate and Frank would be Nathan Nesbit and Franklin O'Conner?"

"Yep."

"Dylan, what are you talking about?" James snapped.

Dylan dropped his fork, then dropped his face into one hand. "Jesus Christ, Dad, he's not some midrange VP for TechPrim—he's the CFO and one of the founders."

James' head snapped around.

"Gabriel Juarez, Nathan Nesbit, and Franklin O'Conner. Cofounders of TechPrim. The Three Wise Men of Silicon Valley."

"Wait until you see Techpix. They'll be calling us the Three Stooges."

"You never mentioned that." James was blinking rapidly and looked more than a little startled.

"I thought you knew. I mean, you were at three of my lectures."

"You never mentioned your title."

Gabe quickly went over his general presentations and realized his title was nowhere in there since people who came to his lectures already knew exactly who he was. "Well, that's an ugly mirror to my ego."

"That does explain why you're nearly surgically attached to your phone," James said. Dylan still looked like he was in pain. "TechPrim's one of the big ones.

"Excuse me." Dylan's voice squeaked as he got up from the table. He came back with a laptop that was geriatric by technological standards. He held it up. "TechPrim?"

"Yeah."

He pulled out his cell phone, which was at least five years old. "TechPrim?"

"Yep."

He grabbed his father's cell phone from the kitchen counter. "TechPrim?"

Gabe squinted at it. "Is that an 8A Phantom?"

James grabbed his phone back. "That's enough. Sit down and finish your dinner."

Dylan sat and took a couple of bites, but he never took his eyes off Gabe. If anything they were harder than before and downright suspicious, possibly even edging toward hostile. It was a look he'd seen on the other side of a negotiation table but not a kitchen table. But then in a way, he supposed this was a negotiation. He'd been selling people on TechPrim for years. Now he needed to sell himself to Dylan as a partner for his father.

"Your dad tells me you're going to my alma mater." He hoped getting Dylan to talk about himself would ease the tension. "What are you planning on majoring in? Other than baseball."

"Majoring in economics, minor in computer science or math. Looking at business for my master's." There was no warming of Dylan's mood as far as Gabe could tell.

"That's a heavy load." If Dylan was the type of kid who read the business section, it explained why Dylan knew exactly who he was.

"I'll manage. May need a fallback position one day and a bullshit jock degree isn't going to help."

Gabe's phone vibrated in his pocket, the little motor humming just loud enough to hear. He really needed to write a memo about that. People put phones on vibrate so they would be truly silent.

"Russia again?" James asked. He didn't seem annoyed by the interruption, but was still looking a bit startled.

"Probably. Excuse me just a sec."

Gabe got up and moved into the living room as quickly as he could, thankful for the brief respite from the interrogation. It was Russia, moving from the panic phase into the "tentative renegotiation to try to get a better deal" phase. Gabe managed to convince them their ideas could be looked at later in the week, once some better data came in from Europe. He hoped it didn't sound like he was blowing them off.

Gabe took his seat at the table, trying to smile.

"Everything okay?" James asked.

"Just some more predeal jitters. Plus it's Monday morning there."

"Is this the *Buduŝie tehnologii* buyout?" Dylan asked.

That was the last comment Gabe was expecting, but he knew he shouldn't be surprised by it if Dylan was half as ambitious as Gabe thought he might be. "You read the business gossip."

"When I can."

"You know what deal he's working on?" James asked his son.

"Bits and pieces." Dylan peered at Gabe like he was trying to x-ray his brain. "TechPrim never went public," Dylan explained, never taking his eyes off Gabe. "They're not on any stock market anywhere, which has actually given them a bit of a cushion in this economy. They also never took venture capital money, so the three founders still have full ownership and control, hence the Three Wise Men. Since they're still afloat, they've been on a buying spree, scooping up bankrupted companies at fire-sale prices, usually folding them into the main company."

"And keeping on as many employees as possible with full pay and benefits for dependents. Better to save half of two companies than let both go out of business." Gabe had been getting a lot of shit in the press about it.

Dylan put up his hands. "I've got nothing against that. Some jobs are better than none. But you've started buying up random internationals as well—transport companies, mineral processing plants, a small private security company—all in weird places like Romania and Kazakhstan. And according to the gossip columns, you're about to pick up, for a not-small amount of money, a third-rate Russian technology company that is basically bankrupt, and no one can figure out why. Best guess anyone can come up with is you're about to go into high-tech weaponry."

Gabe laughed. "Is that what they're saying? It explains some of the looks I've been getting at the club, but no, no weapons. I'm a make-love-not-war kinda guy."

"Still doesn't explain what you're doing."

Gabe grinned. He knew the look on Dylan's face. When he was nineteen, he had won a lunch with some IBM executives. He'd stared at them, trying to somehow bore into their brains with his eyes, that same look on his face. He was suddenly half hoping Dylan wouldn't get picked up by the majors, just to see him jump into the business world still young and hungry.

"Secret negotiations are secret for a reason. Let's say if it all goes well, the production costs of all TechPrim hardware should drop 5 to 14 percent *and* allow us to corner the market on certain emerging carbon-neutral energy technologies, considerably increasing our overall market share and allowing us to move rapidly into other production areas." Gabe thought for a second. "I just sounded like a completely capitalistic prick there, didn't I?"

"A little, yeah," James admitted. Dylan nodded in agreement.

"How about this? I've got half a dozen dominoes lined up. If this Russian deal pans out, then in three years we can plunk a flat-screen TV factory down in the middle of Detroit with a solar panel manufacturing plant right next door."

Dylan tilted his head. "Onshore technology manufacturing jobs?"

"On shore jobs of all kinds. Lots of them, I hope."

Dylan raised his water glass but still had a suspicious squint. "Here's to jobs." Gabe's phone buzzed again. "Going to get that?"

"No. Just a text, and if it's a text, then it's not that important. Probably Tamyra reminding me to do my homework for some meetings tomorrow."

"By the way," James chimed in, thankfully changing the subject. "Why do you have 'Dancing Queen' as a ringtone?"

"Because Tamyra runs my life. I ignored her calls one time too many, so she hacked into my phone and put in an embarrassing ringtone connected to her number; that way I would answer it quickly. I took it off, and she put in something worse. If I take off 'Dancing Queen' she'll replace it with 'California Girls' or 'Genie in a Bottle.' 'Dancing Queen' is at least arguably a classic of sorts."

"That's cold."

"Could be worse. Frank didn't scream for mercy until his phone started playing 'My Heart Will Go On' in the middle of a corporate meet-and-greet with the San Jose Sharks." Dylan and James winced. "And before you ask, no, we can't fire our PAs. They are basically Vice Presidents in Charge of Making Sure Shit Actually Gets Done On Time, Correctly, and By The Right People. A few years back, Nate's PA caught pneumonia and was out for a week. The company lost nearly half a million dollars due to things she normally took care of not getting done. And Nate is basically just Chief Code Monkey. If Tamyra ever bailed on me, I'd be so very screwed."

"Remind me to be nice to Tamyra so she'll let you out of the house."

"She likes you. I wouldn't have asked for your number after

we had coffee if she hadn't stood there, wiggling her eyebrows and making not-so-subtle head gestures."

"I'll be sure to thank her, then."

James' smile was sweet, and for a second, Gabe managed to blank out the fact that they had an audience. He started to reach for James when there was the tiniest bit of throat clearing. Gabe refocused his attention. The interrogation wasn't over.

By the time the table had been cleared, and James brought out a bowl of chocolate pudding, Gabe had sketched out his family, mainly focusing on his sisters, nieces, and nephews, as well as some details on his last few relationships. Dylan was good, but Gabe had more experience being on the other side of a negotiating table, and Dylan didn't manage to wring out any information Gabe wasn't willing to part with, though certainly not for lack of trying.

It was Dylan's phone that rang next and cut the questioning short. He glanced at the number. "It's Coach Frasier."

James gave a quick tilt of the head, and Dylan stepped from the room. Gabe took the opportunity to settle his hand over James'.

"Sorry about the interrogation."

"Completely to be expected. I've got the feeling he's spent almost as much time worrying about his dad as you've spent worrying about him." James smiled and ducked his head. "And I am sorry I never mentioned my job title."

"It's okay," James answered a little too quickly. "It's not like I asked. And I figured you had to be pretty high up the food chain."

"But not at the top?"

"It's fine." Again, James' answer was too quick.

"You know, if I was in your position, I'd be flipping out."

"Give me a few minutes."

Dylan finished his call, but Gabe kept his hand on James', determined to prove he had some balls.

"What did Coach Frasier have to say?" James asked his son, not removing his hand either.

"Nothing much. Practice is going to be short tomorrow, and he wanted to make sure my ankle wasn't swelling. Plus a nag to get some sleep."

Gabe glanced at the stuttering clock on the wall and quickly calculated what time he might be arriving home. And he did still need to look over those projections for the next year.

With great pain he slid his hand away. "Actually, I need to get going. I still have documents to read for tomorrow. Sorry."

"It's fine. Homework comes first."

Dylan gave a small amused cough. Gabe was sure he couldn't begin to calculate how many times James had said those words. He stood and gave James a small kiss. "And dinner was very nice."

"It's a specialty."

Gabe turned to Dylan and held out his hand. "It was nice meeting you again."

"And you."

"I'm sure I'll be seeing you around."

Dylan's eyes flashed again, hard and suspicious. "I'm sure you will."

Gabe gave James another little kiss, gathered up his coat, promised to drive safely, and left.

GABE WAS ABOUT to open his car door when he heard feet moving quickly across the street. He turned to see Dylan approaching.

"Hey, glad I caught you. I wanted to ask you one more thing before you left." Dylan was smiling.

"Shoot."

"Are you enjoying slumming it down here with my dad?"

Gabe jerked as if he'd been struck. "Excuse me?"

"Come on. You're one of the richest guys on the coast and then some, you fly around the world every other week on the company jet, and you just happen to pick up my plain Jane, scraping-to-stay-above-the-poverty-line dad out of a crowd and not mention who you are?"

"Now just a second—"

"No. Let me show you something." Dylan handed over a high school yearbook. "Page forty-seven."

Gabe took the book and opened it to the correct page. There was a picture of a scraggly teenager sitting with his back against a locker, looking half-asleep as he slumped over a book. Wrapped around the teenager's hand was one end of a baby leash. On the other end of the leash was a toddler, maybe two, reaching for something just out of frame.

"That's my dad, junior year. In eighth grade he took the PSAT, got a perfect score. Senior year SATs he barely cracked 1100. He was too tired to do better. He spent his prom night sitting at home playing Candyland. This place." He gestured to the building behind them. "He can do better than this. We could still be living with my grandparents, but this place keeps me *just* inside a good school zone. Hell, he could even upgrade the Lemon Drop to something built this millennium, but he lives like he's taken a vow of poverty so he can save every cent for me. He has this theory that if I lose my scholarship, he'll somehow be able to pay for *Stanford* if he works himself to death. You will not find a better person on *Earth* than my father, and I will not put up with some rich prick from the Valley screwing with him," Dylan ended in a snarl.

Gabe stood his ground despite a desire to take three steps back. He knew he didn't get ice thinner than what he was standing on. "I know how good your father is, and I can assure you I'm not slumming it."

"You know how good he is?" Dylan's voice was thick with sarcasm and disdain.

"Yes, I do. Half the reason I'm making an effort and not treating this like a three-night stand is because he has more integrity than damn near anyone I know."

"And the other half of the reason?"

"I...." Gabe had yet to put it into words, even for himself, how he felt around James, and now he'd have to pick those words very carefully. "He's stable." Dylan snorted at him. "I don't mean like that, I mean... I spend most of my life feeling like I'm juggling knives on a teeter-totter. And since the economy crapped out, it's felt like I've been doing it in the middle of an earthquake as well. Now I'm damn good at it, and I've been doing it for a long time, but that doesn't mean it's easy or exactly relaxing. When I'm with your father, I feel stable. Grounded. I'm still juggling knives, but it feels like it's on solid ground, and I'll be damned if I know why. I can breathe when I'm around him, and maybe it was because he didn't know what I did. Maybe it's because he is a good person, and I'm not waiting for him to try to knock me off-balance. I just don't know."

"Do you love him?"

Gabe looked Dylan dead in the eye and decided to go with the most radical negotiating tactic he knew. He would tell the truth. "Not yet," he answered. "I care for him very much. He has already become important to me, and I'd like what we have to continue and get stronger. I had some lousy relationships when I was younger, then one *very* bad relationship, followed by a string of men who hung around mainly because I was too busy to tell them to leave. I *want* this to go slowly. Partly because your father is in new waters and partly because I'm in waters I haven't seen in a long time."

Gabe's phone rang. He didn't answer it. He kept his eyes locked with Dylan's.

"That's a good answer. I know my father likes you." Gabe held back a deep sigh of relief. "You make him happy," Dylan continued. "There have been other men who have shown interest in him, but he's been oblivious to it. My fifth grade teacher had a flat-out crush on him. Called him in every time I sneezed. He never clued in. Too busy with other things. You are the first person to notice him that he has *allowed* himself to notice back."

"That's good to know. I promise I'll do my best to step carefully with him."

"Good. I want him to be happy. And if you ever hurt him, I'll take a baseball bat to your legs, starting with your feet and working up."

"When I made that threat to my sister's boyfriend, I said I'd use a tire iron."

"Was it a serious threat?"

"Yes."

"Then we're on the same page." Dylan took the book back. "Drive carefully."

JAMES TURNED SIDEWAYS, looking at himself in the mirror. He was thin and not in a flattering way. It was probably the lack of anything resembling muscle definition. He tried sucking his stomach in, but that somehow made it worse.

He heard the front door open and shut, then Dylan coming down the short hall. "Did you threaten him?" he asked when Dylan stopped by his door.

"Only a little."

"You said you wouldn't."

"That was before I found out he's one-third owner of one of

the larger, and still in the black, companies out there. I wanted to make sure he knows you're not someone who can be played with and set aside."

James twisted around, hoping a different angle would somehow improve the view. He wanted to scold Dylan, but lately, scolding had a habit of turning into talking, and he wasn't ready to do that yet. And while he didn't believe Gabe was playing with him, he also wasn't expecting Gabe to stick around and grow old with him. James tried sucking in his stomach again.

"You know, I could set you up with an exercise plan." James gave Dylan a sharp look. "Nothing too hardcore. A bit of stretching, some basic calisthenics?"

"I think that was a lost cause before you were even born."

"Never too late. I just want you to be happy."

"I am." He was, he thought. "But we should both go to bed. It'll be Monday soon enough."

12

Gabe dropped a bunch of papers on Nate's desk. He knew there were a dozen people on this floor whose main purpose seemed to be to move bits of paper around, and it would have taken seconds to e-mail them, but e-mails could be hacked and traced, and low-level employees were prime perpetrators of industrial espionage.

"How's it going?"

Gabe fell onto Nate's couch. It was the same one that had made up the entire reception area of their first office. Nate had refused to get rid of it or move into an office much bigger than a couple of cubicles. It was some sort of reverse claustrophobia. He worked better in small, crowded spaces where at least one coffee cup was growing mold.

"Well, we might end up bribing half the *Gosduma* for the permits, but the dollar is still holding up okay against the ruble."

"I don't mean that. I mean how'd your special weekend go? Keeping in mind that I will interpret any reasonably positive or even noncomment as 'you got laid.'"

"It went fine."

Nate lifted his arms in victory.

"I still don't see how my love life is your business."

"I don't want to see you have a stroke, and sex is a good form of stress relief. Now tell me how things went, because Margaret will want to know."

"How much detail do you want?"

"Broad strokes. Very broad."

"We had a nice relaxing dinner on Friday night. Spent a pleasant evening together. Tamyra showed up with papers before eight the next morning. On Sunday evening I went to his son's baseball game, followed by an interesting dinner where Dylan pointed out exactly who I was and what I did, and also knew who you and Frank were."

"And your boyfriend didn't know who you are?"

"I may have completely forgotten to mention what I did," Gabe mumbled. "It made for a slightly awkward moment."

"I can see that."

"He also threatened to break my legs with a baseball bat if I ever hurt his dad."

"That sounds reasonable. When do Frank and I get to meet him?"

"How about never?"

"Nope. You know the rules."

Gabe ground his teeth. "Those are old rules, and James is a nice guy."

"The rules still apply, and you know it."

Gabe wanted to argue, but the rules about checking over anyone he was seeing seriously were in place for a reason. That reason was named Gregory, and that mess had ended in a two-man intervention, a minor act of violence, and Gabe living with Nate and Margaret for almost three months while he got his head back together.

"Give me a little more time before you two scare him off."

"If he's as nice a guy as you say, he won't get scared off. And if we let the rules slide once, we can work out an excuse for them to slip again and...."

"I know, I know." Gabe got up, sure there was something he had to be late for. It was a chronic state these days. "Oh, by the way, according to Dylan, the online rumors are that we're going into high-tech weapons manufacturing or something."

Nate laughed. "We would be spectacular hypocrites if we did."

"Look around. Hypocrisy is one of the few things people expect from corporations these days."

JAMES HAD one new message on his phone. He hadn't heard it ring or even vibrate. He knew he should be considering getting a new one, but the alignment of the Lemon Drop really needed to come first. He dialed into his messages.

"Hi, it's me. I'm guessing your phone is being antisocial again. If that is an 8A Phantom, you should know we recalled that phone for a reason. Anyway I just wanted to say I had a really good time this weekend. It was nice to meet Dylan, and he didn't threaten me too much. It was also nice to have some time with just the two of us."

Gabe's voice dropped lower, and James felt a warm rush.

"Um... according to my schedule, I've got pretty much nonstop conference calls between now and whenever hell gets around to freezing over, so I don't think I'll be able to make it up your way."

James tamped down the flare of disappointment. He knew there was no way Gabe could have regular lunch dates with him. He was honestly surprised to even have a phone message. He could only guess as to how much responsibility Gabe had and knew if he was in the same position, he'd be lucky to find time to breathe.

"I was wondering, there's a hockey game this Saturday...."

"Hockey?" James said silently to himself.

"...and we've got this corporate box that doesn't get nearly that much use, and there's a game this weekend, and if you don't like hockey or you've got other plans, that's fine, just thought it might be fun. Oh... I'm being told I have to get off the phone and go somewhere, so I'll talk to you later. Bye."

He flipped his phone around. The TechPrim logo embossed on the back in silver had been nearly rubbed away. In truth it was a shitty phone, but the new TechPrim multimedia projection system in the English Department ran like a dream. Half the mail servers were TechPrim, and they'd been chugging along well past their warranty date.

And Gabe wasn't just a part of the company that made it all happen. He was at the fucking top of it. James had spent half the morning running searches on his... whatever Gabe was. There were hundreds of thousands of pages. Some lauding him as a visionary, others completely trashing him. None of them had helped James sort out the confused feelings that had kept him up half the night.

After skim-reading a tenth article about TechPrim profit projections, James decided it didn't matter. He had his own priorities and responsibilities, and his current or possible future dating life would not alter those. And if the 300,000 articles were anything to go by, Gabe had a strong set of priorities and responsibilities as well.

He stared at the ceiling over his workstation. Some former manager had managed to lodge sharp pencils into the tile, and they had yet to fall. He'd once gotten on top of his desk to look at them. They were lodged in deep, and James could only guess as to how much anger or frustration had gotten them stuck up there. He'd tossed a few himself but never managed to stick one.

Dave approached, his newly acquired copy of *What to Expect*

When You're Expecting tucked under his arm. James picked up his phone and dialed Gabe, wanting a quick moment to brace himself before Dave asked some new stupid question. He got Gabe's voice mail.

"Hi. It's me. Soooo…. Never been to a hockey game, but sounds like fun. Leave me another message about when and where, and I'll try to get my phone to work on its social skills. Hope you're having a good day. Bye."

A COUPLE thousand people dressed in black and teal milled around James. Gabe had said to meet him by the VIP entrance, but he hadn't been there, and the man at the door had been unhelpful. James supposed he didn't look like the VIP type despite Dylan squeezing him into a smaller, less warm, but according to Dylan, better looking sweater. He spun in another slow circle, then checked his phone. There was a text.

Running about 15 minutes late. Will be there soon. Sorry.

According to his phone, it had been sent seventeen minutes earlier. He stood on his toes, trying to look over a sea of funny foam hats. He saw an arm waving and moved against the crowd, swimming upstream until he found Gabe.

"Sorry I'm late." Gabe gave him a quick peck on the cheek. He was still in his suit and tie. "I got held up in this thing, and anyway, how are you? You look nice."

James looked down at the too-tight V-necked sweater that had been living quietly in the back of his closet for years. "Um…. Thank you."

"We should go in."

Gabe led him back to the VIP entrance and inside the arena. Outside of Dylan's baseball, James wasn't much for sports, and he'd never seen a sporting venue that had thick carpeting and people standing around sipping wine.

This is how the other half lives was James' thought, quickly followed by a thought pointing out that Gabe was the other half. He was sure five minutes on the Internet would tell him exactly how far into that other half Gabe lived, but he didn't actually want to know.

When they got to the corporate lounge, he rejigged his opinion as to what qualified as posh. There were deep leather seats and a buffet that was more a line of cooks whipping up custom-ordered tidbits. An impressive bar. He did his best to look unfazed.

"Are you hungry?"

"What?" James had been distracted by one of the chefs flambéing something. "Oh, um... I ate before I left, but if you want to eat...?"

"I'll order something later. Let's get our seats."

When Gabe opened the door with the TechPrim company logo over it, he just expected seats on the other side; instead there was a room possibly nicer than Gabe's living room, complete with uniformed staff standing by. He changed his estimate from upper half to more likely the upper 2 percent at least.

"We were supposed to be entertaining a group of potential partners out of Australia this weekend, but the whole thing got pushed back a month."

"And you didn't want all this to go to waste?"

"Well, it would have been a shame. And their pastry kitchen makes a really amazing chocolate cake."

James didn't comment on the very odd idea that a hockey arena had a pastry kitchen. Gabe led them out another door, where there were seats that actually looked down onto the ice. Below them the crowd was a wash of black and teal with occasional splashes of purple.

He was about to take a seat when the suite door opened and

two men stepped in, followed by a woman and a couple of teenagers.

"Shit," Gabe said softly.

"Hey, Uncle Gabe," the teenaged boy called.

Gabe put on a smile that James could tell was completely forced.

"And what are you all doing here?"

"We're here for the game," the taller of the two men replied, grinning from ear to ear.

Gabe made a small noise like he was in pain, then took a deep breath. "James, these are my two oldest, best, and most annoying friends, Frank and Nate. This is Nate's wife, Margaret, and the two brats are my godchildren, Sarah and Harry. Everyone, this is James Maron."

James realized this was his turn to meet the family, as it were. He shook everyone's hand with a polite smile and sharply buried any disappointment that it wouldn't be just him and Gabe.

"Nice to meet you."

Frank smiled. "It's very nice to finally meet you. Gabe's become almost tolerable since you two met."

James tried not to flush even as Gabe rolled his eyes.

Music started coming from the direction of the ice.

"Okay." Margaret herded her children toward the seats, with Frank and Nate following.

"I'm sorry," Gabe said just loud enough for James to hear. "I thought it would be the two of us."

"It's okay. Really." James found himself sitting between Gabe and Margaret as the game started. He had never even watched a hockey game on TV, but Margaret seemed to be a fan and kept a running commentary as to what was going on, who the players were, and why the Sharks were the good guys and the Kings were the bad guys.

He tried to pay attention, despite Gabe's hand on his knee,

making him wish they were alone. He had no idea when his knee had become an erogenous zone, but a week earlier, he couldn't have told anyone a single erogenous zone on his body.

The crowd cheered as there was a particularly brutal crash against the boards. James winced but was also, he had to admit, enjoying himself. Very large men crashing into each other at high speeds was tickling something primal. Unfortunately that primal bit also wanted to rip Gabe's clothes off. By the time a buzzer announced the end of the period, it was becoming a problem.

Everyone else got up and headed back toward the suite. James remained sitting, with Gabe next to him.

Gabe leaned close. "After the game, would you like to come back to my place for some coffee?"

"Yes, yes, I would." Gabe's breath on his skin was doing nothing to calm him down, and he did not want to stand in front of Gabe's friends with wood.

"Good. I'd slip us out now, but it might be a little obvious."

"Just a little."

He brought up an image of Dave's Cheetos-stained fingers, which went a long way to helping him compose himself, then he took a deep breath. If Gabe could face down Dylan, then he could face down a couple of Gabe's friends.

"I think I should try some of that cake."

GABE FOLLOWED James into the suite, only to be stopped short by Nate and Frank while Margaret subtly herded James off to the side.

"You couldn't have waited for me to introduce you?" Gabe hissed.

"Nope, because it wouldn't have happened." Gabe wanted to argue with Frank on that point, but he was possibly right.

"Look." Nate kept his voice low. "Margaret can spot a jerk at a hundred yards. Has she ever been wrong about a single one of your boyfriends?"

"No."

"So if this James is a good guy, then you have nothing to worry about."

"He is a good guy, and he doesn't deserve the whole Spanish Inquisition."

Nate nodded in his wife's direction. "I think he'll be fine."

Gabe looked over his shoulder. Margaret was laughing at something James had said. James took a bite of chocolate cake and for a brief moment got a look on his face close to the one he'd had the first time Gabe had sucked his cock. Gabe sat down on one of the couches and quickly crossed his legs. He wanted to walk over there and accuse James of being a tease except he knew it had to be completely accidental. He grabbed a raspberry tart from a tray sitting on an end table. If he couldn't jump James and lick the chocolate crumbs off his face, he could at least eat dessert.

Harry plopped down next to him, with a slice of cake. "Uncle Gabe, can I ask you a question?" Harry's voice was at a half whisper with a bit of a teenaged squeak.

He bet himself ten bucks it was going to be about a boy. "Sure."

"How do you know if a guy likes you?"

"You're asking me this now?"

"Well... yeah."

"I don't know." Harry pinched his lips. "Honestly. Someone has to slap me on the back of the head with a two-by-four before I notice that kind of thing. You'd probably be better off asking your sister."

"She doesn't know either."

There were sounds of the game starting back up. "Okay, ask me later."

Gabe didn't pay much attention to the second period of the game. He was thinking too hard about what to say to Harry. Gabe hadn't been lying. He was awful when it came to noticing if someone liked him and had to be told directly either by that person or someone else. James was about as close to subtle as Gabe had ever come and he would never have picked up that phone if Frank hadn't told him to.

A horn blared to announce a goal. Gabe quickly glanced at Margaret to see if she was cheering, then looked up at the scoreboard. Somewhere along the line the score had tied up.

Gabe could just make out the standard ring of his phone in his pocket. He pretended like he didn't. At that hour anyone who wanted to talk to him was someone he wasn't up for talking to. Not when James was leaning against him and the Sharks were making the best of their power play for once.

The score was still tied at the end of the second period. James' cheeks were flushed from the cheering and the cold of the arena. As they made their way back into the suite, Margaret cut Gabe off while the guys subtly cornered James.

"I like him," Margaret said before Gabe could comment. "He seems like a good man."

"He is."

"You should be careful, though. I don't want to see anyone get hurt."

"He's not going to hurt me."

"No. But you could hurt him. Quite easily, I think." Gabe opened his mouth to object, but Margaret shook her head. "You wouldn't do it on purpose, I know. But it could still be dangerous. I mean, you said he hadn't had a relationship, not that he was a virgin or damn close to it!"

Gabe sputtered, not believing James would simply tell anyone that.

"Don't worry, I won't tell the boys. I made a little innuendo, and he blushed harder than Sarah when I asked her about kissing a boy. And I don't know a single grown man who blushes once he's been around the block a couple of times."

Gabe didn't mention that he liked the way James blushed. "I'll be careful."

"You could spin his head around very easily, and you know how badly that can end. Even if it's not on purpose."

"It wouldn't happen." Gabe took careful breaths to keep from shouting. "He's a lot stronger than I was or possibly ever will be."

"Just as long as you're careful."

"Promise." Margaret gave his arm a squeeze. "Quick question: how do you know when a guy likes you?"

"Gabe, he likes you."

"I'm not asking for me." He tipped his head in Harry's direction.

"Ah, well, in my experience, if you force feed a boy a live worm, and two months later he leaves a Garfield valentine on your desk, it's love."

"That is completely unhelpful."

"Sorry, but you might want to go rescue the boy who does like you."

Gabe looked over his shoulder. James was having his ear talked off by Harry and Sarah alternately. He quickly interjected himself into the conversation, and with a quick apology, extracted James. Sarah gave him a subtle thumbs-up.

"Sorry about that."

"It's okay. I'm used to talking with teenagers. They seem like good kids."

"Most days. Then there are days when they are spoiled brats, but I don't have to deal with those days. I get to be fun Uncle Gabe."

"Lucky."

"Very."

James looked away under the guise of sipping his drink. "So, have I passed muster?"

"With flying colors, not that it matters to me. I don't need any convincing that you are a good person."

James blushed. "You really hardly know me."

"True." Gabe lowered his voice. "But I plan on knowing you even better by morning."

"If you say things like that, I'm not going to make it through the rest of the game."

"Hey, watching you eat chocolate cake very nearly killed me, so we're even."

"We should get back to our seats, cool down a little."

Gabe paid even less attention to the third period than he had to the second. Margaret's words had sunk slowly into his mind. Half the reason he was sitting in a corporate box seat was due to a man who had spun him around so fast, he hardly knew who he was anymore. But Gregory had also been a manipulative bastard who wanted TechPrim for himself, and Gabe had been too young and inexperienced to see what was really going on until it was almost too late.

He glanced at James, who was cheering and smiling. He told himself to stop worrying. James was older and wiser and so much stronger than Gabe had been in those days, and more than capable of holding his own.

JAMES SHOOK HANDS WITH NATE, Frank, and Margaret as they left, stepping into the stream of happy fans. Gabe lingered near the bar. He let the door close and turned to Gabe. As much as he had enjoyed himself, James wasn't a social person by nature, and he felt tension lift from him as Gabe approached. Before he could say anything, he was silenced with a deep kiss. He pressed his whole body into Gabe's and wondered how much trouble having sex in a corporate suite in a hockey arena would get them in.

He'd been on edge all week, replaying the previous Friday night in his head. He'd gone to bed each night and taken his cock in his hand, slowly teasing himself, trying to build up a little stamina. His usual rush jobs in the shower had not prepared him for long nights of sex.

Gabe pulled away. "Would you like to go back to my place?"

"I think that would be an excellent idea."

"I got dropped off, so I'll order a car around for us."

"I drove. I don't think I can leave my car where it is overnight."

"I guess you can take us to my place, then."

NOTEBOOKS, powerbar wrappers, and a pair of thankfully clean sports socks were tossed in the backseat by James with no little embarrassment.

"Sorry. Dylan drives it most days. I tell him to keep it clean but…."

"Don't worry about it." Gabe got in when the last of the mess was relocated.

James prayed the Lemon Drop would start. Every so often it would get fussy and decide not to turn over. He put the key in the ignition, then pulled it out a couple of millimeters. He tapped the gas with the tip of his toe. Then with great care and a steady hand, he turned the key. The engine didn't exactly roar to life, but it did turn over and begin to hum.

"You'll have to point the way from here."

Gabe did so without much comment until they got onto the freeway. The Lemon Drop shook as they passed thirty, merging into traffic. Gabe gripped the dashboard.

"I know." James preempted any comment. "But my

mechanic promised the transmission *probably* won't fall out or catch fire."

"Probably?"

"Probably."

"So." Gabe tried to cover a squeak in his voice with a small cough. "Why the Lemon Drop Wonder? I'm assuming it has something to do with the color?"

"Actually, no. When Dylan was about three, one of my more senile great-aunts gave him a bag of lemon drops. He spilled them all over the back, and for years, every time I reached under a seat, I'd end up finding a furry half-dissolved lemon drop." Gabe chuckled but still sounded nervous. "I'm sure there are still a few under there, along with a half pound of Cheerio dust, a couple of Super Balls, plastic army men, and God knows what else. There's a distinct possibility that lemon-drop goo is holding parts of this car together."

James spotted a familiar exit and gripped the wheel hard as their speed dropped to thirty-five, then thirty on the exit ramp. Gabe's building rose above the surrounding properties, and he tried to push thoughts of sticky lemon drops out of his mind.

THE ELEVATOR DOORS had hardly closed when Gabe was on him, demanding entrance with his tongue. James granted it, tasting the raspberries of some little pastry Gabe had grabbed on his way out. The doors opened, and they stumbled into the living room. Gabe got his hands under James' sweater and yanked it over his head, flinging it aside.

"Do you want me to slow down?" Gabe asked even as his hands were rushing across James' skin.

"God, no."

"Good." Gabe drove them toward the bedroom, pulling off bits of clothing as they went. He pushed James backward onto the bed and yanked his jeans off. "God, I've been thinking about this all week." Gabe straddled James. "I'd be stuck in meetings about three-year production trends, and all I could think about was getting your cock back in my mouth."

James' breath rushed from his lungs as Gabe's cock slid against his. His skin was already burning, and he reached for Gabe, pulling him down into another kiss. He felt out of control. The nervous tremors and tentative touches of the week before were gone. Now he wanted to rush over that edge he had once feared. He wanted to do all the things Gabe had whispered in his ear.

Gabe ground against him. Smell and taste drowned out his other senses. He squeezed his eyes shut as Gabe started to suck at the pulse point in his neck. He thrust his hips up hard without a thought. There were no words, no thoughts, just a scream building in the back of his throat and a burning tension that curled his toes and arched his spine.

Gabe reached between them, wrapping a strong hand around James' cock. The scream that was building finally pulled loose and didn't stop as Gabe stroked him faster and harder until something in him snapped, and with one more scream, thrashing his limbs about, he came across his belly and Gabe's fingers.

He fought for breath, his heart still racing in his ears as Gabe rolled off him and propped himself up on one elbow. James was aware of being watched as he settled back down. Gabe brushed a wisp of hair from James' forehead. Even that tiny touch sent tremors down his over sensitized flesh.

"That was amazing," Gabe murmured. "If you let go like that from just my hand, wait until I really bring out my bag of tricks." James hummed, not yet trusting his voice. He approved of the thought, though. "I was worried you wouldn't come tonight. That I'd scared you'd off, or you'd decided my life wasn't worth the trouble." There was a sudden thickness in

Gabe's voice. "I spent all week worried that every message was you calling it off."

"Didn't you have more important things than me to worry over?" It was an honest question. He couldn't picture how a date could override everything that must be going on in Gabe's life.

Gabe leaned in and slowly nuzzled at his throat. "I couldn't help it. You've gotten into my head. Every night this week, I jerked off picturing your blissed-out face and all the things I wanted to do to make you make that face again."

James gasped and his cock twitched, already trying to regain interest. The image of Gabe stroking himself in the shower had become part of his own nightly ritual. He felt Gabe smile against his skin.

"Do you like that thought? The thought of me touching myself like a horny teenager, thinking about you?" James nodded, the images filling his mind.

Gabe gathered him gently into his arms, then rolled onto his back, pulling James on top of him like that first night when they had made out on the couch. Except now they were naked, and Gabe was fully hard, seemingly not caring about cum getting spread across his body.

He kissed James softly and ran his hand feather-lightly across James' back, then along his hips. His hips rolled, and James rolled his own in response, despite still being spent. He moaned into the kiss and trailed one hand up into James' hair. James melted that little bit more as Gabe played with his hair. He worked his own fingers into Gabe's hair. It was thick and healthy but somehow softer than it looked. His fingers slipped into it easily.

Gabe's hips continued to roll, but he didn't pick up any speed. He seemed content to simply have James pressed against him, and James did not mind. It felt so natural to have a strong male body under his. Another man's cock pressed against his. If the previous weekend had been the first hit, this was the addiction, the thing he'd been craving his whole life. He'd always told people he was gay, but that had been more theory than fact. One kiss hardly counted. Now he knew what he truly wanted. Now he knew what he honestly craved. Even as one of Gabe's hands gently squeezed his ass, he became afraid. He'd controlled his life as much as possible for years—every cent counted, every minute put to maximum use. His guiding principles had always been responsibility and priority. Now he knew he wanted to feel that out-of-control scream escape from him as often as possible, going against nineteen years of practice and belief.

Gabe started to thrust harder and faster. This time James slid his hand between them, noting how even holding Gabe's cock felt good right now, the smooth skin sliding along his palm. It was an odd angle, but Gabe thrust up into James' hand until Gabe's back arched, a low growl coming from deep in his chest, and he spilled between their bodies, his breath mingling with James' as he did.

JAMES KNEW he liked Gabe's bed the moment he'd touched it, but he was quickly learning to enjoy Gabe's bath just as much. It was deep and large enough for at least three, and with the steam rising from it, he felt there should have been Roman slave boys hanging around, holding towels. He leaned back, resting his head against Gabe's shoulder as Gabe's arms wrapped around his chest. Gabe gently rubbed one of his nipples with the edge of his thumb. It was sending soft waves of pleasure down his body like a gentle tide.

"I don't get to do this nearly often enough." Gabe sighed, giving James an extra squeeze.

"It is nice. I think bits of me that I didn't even know I had are relaxing."

"Do you want to know the only thing better than sex and a hot bath?"

"There's something better?"

"More sex, then a good night's sleep."

"I think I can get behind that idea."

Even as he said that, he found himself starting to half doze in Gabe's arms. In the distance, a phone rang. He started to lean forward so Gabe could get out, but Gabe held him tight.

"I'm not getting that."

"What if it's important?"

"I'd rather be doing this. I have a hard enough time not thinking about work." The phone kept ringing. "The guys are convinced I'm going to have a stroke or a breakdown." The ringing stopped, but Gabe raised a hand and began worrying the pads of his fingers with his teeth.

James had noticed the skin on Gabe's thumb and ring finger was cracked and oddly worn. He reached up and gently removed Gabe's fingers from his teeth in much the same way he'd taken Dylan's thumb from his mouth when he was little. Gabe looked startled, then embarrassed.

"What are you thinking about?"

"Work." Gabe's voice was more than a little irritated. "I shouldn't. I should be thinking about you and this."

"Tell me about your work. What's going through your brain?" James was sure most of it would go over his head, but he wanted a general idea so he could be aware of when Gabe really couldn't afford distractions.

"It's not interesting."

"I reset passwords and set up e-mail accounts for a living. On exciting days I lay cables. Now tell me what has you worrying your fingers off."

Gabe rolled his head back and stared at the ceiling. "There's a guy at the club, Simon, a real tool, and he doesn't like me. But he owns a little tech company. It's had four owners in five years, a dozen employees, and has never turned a profit. It's basically a second-rate tax shelter, and it's almost not that anymore. I want to buy it, but he won't sell. At least not to me."

"Why do you want it, and why won't he sell?" James knew he probably couldn't help directly, but he could at least be a sounding board.

Gabe brought his fingers to his mouth again, and James gently removed them. "I don't want the whole company. Just a couple of the patents they hold."

"And you can't buy those separately?"

"Not without Simon digging into why I want them. Right now I doubt he knows they exist."

"And they're that important?"

Gabe shifted, sloshing water onto the tiles. "Who do you think was one of the first companies to really use the mouse?"

James had never thought about it. "Apple?"

"Try again."

"Microsoft?"

"Xerox."

"Xerox? The copy machine guys?"

"Yep. They had it, they used it a bit, but they just didn't make the grand leap. They didn't bring it into the wider world. Then Apple came along and there was theft and infringements and counter theft, but when that mouse broke free, it was the game changer of game changers. It should be held up with the first Model T. Suddenly there was the Mac and Windows and everyone from grandma to a toddler can use a computer. Graphical user interface. Simon is sitting on a mouse. Two of them in fact, and he either doesn't know about it or doesn't have the vision or resources to do anything with it."

"But you do."

"If Russia works out, it would be the little bell that rings when the last domino falls over. It wouldn't change computers. It could change the world. Technically I don't need it, but oh, dear God, I want it. And even if he did sell it to me, the engineers who built it all have twelve-month restraint-of-trade clauses in their contracts, so they'll have to be unemployed for a year before they can work on their own projects again. And if I try to buy their contracts with the patents, Simon is going to get really suspicious." Gabe briefly clenched his hands in frustration.

"So you need the whole enchilada."

"Yeah. And that is just one of the places my mind has been wandering off to. Sorry."

"Don't be. You've got a lot of responsibilities. Those are important."

Gabe gave a little huff and James another squeeze. "It was never meant to be this—TechPrim, I mean. The guys had a drunken, overcaffeinated idea one night, and their plan was to sell it to some company for a few grand. I held them down and made them promise not to. And when I say held down, I mean I knelt on Frank's back and had Nate in a headlock until they promised." The phone in the other room started ringing again. "Our first office was the size of my shower," Gabe continued. "It had two phone lines and dodgy power. I thought we'd last a year or two tops, and then we'd all move on to other things. Instead we have offices on six continents, and I get alcohol poisoning at least once a year trying to close a deal. I mean, I know I shouldn't bitch. Especially to you."

James rolled over so he could look into Gabe's eyes. They were warm and soft, but they also looked tired. Gabe probably needed a good night's sleep more than he needed more sex.

"You can talk about your job any time you like. I don't mind."

Gabe smiled and kissed him.

The phone rang again, but this time it was playing "Yellow

Submarine." "Okay, that's Nate. That I need to get."

There was some splashing as Gabe got out of the bath as quickly as he could and rushed to the other room. James resisted the urge to wipe up the drips. He reminded himself he was a guest, and that marble didn't curl the way linoleum did. He wrapped a couple of large towels around himself. In the bedroom Gabe was looking worried.

"James, it's Nate." He held out the phone. "He wants to talk with you."

"Me?" James took the phone. He couldn't conceive of a single reason why Gabe's business partner would want to speak with him. "Hello?"

"James, hi, um…. Harry's run off. Well, he hasn't run off—he was supposed to be at a friend's house—but the GPS on his phone says he's in *Berkeley,* and he's not picking up his phone, and his friend's parents are out of town but I didn't know that, and he has never done anything like this, and Margaret is driving up there to find him, but I'm from Salinas, I don't know what kind of neighborhood he's in and—"

"Okay, okay, stop." James cut off Nate, now having a pretty clear picture of the situation. "First, big breath. Don't hyperventilate." He heard the sound of a deep inhale and exhale. "Now, where does your computer say he is?"

"It says he's near San Pablo Avenue."

James tried not to roll his eyes. "San Pablo is twenty miles long. Give me a cross street."

"Um… Gilman Street?"

James let out a quick breath. "Okay, there's an under-twenty-one club there. Mostly punk, some metal. Not the world's greatest neighborhood but could be lots worse."

Nate took a few more deep breaths. James had no trouble being sympathetic. The first time Dylan had snuck away with friends after a baseball game, he'd been in a dead panic. He looked at Gabe, who was looking a bit panicked himself.

"He's never done anything like this before," Nate repeated. "I swear, up until an hour ago, I thought he was a saint."

"He's fourteen. He's probably trying to impress a girl."

"More likely a boy," Nate muttered.

James decided to be kind and not point out that being fourteen and gay would not get rid of the chance he could get some girl knocked up.

"I think Dylan mentioned something about his ex-girlfriend's band playing there tonight. I can call him, see if he's there, see if he can find Harry and sit on him."

"Oh, that would be amazing."

"Hang on." He turned to Gabe, who found James' cell phone in his discarded pants and traded it for the house phone. He dialed and counted through the rings. If any band was playing, the odds were good he wouldn't hear the phone. Suddenly the line was filled with what James could only call noise.

"*Dylan. Go outside so we can talk!*" James shouted down the line, then waited until the noise in the distance became muted.

"Hey, Dad. What's up?"

"I need a favor; are you at the Gilman?"

"Yeah, Catherine's band is on their second set."

"Okay, Gabe's business partner, Nate? His son, Harry, was supposed to be staying with a friend, but it turns out the friend's parents are out of town, and the GPS on his phone says he's at the Gilman."

Dylan laughed. "You kind of have to respect the classics."

"Well, this seems to be the first rebellion, so his dad's in a dead panic. His mother is driving up there, and I was wondering if you could have a look around and sit on him until she gets there."

"What do I get out of it?"

"Dylan!" James snapped.

"Okay, okay. Any idea what the kid is wearing? And don't say black!"

"Um… just a second." James waved for the other phone and held it up to his other ear. "Nate, hi, what's Harry wearing?"

"Jeans, a T-shirt?"

This time James did roll his eyes. Gabe motioned for the phone with Dylan on the other end. James handed it over.

"Hey, it's Gabe. You've got our 880-SA phone, right? Is it set up to get photos?" Gabe grabbed a tablet from his bedside table. "Give me your number, and I'll send you a photo from his birthday a couple months back."

"You still there?" James asked Nate.

"I think so."

"Gabe's sending Dylan a picture of Harry. He'll keep an eye out."

Nate let out another long sigh. "I swear he was an angel until not too long ago."

"He's a teenager. These things happen."

"We've never even had to ground him before, he's been so good. We've been like best friends. I mean, what kind of punishment do I give out for something like this?"

James sat down on the bed. He'd watched plenty of Dylan's friends and teammates crash and burn over the years because their parents were trying to be either best friends or drill sergeants.

"You want my advice?"

"I'll take anything I can get right now."

"Firm but quick; this is a first offense. He'll throw a fit about his privacy. Doors will be slammed. Take his phone, cut off his social networking if you can, and make him be seen in public with his parents. He'll be screaming for mercy in forty-eight hours. Sit down, have a talk about how you were more worried than angry, then move on."

"And that'll work?"

"For a few weeks, two months if you're lucky. What did you do at fourteen?"

"I was trying to get enough XP to dual-class my half-orc fighter."

James remembered who he was talking to. "Right. Just have the safe-sex talk, a lot. Daily if necessary. You don't want grandchildren yet."

"I think he's gay."

"I'm gay. I'm also thirty-two with a seventeen-year-old son."

"Oh, that's right."

Gabe waved at him, then handed over the other phone. "Just a sec." James juggled phones.

"I found him!" Dylan shouted down the line. "He's standing by the wall, looking lame and uncomfortable, and making moon eyes at some guy who's practically dry-humping some girl."

"Can you sit on him until his mother gets there?"

"Sure, but TechPrim owes me one."

"I'll pass that along." Dylan hung up. James tossed the phone back to Gabe. "Dylan found him."

"Oh thank God." Nate's voice was thick with relief that matched the look of relief on Gabe's face.

"Apparently he's looking lame and uncomfortable, and Dylan will sit on him until your wife gets there."

"Thank you, James. I'm really sorry but...."

"It's okay. We've all been there at least once. I'm sure he'll be fine."

"Thank you for the advice."

"No problem."

"I should call Margaret and tell her where she's going. Oh, this is going to be a long night."

"It gets easier from here."

"Does it?"

"No. But if you don't tell yourself that, things can get ugly really quick."

Nate let slip a nervous chuckle. "I'll keep that in mind.

Thanks again. And I'm sure I'll talk to you later."

"You too."

James hung up, then flopped onto his back. Gabe sat down next to him and ran his fingers through James' still damp hair. "Thank you for that."

"Giving out child-rearing advice and being listened to is one of the perks of getting your own child anywhere near adulthood." James mumbled the last few words as Gabe's ministrations started to melt his body from the top down. "So if Tamyra's "Dancing Queen" and Nate's got "Yellow Submarine," what is your ringtone for Frank?"

"'Can't Touch This.'"

"I'm going to assume there's some long, complicated story behind that rather than believing one of you has terrible taste in music."

"Let's just say for Frank's own good, we don't let him near karaoke machines anymore." James chuckled, even as the will to move even a single muscle slowly drained from his body. "You look like you're about to fall asleep."

"I'm sure I could stay awake for certain activities."

Gabe gave him a kiss. "It's been a long week. How about morning sex?"

"I like morning sex. At least I think I do. I like the idea of it."

Gabe pulled away the towels and let them drop to the floor. "In that case, let's crawl into bed so we can be well rested for your first foray into morning sex."

THE FIRST THING James was aware of as he floated awake was the feel of fine fabric against his skin. It was soft and light and covered him except along his left side, where he could feel skin, warm and smooth against his own. It was the smell that came to him next. It was warm like the skin, masculine. It was a nice smell, relaxing. It made him want to slip back to sleep. Instead, he opened his eyes.

Gabe was sitting up next to him, working on his tablet. A tiny sliver of sun broke through heavy curtains and fell across the bed. The sun seemed to be coming from very high up, though, and it felt later than it should.

"What time is it?" he mumbled.

Gabe smiled down at him and smiled. "Hey, you're awake. It's almost nine."

"Nine?" James sat up. It meant he'd slept for over eight hours. That never happened. "Why didn't you wake me?"

"I tried, but you mumbled at me. I figured you needed the sleep."

"I haven't slept until nine in years."

"Then you really must have needed it." Gabe put his tablet aside. "I know I never notice how tired I truly am until I have a day when I can actually stop and breathe." James stretched his back, then Gabe pulled him close. He had the sudden urge to fall back asleep. "Got an e-mail from Nate. Harry is grounded, but he says thank you for the advice."

"Advice is easy," James said through a yawn. "It's a way to sucker other people into doing what you've already done, knowing full well that it's nightmarishly hard."

"I get the impression teenagers are never easy."

"Not really, but the first six months really were the worst. Lots of crying in the middle of the night. From both of us. I think it was a toss-up as to who was more exhausted."

Gabe put a kiss on his head, and James did his best to shake the old memories from his mind. Those days were long gone. Now he was lying in a soft bed, relaxed and happy from more than eight hours of sleep. If there was any time to seize the moment and take some initiative, this was it.

He rolled over and pressed his lips to Gabe's chest. "I think you said something about morning sex?"

"Did I?"

"I do believe you did."

"In that case...." Gabe tipped his head down and kissed him. James kissed back, feeling more confident than ever. Each touch between them was soft but sure. Kisses were gentle and lingering. Gabe slid down James' body, his light beard a contrast to the smoothness of the rest of his skin. He kicked away the sheets as he nuzzled the little stripe of hair below James' navel before taking a couple long licks of cock.

James closed his eyes, letting the sensation wash over him but also tried to disconnect, not wanting to leap off that edge too soon.

Gabe took a couple more licks, then stopped. "James?" James hummed, feeling too good to bother with words. "Would you be up for trying something new this morning?"

"Sure." James was up for trying just about anything right then.

"Good." Gabe kissed the inside of James' thigh. "I want to feel you in me this morning."

That managed to get through the lustful fog of James' mind. He sat up. "You do?"

Gabe had rested his cheek on James' thigh and was looking up at him. "Is that a problem? If you don't want to, that's fine...."

"No, no. Just wanted to double-check." James' cock was behind the idea. James was trying to work out the details. "Um.... How...?"

Gabe smiled and kissed the tip of his cock. "Lay back and let me take care of it."

Gabe crawled back up the bed and rummaged around in his nightstand. James glanced over and was glad to see that Gabe had as much random stuff in his nightstand as James did. He finally pulled out a tube of what James guessed was lube and a condom.

"I know you're clean but no point getting into bad habits."

"Oh, I'm a big supporter of condoms."

Gabe gave him a kiss, then quickly kissed his way down James' body.

James watched in fascination as Gabe opened the tube and slicked up his fingers. He wrapped one hand around James' cock, and with the other hand, reached behind himself. James couldn't see what was happening, but he could guess, and that guess sent a shock of lust through him. He bucked his hips into Gabe's hand.

"Easy there." Gabe stopped whatever he was doing and tore into the condom. "This is less prep than I usually like, but I'm feeling very impatient this morning."

James nodded as the condom was rolled on and Gabe straddled his hips. James closed his eyes and tried taking long, deep breaths. He felt a pressure against the tip of his cock, then a tightness, then suddenly an all-enveloping heat. He snapped his eyes open as Gabe shut his, his head tossed back and a smile on his face.

"Oh God," Gabe breathed. "Oh."

James watched in fascination as Gabe slowly rose, then pressed himself back down. The squeeze around his cock was on the edge of painful, but every nerve in his body seemed to be connected to that one point. Every tiny shift of Gabe's body telegraphed itself into James.

Gabe slid up and down a few more times. "You can move if you like." His head was still thrown back.

James had been fighting to keep as still as possible, but with that one comment, he thrust his hips up hard.

Gabe gave a small cry.

James froze. "Are you okay?"

"Fucking perfect."

James grabbed Gabe's hips and thrust again. He tried for some semblance of control, but it was the first time he'd been inside someone in over eighteen years. His body screamed in pleasure as what he'd been missing was finally delivered.

"Wait."

James froze but whimpered, struggling to keep himself still.

Gabe leaned forward, kissed him, then rolled them both over. James scrambled up onto his knees, trying to stay inside Gabe. Gabe raised his hips and wrapped his legs high around James' body. James pushed back in slowly, looking down to watch his cock vanish.

"Nice and hard, James." Gabe's voice was thick and rough, with an edge of command.

James pulled back and thrust hard. Gabe cried out, his voice filling the room. He grabbed his cock and started stroking it fast. The sight broke something loose in James' chest. He grabbed Gabe's hips and let all control go. His thrusts were as deep and hard and fast as he could make them. The slapping of his body against Gabe's gave rhythm to their cries.

James felt it coming to an end too fast. He wanted to slow down but couldn't; he felt locked into a race with no slowing down or turning back. Then with a deep bellow, he came, driving himself into Gabe with five strokes, each as hard and deep as he could go.

He held on to Gabe's hips, afraid of tipping over, then Gabe arched his back, squeezed down on James' cock, and spilled across his body.

He lay there gasping for breath, his legs still wrapped around James.

"Are you okay?" James asked. He felt himself starting to get soft but still didn't quite trust himself to let go or move.

A huge grin spread across Gabe's face. "I am fucking fantastic. You've got a bit of fire buried down deep, don't you?"

James didn't answer. His body was suddenly sending in general status reports, most of which were pointing out that he'd never done that before, had some rather underused muscles, and he didn't get nearly as much exercise as he should.

Gabe dropped his legs, and James slid out. He must have realized James was still processing and slipped the condom from James' cock for him, chucking it into the basket under the nightstand. Only then did James fall face-first onto the bed under him.

Gabe rubbed the small of his back. "How was that for morning sex?"

He managed to give a thumbs-up.

"Good."

Gabe's phone rang.

"Are you going to get that?" James already had a pretty good idea as to how lucky he was getting so much uninterrupted time with Gabe.

"Nope."

"Might be important."

"Don't care. It's Sunday morning, and I'm naked in bed with my boyfriend."

James pushed himself up. He'd guessed they were at boyfriend stage, but he'd yet to hear anyone use the word. "Boyfriend?"

Gabe frowned. "Is that okay?"

"Yeah, yes.... Still not quite sure how this all works."

Gabe kissed him. The phone was still ringing. "This works however we want it to work, as fast or slow as we want."

The phone stopped. James looked over at where it was sitting on the bedside table. The screen said seven missed calls and five messages. "I shouldn't be distracting you from work."

"I'm the boss. Sometimes I get to decide how I spend my Sunday mornings, and right now I want to spend it taking a long shower with my *boyfriend,* then having a nice breakfast. How does that sound?"

James felt warm under Gabe's gaze. "It sounds great."

13

It was after noon when James slowly unlocked his front door. He wasn't sure why he was trying to be quiet. It wasn't like he was sneaking home at two in the morning or had anything to be ashamed about.

He slid inside and shut the door silently. Dylan came out of the kitchen with a sandwich in each hand. He grinned. "Looky who finally made it home."

"There was traffic," James mumbled, still not sure why he felt the need to make excuses.

"At noon on a Sunday. Sure." Dylan crashed on the couch, tearing into one of his sandwiches as he did.

"Thank you for taking care of things last night, by the way."

"Oh, no problem. Harry and I had a long and *interesting* conversation about your boyfriend, covering many topics, while we waited for his mom."

"Really." James tried to sound like he didn't care.

"Oh yes. Has he mentioned a guy called Gregory?"

"A few times. Old business manager, I think he said." James tried to downplay it, but Gabe hadn't really talked much about any past boyfriends.

210 | ADA MARIA SOTO

"An old boyfriend."

"Yeah, he sort of mentioned that."

"Well, according to Harry it was a *very* bad relationship, and the adults only talk about it when they think no one is listening. Best he and his sister can put together is the guy was trying to steal TechPrim, seriously screwing with your boyfriend's head in the process. It might have even gotten a bit violent toward the end." That thought pulled James up short. "No one will talk about it, but he does know that Gabe lived with his parents for a few months after the breakup. Bet you didn't know about any of that."

"No, that was never mentioned." James tried to picture Gabe in any situation where he'd let someone take control like that. But then he couldn't picture Gabe in any situation where he wasn't in control, where even if he didn't have the upper hand, he at least knew what was going on around him. But he couldn't blame him if the relationship had been that bad. And James knew he wasn't one to talk about control. His whole life was about trying to bring order to situations that were out of his control or where people were trying to take control from him. He was learning that one of the things he found appealing about Gabe was that he felt he could trust Gabe to take control for a bit, allowing for things like eight hours of sleep.

"He also mentioned you got the seal of approval from his parents, so you're in. Though TechPrim owes me an internship, paid."

"I'll be sure to pass that along."

NORMAL, rational people did not spend their Sunday afternoons trying to go over badly translated Russian business law, half of which seemed like dusted-off leftovers from Czarist days, and Gabe knew that.

He read Tamyra's proposal for the hundredth time. So far he'd moved a comma and fixed one misspelled word.

He knew he should be letting the lawyers handle the entire thing. He knew he should stand in front of a team, hand them a memo, and say, "I want to buy *Buduŝie tehnologii*. Make it happen."

But the fact was the whole project had been his idea. A randomly accessed late-night article on rare earth elements had settled into his brain. It turned into an idle search through mineral deposit maps, more as a time waster than anything else. Three days of no sleep later, he'd had the list and the idea. If Hershey could own the cocoa farms and almond orchards for their chocolate bars, why couldn't TechPrim dig up their own indium and neodymium from newly discovered deposits? Okay, the deposits were literally at the ass-end of nowhere, and half the mineral rights were already owned by random companies lacking the resources to get to them, but after three sleepless nights, these sounded like minor problems, and he'd pitched the whole thing to Frank and Nate.

He leaned back and felt an ache from the morning's sex. He really hadn't prepped himself enough, but it had been a long time since he'd had a good fuck. It had been a long time since he'd felt comfortable letting anyone do that, and the sudden desire had startled him more than a little. James had seemed to take to it well. He'd seen the moment when something in James' head flipped over. When the mild-mannered single parent had given way to something raw and primal.

His cock twitched at the memory, and if he hadn't already forked out cash for a half-dozen other companies, he'd be tempted to just chuck the idea, buy his neodymium from the Chinese like everyone else, and drag James back into bed.

He picked up his cell phone.

Russian property law is really boring. Can I come up there so we can make out? ;-)

Gabe sent the text and hoped James' phone was feeling social. He'd gotten through another two paragraphs when his phone bleeped.

Only if your homework is finished. Tamyra would never forgive me otherwise.

Gabe wasn't sure if he should be amused or annoyed. He'd never had a response quite like that. He decided to go with amused and went back to his homework.

JAMES WAS PULLED into a rough hug when he stepped through his office door. That was startling enough, but the fact that it was Dave hugging him put it well into the weird category.

"Congratulations, boss!"

"Thank you. For what?" James looked over Dave's shoulder. The rest of his team was gathered around one workstation, grinning at him. He wasn't sure what could have happened in the half hour he'd stepped out to eat his lunch to get that kind of response out of Dave, but he hoped it was some internal memo stating that everyone at his pay grade was getting a raise.

Dave slapped him on the arm. "For getting engaged. You should have told us."

"What?" James was sure he could not have heard right. "I'm what?"

"Getting married, or I don't know, commitment ceremony or something?"

"What the hell are you talking about?"

Dave pointed at the computer. James sat down with caution. There was a gossip blog from a local newspaper up on the screen and a line of bold text that read "TechPrim Family Day." Below was a picture that looked like it had been taken with a long lens from the other side of the hockey rink. He could clearly make out himself, Gabe, and Margaret in the front row, and Frank, Nate, and the kids behind them. James read the full-paragraph write-up.

The Three Wise Men of Silicon Valley spent an evening out with their families at Saturday's Sharks v. Kings game. Included was UCB Academic James Mazon, longtime partner of CFO Gabriel Juarez. Sources inside TechPrim say to expect wedding bells before the summer is up.

James put his face into his hands. "Who else has seen this?"

"It's going around campus, and we might have sent it up to the Lawrence guys."

James took a deep breath and counted to five, then kept going until he hit thirty.

"First, they spelled my name wrong. Second, as I'm sure you are all aware, I am not what you would call an academic around here. I fucking work for a living. Gabe and I have only been dating a couple of months. We are not at the partner level —we've barely hit the boyfriend level. And whoever their inside source is, is smoking crack."

"So you're not getting married?" Dave asked. "'Cause if you were, we'd all be totally cool with it."

"I'm not." James looked around at his team. They didn't look like they believed him. "How about if I ask someone who would know?"

James dialed Gabe's number, then hit a couple of buttons that were supposed to turn it into a speaker phone. It was a feature he'd never used and to his surprise, it worked.

"Hello."

James put his phone on the workstation desk so everyone could hear. "Hey, it's me. Got a second?"

"For you, about five of them."

"Great. Are we getting married?"

"No!" Gabe snapped. James tried not to feel hurt. "I mean… no, wait. That didn't come out quite right. Am I on speaker phone?"

"Yes."

"Who else is there?"

"My team, who doesn't believe I'm not engaged."

"Oh. Hi, James' team." There was a chorus of greetings from his people. James heard Gabe take a deep breath. "I know which website you're looking at, and the guys and Tamyra have been giving me shit nonstop all morning. That crew just makes shit up. They've reported Tam and I getting engaged a half-dozen times, and she's a golden lesbian." James chuckled, feeling a little better. "And I promise that any sort of commitment ceremony that may possibly occur in the future will not be announced via a gossip column, nor will I ever propose at a hockey game. Is that all right?"

"That's fine."

"Hey, rich guy dating our boss," Clare piped up. "You totally should marry him because he puts up with us and this place, so that makes him like a fucking saint. You could do a lot worse." There were some general murmurs of agreement. James bit back a sudden urge to cry, since it was easily the nicest thing anyone in the department had ever said about him.

"I will certainly take that into consideration." James heard the smile in Gabe's voice. "Okay, I've got to go. I'll talk to you later?"

"Sure. Bye." James ended the call and turned to his team. "Okay, everyone, you've had your amusement for the afternoon. Go do something that at least looks like work." He made little shooing motions and most everyone wandered off, except for Dave.

"Um… speaking of weddings. Here." Dave shoved a postcard showing Golden Gate Park into his hand. James flipped it over. On the back, where a vacation greeting would usually go, was an announcement for the wedding of Dave Melinick and Karabi Parthasarathy. "Kara and I decided we should get married. You know, for the kid and all, and Kara wants to do it kind of quick so she doesn't look totally pregnant in all the photos. Plus, I mean, when the hell am I ever going to find a girl like Kara again? We can't really afford a big wedding, even though her folks are helping out a bit—well, basically taking it over—but that's why we're just having it at the park and using postcards for invitations and stuff, because it's kinda cool and different. And since you're giving me all the baby advice, you're totally invited."

James looked at the postcard. It was kind of a cute idea as far as cheap wedding invites go, and he had to admit he was curious as to what kind of woman would not only sleep with Dave, but marry him and bear his children.

"And you can totally bring your boyfriend," Dave added.

James gave Dave a pat on the arm that he hoped was reassuring and supportive. "I'll take a look at my schedule and definitely try to make it."

THE ENGINE of the Lemon Drop Wonder ground and refused to turn over. James pressed his forehead to the steering wheel and tried to take long, cleansing breaths. His phone rang midbreath.

"Yes," he grumbled into it.

"Hi. It's me." Gabe's voice sounded cautious, and James pictured the little flashes of half smiles Gabe gave when he was treading carefully.

"Hey."

"Before you say anything, let me start with apologizing

about being snappy earlier. It's been a really long Monday, and the guys were teasing me about it, and please don't take it as a sign of lack of affection or commitment-phobia or something." Gabe's words had all come out in a rush, but they were comforting to hear.

"It's okay. I'm having a bit of a Monday myself."

"Anything I can do to help?"

James turned the key again and winced at the noise. "Not really."

"Is that your car?"

"Yeah. She gets fussy once in a while. I just need to sit for a few minutes, and she'll turn over."

"Do you need a lift anywhere?"

James laughed. "Thank you, but last I checked, you're at least an hour away."

"Yes, but I'm an hour away in a car that works."

"I'll be fine." James leaned back. He wasn't going anywhere for at least five minutes. "How was your Monday?"

"It was a Monday. I've been putting out all the fires that flared up over the weekend." Gabe sounded as tired as James had to admit to feeling. "Spent a fair amount of time wanting to be back in bed with you instead of sitting in asset allocation meetings."

"I'm sure they were important meetings."

"Technically, all my meetings are important. At least that's what I keep getting told. Doesn't mean I don't want to be somewhere else with far more interesting company."

That made James laugh. "Well, then, you must have been thinking about someone else, because I am possibly the least interesting person on the planet."

"The least interesting person on the planet is a man named Traian Zgonea, who works for the Romania Ministry of Economy, Commerce, and Business Environment. This man can suck the color out of a room just by standing quietly in the corner. He makes you want to open a vein just to see if you still bleed red. You, on the other hand, James Maron, are a very interesting person."

"I'll take your word for it." James gave the engine another try, but she just complained.

"Are you sure you don't want me to come up there?"

"It's fine. She'll get there. She always does. Oh!" James wanted to turn the conversation away from the car. "Dave has invited me to his wedding."

"Dave? Knocked-up-girlfriend Dave?"

"Yep. It's in a couple of weeks, and I've been told I can *totally* bring my boyfriend if I want."

"Are you going?"

"Well, I have to admit I'm curious about what kind of woman would marry Dave."

"I'll see if I can clear a bit of space in my schedule. Might be nice to go somewhere where there are good odds we won't end up in the gossip blogs."

"Yeah." A thought suddenly popped into James' head. "Shit."

"What?"

"Dylan reads the gossip blogs."

"Is he likely to believe it?"

"No."

"Oh, good. I'd hate for him to think I proposed without asking him about it first. He'd kill me."

"I'm sure he'd forgive you." James gave the key a twist, and after a quick grinding sound, the engine came to life. "There we go."

"I guess I should let you get home. I might be up there later in the week. Can we do lunch?"

"Sure. Have your people call my people."

Gabe chuckled, and James pictured the little crinkles around his eyes. "No problem. I'll talk to you later."

"Bye."

He hung up, then carefully shifted the Lemon Drop into reverse. There was a squeaking noise, but he knew that was normal. He sent up a prayer to the automotive gods that both he and the car would get home in one piece.

JAMES WAS JUST STEPPING through his front door when a printout of a particular web page was shoved in his face. "I'm not getting married," he sighed.

"Good. 'Cause if Gabe proposed without asking me first, I'd kill him."

He dropped his keys on the plate by the door. "Since when do you get that much of a say in my love life?"

"Since I was six, and Tommy Blair's creepy uncle asked me if you were single, and I told him it was none of his business."

James tried to remember Tommy Blair. The best he could come up with was a particularly skinny redheaded kid. He did have a somewhat clearer memory of little Tommy's uncle, who would come to T-ball games and whom none of the parents particularly liked.

"Thank you for that." He took a deep breath. "How was school?"

"It was school. How was work?"

"It was work."

Dylan smiled at him. James understood. There was comfort in those stupid words they'd said to each other thousands of times. It was changing the subject and allowing the subject to be changed. It was shelving things to be handled or examined at a later date. James knew that was one of the things he would miss when Dylan went off to school. Their shorthand, developed over years, which allowed them to handle big things or scary things that their relative youth had yet to fully prepare them for, but in their own time.

Dylan gave him a pat on the arm. "How about if I make dinner tonight to celebrate the happy announcement?"

Dylan's cooking was no worse than James', and he didn't offer often. "Knock yourself out."

14

As soon as Gabe climbed into the car, he pulled James into a kiss and felt his whole body relax. All the stress of the week simply melted away as he tasted James' lips for the first time in a million years, or four days, depending on how you counted.

Gabe knew he was falling hard and fast. Every day he tried to find a minute to call or text James, to reach out in some little way. Mostly he got James' voice mail and would make yet another note to himself to get James a new phone.

He moaned as James pulled back from the kiss. He was tempted to grab James again and skip lunch, but he was pretty sure James wasn't an exhibitionist, and there were things Jared didn't need to be subjected to.

"Hi," James breathed at him.

"Hi. I was thinking something different for lunch."

"Different?"

Gabe lifted a basket from between his feet. He was very proud of himself that he'd managed to make some little arrangements. "It's a nice day. Picnic?"

"Okay." James looked surprised but was smiling. "Sure. A picnic." Gabe had found a small, secluded park up in the hills that wouldn't have many people around in the middle of the day. He laid a blanket under a tree and motioned James to sit. He hadn't done anything as silly as a picnic for a long time. Possibly since college, but it was high on his list of "fun things to do with James that James has probably never done before." That was a long list.

He flipped open the folding picnic basket. He pulled out containers of sliced fruits, cheeses, and little sandwiches, as well as some quality sparkling cider, since they both had to go back to work.

"This all looks really good."

Gabe popped the cork on the cider and poured them both a glass. "Here's to a few minutes of peace."

"I'll take that."

Gabe sipped the cider, enjoying the feel of the bubbles across his tongue. He watched James drink and swallow. He was starting to have a possibly unhealthy fascination with James' neck. When he closed his eyes at night, one thing he thought about was the way James smelled at the spot between his neck and shoulder, the place that seemed custom-made for him to rest his head for a moment. He took another swallow of the cider and tried to focus on something else, since he could feel himself getting wood already.

He plucked a slice of firm white peach from the fruit tray. "Here, try this."

James took the peach. He was a little disappointed James didn't try to eat it from his fingers, but that was a somewhat advanced maneuver. Still, the look on James' face was compensation enough. He closed his eyes for a moment and a bit of juice smeared across his lips.

Not an exhibitionist, Gabe reminded himself. He took a slice of peach and ate it, making sure to lick the juice from his fingers with particular care. James flushed and shifted a little.

"I checked my schedule. Barring an emergency, I should be able to make it to Dave's wedding with you."

James cringed. "Thank you. I think I'll need support. I keep trying to picture what kind of wedding Dave could possibly have, and it never goes anywhere pretty. I'm crossing my fingers for a rented tux and nice dress and a friend with a Universal Life Church certificate."

"I'm sure it'll be fine. And even if it isn't, it'll be nice to get out somewhere where I know no one is going to talk to me about business."

"Most of the team is going, so that means you'll be there as the boss's date. I'm expecting very polite conversation and good behavior out of all of them."

"Really? I figure I'm going to be cornered at least once and told to make an honest man out of you." Gabe could honestly say he'd never had an entire Tech Support team voice an opinion on one of his relationships.

James ducked his head, blushing hard this time. "I am not expecting them to say anything like that. I'm mostly the guy who signs their time sheets."

"I think you sell yourself short." It seemed to be a habit of James'. "As a head of a major multinational corporation, I like to think I can recognize leadership and management skills when I see them."

"Yes, letting them spend half an hour watching dancing-cat videos online is a great management skill."

"Sure it is, if it's just a half hour. It makes them happy, it makes them loyal, it makes them feel like you're on their side, and happy, loyal employees are the ones who are willing to put in that extra shift when you really need it, spend those extra few minutes finishing up a project instead of clocking out and putting it off for the next day. I bet you do more asking than ordering."

"I don't think my team would follow an order."

"Sure they would. They want to keep their jobs. They'd probably just halfass it."

James chuckled. "Are you sure you haven't met them?"

"I've bought up a lot of companies. I've seen pretty much every flavor of group dynamic and leadership method. TechPrim has a whole management re-education process for when we get in lots of new people. We try to teach them that happy, healthy employees with happy healthy families are loyal, productive employees. And I bet if I asked around, I'd find out you are a reasonably bright spot in what I'm sure is a pretty dreary job for most of them."

James stared into his glass, his face still red. "I floated up into my spot because I'd been there the longest and knew where most of the bodies were buried."

"I got my job because the guys didn't know how to use a spreadsheet and didn't want to fill out the business loan applications themselves."

"I hope they're grateful."

"They are. But it's been a long road. We're kinda like brothers now. We know exactly how to piss each other off. The three of us once did a press conference on how good our next product was going to be and how stable TechPrim was, at a point when we hadn't actually spoken to each other in a week and were passing bitchy notes around via our PAs."

James was trying and failing to hold back a grin. "Sounds very mature."

"That's us. Mature as anything. Two code monkeys and a business school wannabe. Believe me, I regularly look around at the company and the guys and think, 'Who the hell was stupid enough to put us in charge of all this?'"

"Day I took Dylan home, I had the same thought. 'What the hell am I doing?'"

Gabe felt a flash of shame, even though he knew James had had no intention of making him feel that way. He was griping about running a company, something which, frankly, a lot of far less talented people than him did perfectly well, but the idea of having a kid had only crossed his mind on a few occasions and the thought of raising one on his own was the thing of nightmares.

He leaned forward, closing the space between them, and pressed a hard kiss to James' lips. "Whatever it was you did, you did it right."

JAMES NUDGED open Dylan's bedroom door with his hip and set a full basket of laundry on the bed. He'd trained Dylan to mostly pick up and put away his own clothes years earlier, but lately James had found himself doing it again, this time with more nostalgia than annoyance.

He opened the top drawer of Dylan's dresser to deposit some socks and found a pair of glass eyes looking up at him from a face of matted, off white fur.

He pulled Squiggle Bear from the drawer and sat down on the bed. The blue felt on the paws, with the strange abstract pattern that had earned Squiggle Bear his name, was rubbed nearly smooth. James noticed his left ear was coming loose. He was overdue for a repatching after a savage teacup poodle attack.

He wrapped his arms around the bear, holding it to his chest the same way Dylan had only moments after shredding through wrapping paper with the number three printed all over it. He'd gotten a dump truck and another stuffed bear that birthday, but the white bear with strange blue felt paws had been his instant love.

"Do you two need a moment?" Dylan was leaning against his door, looking amused. James loosened his hold on Squiggle Bear but didn't put him down.

"Are you taking him with you when you move into the dorms?"

"Well, not if you want him."

James didn't rise to the bait. "You used to take him everywhere."

"I stopped that a while ago."

"He'd miss you."

Dylan didn't reply, but he did sit down on the bed next to James. He took Squiggle Bear from James' hands and stared at him in quiet contemplation.

"His ear is getting loose again."

"I've been meaning to get to that."

"I never thought you'd stop crying that day. Thank God your grandmother is quick with a needle and thread."

Dylan ran his thumb across the chronically lopsided ear before a slight frown pulled at his face. "That day I left him at the merry-go-round up at the park, how did you get him back? I mean, it was after dark by the time I noticed I didn't have him, and they shut down the park at dusk."

James sighed. It had not been one of his better evenings. "I may have hopped a gate, hiked a couple of miles, and jimmied open a door with a pocketknife. Thankfully, carousels aren't known for high security."

Dylan put Squiggle Bear aside and pulled his dad into a hug. "Thank you."

"You refused to sleep without him. Didn't leave me with a lot of options."

"Sorry about that."

"It's okay. I'm sure Squiggle Bear didn't want to spend the night in the ticket booth anyway."

THE SUN WAS WARM, and there was a cool breeze. The morning

fog had floated away from Golden Gate Park, and it was looking like a beautiful, picture-perfect day for a wedding. As Dave's big day approached, James had found himself looking forward to time out of the house, possibly with Gabe. That it would involve watching Dave get hitched added a level of amusement.

He strolled slowly along as the path twisted around trees as old as the park. They felt like a pinprick of wilderness in the middle of the city. He'd given himself plenty of time to find a parking spot and gotten lucky, finding one right away, so he was comfortably early. He heard steps moving quickly up the gravel path behind him and stepped to the side.

A hand landed on his shoulder. He yelped, jumped, and whipped around. Gabe stood less than two feet from him in a light cream suit with no tie.

"Jesus!"

Gabe raised his hands. "Sorry."

"You nearly gave me a heart attack."

"Sorry about that." Gabe dropped his hands and put a quick peck on his lips. "But I made it."

James smiled. "Thank you. I know you've got work on—"

Gabe shook his head. "I always have work, but it can be shifted around a little to witness shotgun weddings with my boyfriend." James was still getting used to hearing the word "boyfriend" applied to him, and it gave him a little thrill. Gabe gave him another kiss. "Come on. Let's get good seats."

The path twisted around until it opened up onto a meadow. There were a couple of pavilions set up and a gazebo people were gathering around. The gazebo was draped in long strings of orange and white flowers, and golden fabric. A fire was burning in a small pot in front of it. Men with large drums were getting settled, while three very serious-looking older men waited in the gazebo. There were maybe fifty guests. About a quarter of them looked like they had dug out and dusted off old job interview clothes; the other half were in well-tailored suits and saris. James wondered if perhaps they had wandered into the wrong wedding.

"You should have told me it was an Indian wedding. I would have worn my *veshti*."

"I had no idea. I was honestly picturing ten people and a shotgun."

Gabe grinned. "Oh, this could end up being way more interesting than that."

As they approached the gathering, James spotted a couple members of his team, who waved at him. There was a bit more waving, and eight people slid their way through the crowd to meet them.

"Hey, boss," Clare greeted them. A child of radical labor activists, she was usually the spokesperson for the team when they were all together. "Hey, boss's plus one."

James gave her a quick, hard look. "Gabe, this is my team—Clare, Sasha, Ying, Martin, Chris, Alex, Elijah, and Zippy. Everyone, this is Gabe Juarez. My boyfriend." Those last words felt odd coming out of his mouth, like his lips were still trying to feel the shape of them. Gabe, always the professional, made a quick round of handshakes.

James looked his team over while Gabe was shaking hands. He seldom, if ever, saw them outside the stifling confines of work. Clare, Ying, and Chris were actually in dresses, and the guys were all in shirts that had at least a few buttons. Zippy had gone all out and found a tie. A hideous, avocado-green one, but a tie nonetheless.

"Wow. You all scrub up pretty well."

Zippy adjusted his tie. "Dave begged us. Like properly begged."

"Did you all know about…?" James waved his hand toward the decked-out gazebo and the bride's side of the aisle.

"Nope," Clare answered for the group.

Zippy was shaking his head. "We knew Kara was Indian, but we figured Dave would have a gaming buddy get one of those online priest things, and just do it."

An old man approached the fire. People started taking their seats. "I think it's going to be more complicated than that," James said.

"Yeah."

Everyone started moving toward their seats. A young Indian man of maybe twenty-five approached as James headed toward a pair of empty seats. "James Maron?"

"Yes?"

"Your seats are up here."

James gave a quick shrug to Gabe before following the young man. In the front row, there were two seats with neatly folded name cards, bearing his name and Gabe's.

Gabe smiled at him. "It's good to be the boss."

James took his seat with a chuckle. Being the boss might get Gabe front row seats at weddings, but it was new to James.

The old man began speaking. James didn't understand a word. Gabe leaned close. "I've been to a few of these. This is going to take a while."

"How long is a while?"

"Last one took about three hours. Though I'm told you can squish it down to two if you really need to."

James had only ever been to one wedding. He'd been ten, it had been for some cousin, it had taken all of fifteen minutes, and his abiding memory was of being allowed to have cake even though it wasn't his birthday.

"You're kidding."

"Nope."

He looked over his shoulder at what he assumed were Dave's family and friends, including his team. They all had the same looks on their faces: polite interest, masking total confusion. After some time there was music, and everyone looked over their shoulder. Dave was being led up to the altar by an older Indian man who didn't look terribly happy. Dave was as clean as James had ever seen him, in a white shirt, white silk scarf, and a white sarong-type thing. There wasn't an orange stain in sight. Dave was deposited in his place to the right of the fire pot, where he stood, looking uncomfortable.

Then everyone craned their heads back around. At the far end of the aisle was a young woman in a deep red sari trimmed with gold. Her hands and feet were covered in intricate *mehndi* patterns of henna, and her fine-boned face was framed with gold jewelry. James looked at Dave. Dave, with his mushy, white-bread complexion and bad posture. He looked shell-shocked.

James looked at the bride, then whispered to Gabe. "Am I hallucinating, or is she attractive?"

"Yes. She falls under the category of hot."

James took one more look at Dave. "Okay. Just checking."

The bride was brought up to the altar by her family, and the old man began to speak again, still not in English. James quickly lost track of the ceremony. He didn't feel too bad about it. Dave looked completely out of his depth, but so did his almost-wife, who was receiving as much nudging and whispered instruction as Dave. The people he assumed were Dave's parents looked just as confused.

Gabe, on the other hand, was keeping up a soft running commentary as the ceremony progressed. "They're exchanging the garlands as a sign of unification of souls. But they're really supposed to be on their uncles' shoulders to do it." James tried to picture anyone lifting Dave to their shoulders and was glad that bit had been skipped.

"That's milk they're washing their feet with, as a sign of respect."

"Ah."

More hymns were sung, which James couldn't follow.

Drums were played. There was a lime taken out of a bucket. Through all of it, he kept a sharp eye on Dave. Maybe it was because Dave was the first member of his team to get married, but he couldn't help feeling that if Dave blew this, it would somehow reflect badly on the team and his management skills. Dave looked nervous and confused, but every time he caught Kara's eye, they both smiled in a way that made them look painfully young.

James chastised himself for being a cranky old man. He'd sat in enough single-parent support groups to know Dave would not have been in a minority if he'd simply run for it. The fact that he was standing there being talked at in a language he didn't understand, while milk was poured on his feet, spoke volumes about his intentions of making a go of it. He felt the warmth of Gabe's fingers lacing with his as the ceremony continued.

From the looks of it, they were up to knot tying.

"They're not allowed to touch each other until those knots are tied," Gabe whispered as Kara tied a cord around Dave's wrist. James did his best not to snicker. Dave placed a necklace around her neck.

There were loud, fast drums that must have echoed across the park. There were more whispered instructions, then at some unseen cue, Dave linked pinkies with Kara. James saw his hand shaking, but he was also smiling. They started to walk.

"Seven steps, most important bit."

James carefully counted their slow steps, as he was sure everyone else was. At seven Dave positively beamed. James turned to Gabe, grinning.

"There's still more to go."

"More to go" apparently meant feeding the fire with things that caused it to flare and pop, but Dave didn't seem even slightly fazed. There were prayers and blessings and uncomfortable-looking family members, but the grin on Dave's face hadn't faded since the seven steps, and it was contagious. James took a quick look over his shoulder. Ying, Alex, and Zippy had grins as big as Dave's. James turned back to Gabe and gave his hand a squeeze, getting one back in return.

Finally things came to some sort of a head. James wasn't sure what signal he'd missed, but there was applause and hugs. Dave gave Kara a peck on the cheek and held her hand tight.

The two made their way back up the aisle together, but as they passed James and Gabe, Dave gave him a thumbs-up. James made sure to give him a smile and solid nod in return.

Gabe took a glance at his watch, then his phone. "That wasn't so bad. No fights in the middle, and Dave didn't pass out."

"There's still the reception." The wind shifted, and the smells of savory food came down from the pavilions. James' stomach rumbled. "Oh, that smells good."

He followed his nose and the rest of the guests to the back of the reception line. He stood on his toes for a second to gauge how long the line was.

"I was at this one wedding in Indore, over a thousand guests. The total party took three days. This is tiny."

"A thousand?" James couldn't even picture that. The line was moving at a good pace, and James shifted them around so they'd be the last through. James gave Dave a good handshake first. "Congratulations."

"Thanks, boss." He turned to his new wife. "Kara, this is my boss, James."

Kara took James' hand in a good professional grip. "It's so nice to meet you. Dave's told me all about you."

"Good things, I hope. It's nice to meet you. This is Gabe."

"Hi." There were more handshakes.

James reached into his coat pocket and pulled out a piece of paper. "Figured you should get this gift first. Congratulations."

Dave unfolded the paper. "A shift schedule?"

"Look closely." Dave squinted at it, then his face broke into a grin. "I moved some things around—you don't have to be back at work until Thursday."

Dave pulled him into a hard hug. "Thank you."

He pried Dave off. "Use it well. It was nice meeting you," he said to Kara before following his nose to the food.

Gabe touched his arm, then pointed at his phone. "Can I deal with something really quick? It'll take two minutes, tops, I promise."

"No problem." James was amazed Gabe hadn't needed to slip out midceremony. His phone must have been completely on silent. He headed toward the food. There looked to be enough to feed a thousand.

He loaded up a plate with curries, breads, spiced rice, and funny little pickles. He spotted most of his team doing the same. He also watched as some relative of Dave's dished up the absolutely minimum amount that could be considered polite.

He went to find a seat, only to discover there were actual place cards. He circled around four tables before he found his name and Gabe's near the head table, seated across from Dave's grandparents. He took his seat and prayed they wouldn't ask what kind of a worker Dave was. He wasn't a very good liar and was really quite horrible at small talk in general. He introduced himself, shook hands, then shoved a spoonful of something made with chickpeas into his mouth. It took more self-control than James thought he was capable of not to simply melt into the floor, rolling around in culinary bliss. He really needed to learn how to cook. He wondered if he could get the recipe off the grandmotherly Indian ladies, who seemed to be taking a particular interest in exactly what people were eating and how much.

It looked like he was about to be forced into small talk when Gabe sat down with his plate, giving him a peck on the cheek.

"Everything okay?" James asked.

"Just some minor fires. Tamyra put out the worst of them. I swear if we paid her what she was worth, the company would go broke." Gabe turned to the other occupants of the table and flashed them a bright smile while introducing himself. In a matter of minutes, he was steering the small talk away from James and himself. He had Dave's grandmother, a restaurant bookkeeper, talking about rising produce prices, and Dave's grandfather, a nearly retired supervisor out at the Port of Oakland, talking about the newest software—made by TechPrim—for tracking shipping containers, leaving James to eat his food, watch people go by, and smile and nod at all the right places.

James was on his second helping of he wasn't entirely sure what, but it certainly was good, when there was a *clink*ing of a fork on glass. Everyone turned to the head table; Dave stood up.

"Um, hi, everyone. We're not going to do lots of speeches, so don't worry, but there are a few people Kara and I want to thank for this day. Well, first I've got to thank Kara for letting me marry her." He smiled down at his bride. "I promise I will do my best not to screw this up."

A few people chuckled; many didn't.

"I have to thank Krishnaswami and Lalitha for arranging and gifting this all on really short notice. It is amazing, and Paati Jayam and Athai Radhai and Athai Bharati for the food. They've been working on it for three days. I need to thank my parents, Daren and Kate, for being amazingly supportive about the entire situation. I know in their shoes I don't think I would be nearly as cool about it. Um…. And I really need to thank my boss over there, James Maron."

James sat up straighter.

"He got the joy of listening to me whine a while back, and he… well, he told me the same thing people have been telling me for years: time to grow up, get my act together, take some responsibility, but he also added a pretty solid whack on the side of the head and a lot of yelling, so I guess it finally sank in."

James smiled even though he'd just been thanked for doing something that could have easily gotten him fired.

"And we'd like to thank the rest of you for coming and making this a really memorable event." Dave raised his glass one more time, and people drank.

James finished his glass of mango juice as a white cake was produced from somewhere and placed on the head table. It wasn't large, but it was accented with little sugar flowers the same orange color as the strings around the gazebo. Kara and Dave linked hands together and cut into the cake, then fed bits to each other before the whole thing was dismantled for the guests.

"That was nice that he thanked you," Gabe said softly in his ear.

"Considering he could have gotten me fired for assault, it was very nice."

A selection of marbled cake made its way to their table, and someone turned on music.

Gabe jumped up and held out his hand.

"Oh no, I don't dance."

"Everyone dances."

"Not me. Not at a wedding. Especially not in front of a bunch of strangers and my team." Dave and Kara were moving as best as they could to the fast, bouncy Indian pop that was playing. Dave especially seemed to be throwing himself into it before other people got up and joined them.

"Fine, then. But you owe me a dance in private."

"Deal."

Gabe joined the group in the little dance area of the pavilion. He moved perfectly to the music, joining in with everyone else, his cheeks flushing and a grin covering his face. He spun around and sent James a wink.

James crossed his legs but also made a show of eating his cake. It was nice being out with Gabe and even socializing a little, but his body was sending demands for a private moment or ten.

As one song morphed into another, Dave extracted himself from the crowd. He sat down in the empty chair next to James and pulled a neatly folded piece of paper from somewhere up his sleeve.

"Hey, boss, I wanted to show you something." Dave unfolded the paper, revealing a sonogram printout. "Look. You can totally see the head, and the arms and legs and tiny little hands and stuff." Dave's grin was as big as James had ever seen it. "I mean, it didn't feel real, like really real, then we got this done on Thursday, and I could totally see it moving around on the screen, and I mean, there's like a Dave or Kara junior in there. They don't know which yet."

"Everything looking good?"

"Yeah, totally. The doctor said everything looked fine, and there weren't extra arms or anything, and Kara's totally healthy. Man, it's just up to me to get my act together. Those two have got their bits all worked out."

James took out his wallet and removed a small black and white photo he'd carried every day for almost eighteen years. He handed it to Dave. "That's Dylan at six months in. That was the day they told me I was going to have a son. He was already sucking his thumb. Took me years to figure out how to get him out of that habit."

"He's totally cute."

James took the picture back. He didn't need to look at it. It was burned into his memory. "Day after this was given to me, I found out his mother's parents were basically going to sell him to a couple out of state who already had eight kids and believed Jesus wanted them to take in the children of fornicators."

Dave blinked a few times. "Suck. Ass."

"Yep."

"Dude, what did you do?"

"I sued."

"You sued?" Dave laughed. "That's kinda awesome."

"Yeah. It was an interesting road to fatherhood. I'm not sure if I would have given me custody at that age."

"Yeah, but your kid ended up just fine. I mean he's going to college and everything. People who have it way easier totally fuck up their kids."

"I think a lot of it was luck."

"Bullshit. You need to write a book."

James gave a bark of laughter. "A book? About what?"

"Raising kids. You could write an awesome book."

"It would be called *The Stupid Teenager's Guide to Parenting*, 'cause that's what I was."

"Boss, do you know how many stupid teenage parents there are? You absolutely need to write that book. Put in stuff like how to graduate high school with a toddler."

"Start drinking coffee at a young age. Lots of it."

"I already do that."

"Then get yourself off it now, so it'll have the right amount of kick when you need it."

Kara danced her way toward the edge of the crowd and threw Dave a smile. "Isn't she amazing!"

"She is certainly an attractive young woman."

"You know, I knew her for like five years before we ever met. She was GrenadeChick87. She spent years kicking my ass and trash talking. When she moved down here from Seattle, she ended up moving like a block from me."

James had wondered where a guy like Dave would meet a girl like that. "Must have been fate."

"Actually the pregnancy has totally screwed up her game. That's how she figured it out. Every time she loaded up a first-person shooter, she could only stare at it for like a minute, then she'd get sick."

"I'm sure that'll pass."

"I hope so. She's supposed to be in a competition in a few months. Ten-thousand-dollar prize. I mean, I'm pretty good, but I wouldn't stand a chance at a competitive level. GrenadeChick87 totally plays with the big boys. She's like their dream girl."

"And you just married her."

Dave frowned in thought, then grinned. "Yeah, I totally did. I married GrenadeChick87. I am so bragging about that next time I'm on."

A man with a particularly charming smile danced up to Kara. "Better go remind people who GrenadeChick just married."

Dave grinned again before heading back to the dance floor with some purpose. James went to indulge his seldom-used sweet tooth and grabbed a few of the pastries someone had set out next to the cake.

When he got back to his seat, Kara was waiting for him. She was looking a bit rumpled and was adjusting her sari. "This is only the third time I've worn one of these. I don't know how people live in them."

"It looks very nice."

"Thank you. And I wanted to thank you, Mr. Maron, for all the advice you've been giving Dave. It's been a big boost to his confidence."

"James, please. People only call me Mr. Maron when Dylan's in trouble."

"Okay. Still, thank you."

"My pleasure. Any advice I have to give is yours." James looked at the dance floor, where Dave was trying very hard not to trip over his own feet. James took a deep breath. "Okay, I've got to ask."

"Why Dave?" Kara asked.

James tried not to cringe.

"He's sweet."

"Sweet?" That didn't sound like much of a reason.

"I've been around the block a few more times than my parents know about. I've been out with *appropriate* men my family set me up with, and less-than-appropriate men my friends set me up with, and really inappropriate men I've met through other means. And at the end of the day, they were all some flavor of bastard. Dave... he's a little flaky and has some bad habits, but I don't think he has the capacity to be cruel. He can be dumb on occasion, but never unkind."

"Trash talk online doesn't count, I'm guessing?"

"No, it doesn't."

James thought on it and realized, for as much as Dave was a second-rate employee, he'd never once heard of him doing something malicious. If he screwed up, he took the blame. He didn't even pull pranks.

"I guess kind is worth something."

"It's worth a lot." Kara leaned in and put her lips to James' ear. "He's also really good in bed."

James closed his eyes. If there was one thing he didn't need to know about Dave, that was pretty much it. Kara giggled and moved back to the dance floor. Gabe stepped off it. He was flushed and a bit rumpled, and had undone a couple buttons on his shirt.

"I'm going to get some air. Come with me?"

James accepted Gabe's hand as he led them quickly out of the tent. The sun was going down, and the wind had shifted and was coming off the ocean. There was a hint of sea salt in the breeze. James took a deep breath and let it wash over him. Even though he hadn't been dancing, he felt overheated.

"Where'd you learn to dance like that?"

"TechPrim has some major contracts in India these days. A few years ago, I was out there every couple of months."

"Don't you have teams that, I mean...." James kicked himself. Gabe did not have to justify his work habits to him. "Sorry, that didn't come out quite right."

"I know what you mean. CFOs should not be jetting around basically doing sales and acquisitions and personally delivering contracts. I guess I got in the habit back in the day. When we were starting out, the guys handled the computer stuff, and I handled all the other stuff. Sales, marketing, banking. I even picked the name and designed our first logo. I'm even responsible for the typo that made us TechPrim instead of TechPrime. And once we had staff, I never really figured out how to let go of all of it. The guys nag me about it a lot. Of course, other CFOs are being crucified in the press for arranging executive bonuses and tax shelters while their companies go under."

"Good thing you didn't let go, then."

"Tell that to my doctor."

Gabe had led them toward a semisecluded area near the trees. They could still hear the music coming from the tents. It had switched to something slower.

"I'm calling in that dance now."

"Now?"

"Yep." Gabe pulled him close, then put one hand on the small of James' back while holding the other. "We don't have to do anything fancy. Just sway to the music."

James tried to find a bit of rhythm, but mostly he followed Gabe's lead. They swayed back and forth. The music changed to something more poppy, but Gabe kept the slow rhythm. He laid his head on Gabe's shoulder and closed his eyes. Gabe held him tighter. The more time he spent with Gabe, the more addicted he became to these quiet moments of peace. It scared him, something so pleasant and so out of his control.

"Thank you for coming today."

"Thank you for inviting me."

They danced in their own way through another song before Gabe stopped. James looked up in time to be kissed, soft and slow. Gabe tasted of cake frosting and mango juice and smelled of clean sweat.

Gabe pulled away. "Want to get out of here?"

"I think I could make my good-byes."

"Good. How about if I get us a hotel in the city? We can drive back in the morning."

James felt heat flood him despite the cool air. "I'll just go say good-bye, and get our jackets."

Gabe pulled out his phone. "I'll wait right here."

JAMES TOOK out his phone to send a text, even as he handed the keys to the Lemon Drop over to the valet at the St. Francis Hotel. Gabe had somehow gotten them a room on a half hour's notice.

Staying in the city tonight. Be good.

He stepped through the front doors of the grand hotel. His phone chirped at him.

No problem. Don't be good.

He was glad Dylan seemed to be warming up to Gabe. He had little doubt that Dylan would find a way to nag and pry into James' love life even from his dorm room.

Gabe was waiting for him by the main desk on the far side of the lobby, resplendent with marble floors and vaulted ceilings. He gave James a quick kiss. "I got us the MacArthur Suite for the rest of the weekend if we like."

"Don't most people just get a motel?"

"I'm not most people." James couldn't exactly argue with that statement. "Come on."

Gabe led him to the elevator. They got in with a tourist family that included a young teenager and a toddler. They looked haggard.

"What the fuck are we doing here, Mom?" the teenager moaned. "Why couldn't we have gone somewhere cool like LA? You always pick the lamest vacations."

James bit his tongue, hard, partly from Bay Area pride. He'd been born and raised in the Bay Area and was not about to hear it compared negatively to LA of all places. And partly because the mother looked like she was about to apologize. Dylan had gone through a rebellious, smart-aleck phase that started at age ten, but he would have never spoken like that, and if he had, James would not have tolerated it for one second. While James knew Dylan could swear with the best of them, he would never have sworn at his own father like that.

"I'm gonna pee my pants," the toddler stated with absolute certainty. Luckily the door opened, and the family got out before James could hear the reply to that particular statement.

The door closed behind then. James relaxed.

"Glad Dylan is past that?"

"Dylan never was that. Or if he was, he was smart enough not to do it around me."

The elevator crawled up several more floors before letting them out into a large hallway. "I heard the halls were made large enough to accommodate two women in hoop skirts side by side."

"Those must have been very large hoops."

Gabe slid a key card into a pair of double doors that opened into a foyer. It was a hotel room with its own foyer. He dragged them through, closed the doors, then kissed James deeply.

"Let me take you to bed. It's been way too long since I've seen you naked."

"I can get behind that."

Gabe grinned and led them down a hallway. From what James could see, peeking through doors, the suite was at least double the size of his apartment. "You got all this for us?"

"I told them I wanted a suite. Most of them were booked up." Gabe pulled him to the end of the hall and into a large bedroom.

Gabe took off his shoes and dropped his jacket over a chair before turning to James. James swallowed. On occasion Gabe would get a slightly predatory look in his eyes. It heated James up faster than almost any other look.

Gabe stalked toward him. James toed off his own shoes and started unbuttoning his shirt. Gabe stilled his hands and took over, carefully undoing each button while dragging the tips of his fingers across James' body. He leaned into the touch, allowing Gabe to undress him and guide him into bed.

WHEN JAMES OPENED HIS EYES, he was instantly aware the space next to him was empty. The bedside clock told him it was just after one. He strained his ears to listen for any sound. All he could make out was a very distant siren coming through the window. He got up and pulled on a bathrobe the hotel had provided, then went looking for Gabe. The hallway was dark, but he followed a faint glow coming from under a door down the hall. Pushing it open, he found a dining room that could seat at least ten connected to a large living room illuminated by a single lamp.

Gabe was seated on one of the couches, his phone tucked between his ear and shoulder. He was talking quietly. James must have made noise because Gabe looked over his shoulder and smiled at him. He said something to whoever was on the other end and hung up.

"Did I wake you?" Gabe asked.

"No. You didn't have to stop," James replied.

"It wasn't that important."

Important enough to get up at one in the morning, but not important enough he can just hang up, James thought.

Gabe, also wrapped in a bathrobe, patted the couch next to him.

He sat, and Gabe put an arm around his shoulder.

"You should be asleep," James said.

"My sleep patterns are nightmarish these days."

James stared out the window, down onto Union Square, its stone paths softly lit by the nighttime city. "Have you ever been ice-skating down there?" he asked with a sudden need to fill the silence. "They turn it into a rink at Christmas."

"No."

"We took Dylan when he was little, when we were still living with my parents. I was terrible. Fell on my backside five times in four minutes. But not Dylan. He was zipping around the rink, skating backward. Even when some older kids pushed him over, he got right back up. No fear at all."

"You miss those days."

"I miss the edited version. The one that doesn't involve lawyers or food stamps or chronic ear infections. When he was too young to understand how hard it could get, and he didn't want anything but Squiggle Bear and apple juice."

Gabe gave him a gentle squeeze. Looking down at the statue of Victory atop her hundred-foot plinth, she seemed small from above, but James felt small curled against Gabe's side. Small in the grand room of the famous gilded hotel he would never have thought to step foot in on his own.

"And what do you want?" Gabe asked.

"Hm?" James had been lost in reverie.

"What do you want? If you could have anything at all right now, what would *you* want?"

"Nothing," James answered immediately. He wished Gabe wouldn't ask him things like that.

"Everyone wants something."

"No." James' voice was hardly more than a whisper. "Wants are too dangerous. Wants make you live beyond your means. They shift your priorities away from your responsibilities. Needs are fine. I know what I need, but wants cost too much."

Gabe brushed his fingers through James' hair. "There must be something acceptable to want?"

What he wanted to say was he wanted to stay in this suite even if it made him feel small. Gabe made him feel warm and safe and quieted his mind, and he wanted to keep that feeling. He wanted to say "thank you" for giving him bits of time from a busy schedule, and he understood Gabe wouldn't be able to do that forever. He wanted so many things, but wants were dangerous and terrifying in their own way. A want given into at the wrong moment could ruin everything.

He shrugged. "I want Dylan to get a good education. I want Dave to stop leaving orange residue on his workstation. I want Melinda to realize Eduardo is the one who loves her and Ronaldo is just using her to get to her father's money."

"*Siete Palomas?*"

"*Tres Corazones de Fuego.*"

"Of course." Gabe pressed a kiss to the top of his head and squeezed him tight. "Let's get back to bed, before I have an excuse to pick up my phone again."

A DELICATE GRAY light was coming through the morning fog when James woke. Gabe was curled next to him, breathing softly. For the first time, James had been the first to awaken. He studied Gabe's face, relaxed in deep sleep. There was a small scar right by his ear he'd never noticed before. The light caught a few strands of silver at Gabe's temples and in his day-old beard. James had found his first gray hair at twenty-eight, but it was truly gray, not the luminescent silver Gabe was sporting. It was still odd waking up next to someone. It was odd sharing a bed. There were things he didn't know about himself that worried him. Like did he snore or kick in his sleep? Gabe seemed to sleep peacefully, and he liked to cuddle.

He let his gaze slip downward to Gabe's neck. He wanted to lick it, to bury his face in it and simply inhale Gabe's scent.

James brushed a curl away from Gabe's face. He did have impressive "bedhead," with curls that went in every direction. He must use several gallons of hair products daily to keep up his perfectly assembled appearance. Gabe shifted in his sleep, his eyebrows pulling together. And even in sleep, he brought his fingers to his teeth.

James slid his hand into Gabe's. It would not do for the CFO of a multinational corporation to go into meetings with chewed fingers.

Gabe opened his eyes and looked at their intertwined hands.

"You chew your fingers in your sleep."

"I wake up before drawing blood." Gabe's voice was rough, but he had a sleepy half smile.

"I painted Dylan's nails with chili oil before he went to bed each night. He stopped sucking his thumb in a week."

"I like chilies."

"Maybe vanilla extract. It tastes terrible by itself."

"I'll dream of cookies all night."

"Is that a bad thing?"

Gabe smiled. "No." He stretched his arms over his head, working every inch of his long frame.

"How many messages do you have to answer?" James asked as Gabe peeked at his phone.

"No clue." He held up his phone to show a blank screen. "Battery died sometime in the night."

"Do you think the hotel has a charger you can use?"

"Almost certainly." He pressed their bodies together. "But I have better ideas. Work will always be there, but what isn't always there is my boyfriend, a hotel suite, and a dead phone. And I don't want to waste this chance on work."

James closed his eyes. Work *would* always be there. Responsibility and priorities would always be waiting. What wasn't always waiting was a boyfriend in a hotel suite. Or a warm body to wake up next to. Or that sense of peace when he tucked his head against Gabe's shoulder. And one day those things could vanish altogether. But maybe Gabe was right. If for one morning Gabe could let his responsibilities slide, maybe James, for just a few hours, could be brave enough to give in to some wants as well.

GABE AND JAMES WILL Return in Bowerbirds

ABOUT THE AUTHOR

Ada Maria Soto is a Mexican/American expat living in the South Pacific. She's a veteran of the theatre and film business as well as all the lousy jobs that come with two liberal arts degrees. A psychologist once told her she has a fantasy prone personality, but since she's trying to be a writer that's not a bad thing. She is a fan of rugby, cricket, and baseball, who loves to cook, knit, and poke around her garden. She loves to hear from her fans, or really anyone who has read her work.

Join her newsletter to stay up to date with new releases.

https://adamariasoto.com